BOOKS TO BLOOD

Published by:
SHB Books
Brisbane, Australia
First Published 2021
Edition 3

ISBN: 978-0-6453929-8-2

A catalogue record for this book is available from the National Library of Australia

BOOKS TO BLOOD

HARRIE BLAKE

SHB BOOKS

one word at a time

To all my friends and family who have listened to me talk about writing.

1

Greer

People expect far too much before the first cup of coffee. She could barely make herself smile and mumble hello, never mind engage in actual conversation. Which was why Greer forgave herself for not seeing the dead body until she stood on it.

Her footing slipped and stiff fingers struggled to grip the brick wall. Keeping herself upright, she looked down at her boot caught under the body of a man, face-down and spread-eagled across the lane. The stillness of the body gave a sense of absence. The concave shape of the skull was also a clue.

She pulled her foot out from under him and took a breath. Why her? She wasn't even supposed to be here, and if she had gotten the paperwork done on Saturday—as she planned—this would have been someone else's problem.

However life didn't work that way, so she knelt and reached out to touch his wrist. Presumably she would feel cool and clammy dead skin. *Yep, that is what she felt.* She used her hands on her knees to push herself to her feet and took several steps back while reaching for her phone and calling the police.

She looked at the man, or was it body now? Her chest tightened.

"Now Ms Roberts, Greer, what is your exact location?" said a tinny voice from some office with central heating and probably a coffee sitting next to him.

"Lake's End, Merchant Lane." She probably knew the dead man but when she forced herself to look again nothing twigged. Admittedly, her brain wasn't working at its usual capacity.

"Thank you. I know that this is a stressful experience for you, so I appreciate your patience with me on this."

Sure.

The operator waited for Greer to respond but after a brief silence he asked a series of banal questions. Each question somehow linked directly to her blood pressure. What was the point of them? Presumably, someone was on their way and would give a much better description than she could.

She moved to find protection from the wind, changing her spot three times before settling on one about four meters away on the opposite side of the lane. Even her skin didn't know where to be in this situation.

"Did you see anyone when you entered the lane?"

Greer didn't want to be involved. She moved to Lakes End to escape death. Lakes End, a town with no traffic, cobblestone laneways and old sandstone buildings hugging the edge of Lake Divan, a pristine mountain lake. The travel guides described it as picturesque. Not where you expect a murder to occur, despite what they show on TV.

Greer's stomach dropped, and she looked down at her bright blue boots with their green wingtips.

No blood.

She breathed in and felt some of the tension leave her body.

"And you don't recognise the man?"

Greer glanced around the lane for anything that might give her a clue as to who he was.

The questions continued, and by the time the police arrived she was leaning against the wall with the phone propped up on a ledge. In every retelling of this moment, Greer argued she was just resting her eyes.

Greer expected the police to arrive with speed and style. Maybe not the whole shebang like on TV, but still, with numerous cars, vans, and a crowd of people.

Her hands were icy, and she had put her left back in her pocket. On her right hand the feeling of dead skin lingered, spreading across her fingertips like bacteria, and she wasn't letting it near her favourite coat.

A patrol car and an ambulance eventually turned up. Two paramedics whom she was familiar with, Lucinda and Isaac, glanced her way, but ultimately focused on inspecting the body. Two uniformed officers—a woman with thin pale hair pulled back in a tight ponytail and a younger man with his black hair styled in a mohawk with pale tips approached her, establishing her identity and kindly asked her not to move, before putting up a crime scene perimeter. And then a sedan arrived with one of her regular customers, Senior Constable Hugh Stephens, who came straight to her, tablet at the ready.

"Greer Roberts?" Stephens had a face like a car set in neutral. A car covered in well-groomed greying hair.

"Yes." She supposed the question was for the record.

"I'm Senior Constable Stephens."

Right, so discovering a dead body meant she had lost her memory?

He stood there, coat and scarf wrapped tightly around him, angling himself as close to the wall as possible. "Do you know the victim?"

"No, or at least as you can see, he is facing down. I am not sure who it is."

Hugh, or as he was better known, Stephens, ignored or didn't get the sarcasm in Greer's tone.

"Where were you heading?"

Was he kidding? She wasn't sure whether to humour him. Still, there was a dead body.

"Senior Constable Stephens," her voice was as pointed as her finger, "that is my bookstore."

His gaze followed her gesture down the lane to a doorway with two signs—*Book Distillery* and in smaller font *deliveries here*—hanging discreetly off a metal bracket.

"What's your reason for being here this morning?" Stephens returned to his tablet, poised ready to enter details.

Okay, he had to be joking.

"I was on my way to work. I own the Book Distillery," she said, pointing at the sign again. "And just to be clear, I was on my way there to do said work at the Book Distillery." She figured that should cover it.

"At seven in the morning?" He glanced around at the streets empty except for death and the first responders. "Wouldn't get much traffic around here at this time of the morning."

Greer tilted her head examining him. Death was no small thing and she supposed she had to respect him taking his work more seriously than normal.

"Paperwork doesn't care what time of the day it is, Senior Constable Stephens."

Stephens kept making notes. "Where were you when the attack happened?"

"I don't know, as I don't know what time the unfortunate event occurred."

"Okay, Ms Roberts," Stephens paused. He looked up at her again, and she raised what she hoped was one eyebrow and looked down her nose at him. He shifted his eyes back to his tablet and his left thumb started a tapping rhythm. In a low voice, he said, "I will ask you to describe what happened as best you can remember."

Greer blinked. "From when—"

"Before you do that..." a voice called out.

Stephens and Greer turned to find the two paramedics, both with big beaming smiles and cheery it-is-going-to-be-all-right vibes, standing behind them.

Greer had gotten to know Lucinda and Isaac, with their endless energy, on a few call-outs for some of her elderly customers. They were brother and sister and saw themselves as future stand-up comedians with patients as a captive audience to practice on. The few times all their paths had crossed at the bookstore it had quickly become apparent however that Stephens and Isaac had different senses of humour.

"Lucinda, thanks for coming out so quickly," said Stephens.

"Not a problem," said Isaac, giving Stephens an enormous grin. Which was ignored.

The siblings were both tall with large amounts of curly hair and, when they weren't driving ambulances or cracking jokes, they were outdoors, snowboarding or windsurfing.

Isaac's attention moved to Greer, and his weight shifted forward. "Greer, you discovered the body?"

"Yes."

"Are you okay? You look peaky."

She was oscillating between warm and cold while fighting off a strong desire to nap. 'I'm not sure.'

He glared at Stephens. "Did you even check she was okay?"

Stephens bristled. "Greer looked pretty relaxed when I arrived."

So, he did remember who she was.

"Come, my lady, to the chariot. We need to make sure you aren't going into shock over the rudeness of our police officers, the discovering of a dead body and all that."

Greer's lips briefly attempted to move into a smile. He led her to the ambulance, and she crumpled a little as she sat down. While he was taking her blood pressure, she could hear Lucinda say that with the coroner on their way, they would head off once they had confirmed that she was okay.

"Greer, Ms Roberts, I have a few more questions," said Stephens, ignoring Isaac.

"Of course." Greer knew that what had happened so far was only the beginning of the endless questions heading her way.

"Can you tell me how you came to discover the body?"

She wondered exactly what he was looking for. Should she say that as she walked down the stairs leading from her cliff-side house, the winter sun reached over the mountains giving the lake a silver sheen while leaving the town in shadow? That her ears buzzed with cold as she watched, with perplexed curiosity, a few brave souls out jogging with the wind? Or that the glow of a streetlamp captured a stocky shape walking a dog whose ears flapped as it bounded off.

Or should she talk about how she was feeling sorry for herself, shuffling her feet and wishing she was sitting in her armchair, gazing out over the lake savouring her one coffee of the day? That her accountant kept emailing her, asking for things and pointing out certain government deadlines approaching with increasing urgency. That this, combined with hitting the snooze button twice, resulted in a lack of breakfast and coffee, and ultimately a dead body?

"I entered the laneway. I didn't see the body until I tripped over it...the man. I touched his wrist to see if he was alive and called you."

Did he really need to hear about what it felt like for her foot to slip under a body? Or that after realising he was dead she hadn't known what to do with herself, and had the strange feeling of being overly hot and too big for the space? *Maybe not.*

Stephens just stared at her. "Any movement? Anyone else—"

"Your blood pressure is higher than I would like. Perfectly understandable though, considering you're sitting next to me," said Isaac, grinning.

Greer stared at him. It took her a moment to understand what he said and even longer to decide whether or not to smile.

"Not the right time?" said Isaac with a grin. It disappeared when Lucinda gave him a whack on the back of the head.

"That's it, we're off." Lucinda helped Greer up, and Isaac patted Greer's shoulder.

"Good luck," he said.

She watched the paramedics leave, wishing she could go with them. Having to listen to their jokes would have been a small price to pay. If her brain had been working, she could have pretended to be in shock.

"Ms Roberts." Stephens tapped the side of his tablet.

He was exceptionally annoying this morning.

"Sorry, I wasn't awake yet, and the light wasn't good." She had enough light now to tell her answer did not impress him.

Stephens' eyes shifted over her shoulder, and Greer's muscles instinctively tensed.

"Morning."

Greer turned and took in the new arrival. A solid woman dressed in a coat that wasn't quite on right, casual, unironed trousers and a loose shirt. The only sign that she was with the police was the wallet she held open in her hand showing her identification.

"I'm Inspector Mauzer. You discovered the body, right? Ms…"

"Ms Greer Roberts," said Stephens. His hands loosened on his tablet and the other two police officers straightened up and gave quick tugs on their clothes.

"Ms Roberts, I understand you walked up to the body and touched it?"

Inspector Mauzer gazed so intensely at Greer that she had to stop herself from instinctively stepping back.

"Yes, I had to be sure—"

"I think we can all agree from the state of his skull he was dead, Ms Roberts."

Greer kept her face as bland as she could. "Just doing what I thought was right."

"Do you have somewhere to go nearby?"

"The bookstore…I own the Book Distillery."

The inspector looked like she had never heard of anyone owning a bookstore before.

"Can you access it without going down this laneway?" she asked. After she received Greer's nod of confirmation, she stated, "You can wait there. Don't go home until I have talked to you."

With that, Inspector Mauzer turned to the body on the ground.

Greer seethed as she avoided the police tape and headed around the block to the front of the Distillery.

Thug.

The sound of the door closing and the familiar scent of the bookstore worked its magic. Tension melted off her shoulders. She moved to the kitchenette at the back of the store and washed her hands several times.

Greer threw herself into getting everything ready for her accountant. He was delightful, despite taking his work way too seriously. As was often the case once she started working on it, the paperwork didn't take that long to finish, so she turned her attention to her monthly newsletter.

This month, she had been wondering what to recommend as the focus of the Whisky Infused Reader. Now, with a dead body just outside her bookstore, she would have to have an iconic whodunnit, and as a bonus, it would annoy the head of the local book club who only seemed to value epic love stories where everyone was cold and miserable. No one would want to read about romance when murder was in the air.

Once upon a time, the newsletter had just been her reflecting on a week's reading with a whisky in hand and publishing inebriated posts online. Now it was a proper newsletter from a proper bookstore. Dreams, as well as nightmares, can come true.

2

Alba

Alba exhaled as she looked down at the body with its head bashed in at her feet. This was going to be a shit show.

"Everyone, just secure the scene." She hadn't been surprised to find out that Lakes End didn't have its own crime scene unit. But it also meant they would have to wait until the one from their neighbouring town Mountview got here. Which meant preserving a crime scene already destroyed by a handsy bookshop owner.

Stephens huddled against the side of the building. He would want to head back to the station as soon as she let him. She glanced at the constables attempting to establish a barrier. Too many names too quickly, she would have to ask Stephens who they were later, but at least they had done a decent job with the scene, even if it was their first homicide.

She examined the laneway, wondering how the store owners made their living. Could there really be enough people wanting this stuff? One window displayed bits of metal and stone, which she assumed were jewellery, though it was hard to tell with some of it. So far, she had stuck to the newer side with its chain stores and fast food, as evidenced in her recent, more relaxed wardrobe.

"Stephens," she said.

"Yes, Inspector."

Stephens pulled his coat closer around him, no doubt hoping she would notice his not-so-subtle clue that he was cold.

"Any idea of who he is?"

"The coroner's office—"

"I'm not asking for a formal ID."

What little she could see of his face beneath the scarf appeared to be frowning.

Alba just stared back at him.

"Michael Williams, owner of the Hidden Gem," mumbled Stephens.

"Thanks." She gave him a brief nod and noticed he unwound a little. "The Hidden Gem? I've seen it, I think."

"It is a gift store in the central part of town, in that little mall opposite the cookware shop and next to the shoe store."

"Right," Alba said, looking around. "What would bring him here?"

"Coffee? Elvira's Cravings is the best coffee shop in town," said Stephens, a bit more animation coming into his face. "But even then I don't see it bringing him here from on the other side of town." Stephens pointed to the street at the far end of the lane.

Alba tried to remember the street's name — Lakes Way or Lake Lane or something Lake anyway. Like yes, she got it, there was a lake.

"Find out what businesses are around here, and everyone's contact details. If he had a car, locate it."

They should at least be able to do that without getting into too much trouble. Alba pulled out her phone and called the superintendent to bring him up to speed.

Alba did her best to look pleasant as the techs arrived. A bunch of people in various uniforms fell out of cars and vans and the hum of productivity replaced the lethargy over the scene.

After the liberal use of dust and swabs, Michael Williams' body was taken away for further invasive investigations in a more private setting. The techs couldn't find a wallet or a phone. But they did bag some rocks that fit the size of the head wound.

"I don't know much about homicide," said Stephens, watching the techs pick up another clean rock. "But...well, wouldn't you expect to find blood on a murder weapon left beside the body?"

"It's certainly easier when they do," said Alba.

By the time they had wrapped up the scene, it was close to lunchtime. No murder weapon that she could see, and in her experience the window for time of death on a chilly morning would be so broad as to be meaningless.

"A robbery gone wrong?" asked Stephens.

"Perhaps," said Alba. She looked at the quiet streets around them. Even with all the police activity only a handful of people had come by to see what was going on. "Do you get much of that around here?" asked Alba.

"First time for everything." Stephens' lips and eyes drooped even more than usual.

"Maybe, but statistically unlikely." Alba kept her face straight.

There was silence. She didn't expect them to laugh, but a smile would have been nice. Made her doubt her sense of humour. She studied the three from Lakes End. The constables looked like they were about to go on a field trip, while Stephens' expression suggested he was preparing to trek through hell.

"Constables, I want statements from everyone along this laneway and any shops or offices in the area. We want to know where they were this morning from midnight to now. It's a Monday morning, so if they were up and going to work, there should be some movement, and if we are lucky, someone saw something. Stay together and check in with Stephens regularly."

She turned towards Stephens, huddled against the wall.

"Go back to the station, get the CCTV footage in the area and start the background checks." She liked to think that he smiled on the inside. "There can't have been many people around at this time of morning and if we are lucky, this will be over by the end of the day."

Alba pulled into the car park next to a grand old building wedged between two others, the post office and the town hall. The fronts of all three buildings were as Gothic as sandstone could get.

It had only taken a few minutes to get back to the station. Traffic was something that happened in other places, not that it stopped people from bitching about it. She had once heard Stephens complain about a group of elderly people crossing the road making him late home from work. She had never heard him complain about being late *to* work however.

The main doors of the police station led into a large central foyer. Two sets of stairs curved up the walls, leading to a second level. Alba hadn't explored up there yet, so she wasn't sure why they needed two stairwells to get to it. The department had cordoned off a reception area which was staffed by another police officer she couldn't remember the name of as a gatekeeper. No metal scanners or locked doors here.

She used to be a person who could enter a room and use everyone's name by the end of the meeting. Now she struggled to pay attention for more than a few minutes, the faces a blur.

Alba surveyed the police station, reminding herself that she had chosen this place. To her left stretched the central hub with its cluster of desks pressed tightly together. The original floor plan had long disappeared, replaced by a maze of personal preferences creating organised chaos that demanded careful navigation. To the right extended a waiting area flanked by several interview rooms, though Alba had noticed the cleaners visited these spaces far more frequently than any actual suspects.

She headed through the sea of desks towards the superintendent's office.

"Inspector," said Russell, turning away from his computer screen when Alba walked in. "What have we got?"

Alba hadn't quite worked out Superintendent Russell yet. A solid man with short hair and deep lines on his face that accentuated his emotions. Not that she had seen many yet.

"As I mentioned on the phone, sir, we've got a body with a blow to the head with no wallet or phone. Stephens gave a preliminary identification of Michael Williams, and I am waiting for the coroner's office to verify it. I am assuming the coroner will notify the family and ask his next of kin—"

"No need. I have known Michael for years, and I will verify before calling in the family. I wouldn't want to put Fran, his wife, through that if there has been a mistake."

Fuck, just what she needed. A dead body that was a close friend of the superintendent. This was going to lead to all sorts of shits and giggles.

"Thank you, sir. Once verified I was going to interview his wife—"

"No, if it's him, I will visit them. Give them a little time to adjust to this shock."

Alba could feel her face freeze.

"We care about the people in our town, Inspector." His forehead creased in the centre. "How are you settling in? I hope Stephens has given you everything you need?"

A pity his concern didn't extend to the integrity of the investigation. Alba forced herself to nod. "Yes, thank you, sir."

"Good, good. We're lucky to have someone of your experience here. Especially in light of today's events."

"Happy to be here, sir."

Alba didn't think anything she was thinking about slipped through in her tone but he tilted his head and examined her intently.

"It might seem strange at first, but things are different in a smaller community, and I need to see that you respect that."

Sure.

"Yes, sir." Alba tried to stop there but couldn't. "It's just that time to adjust might also give time to destroy critical evidence."

Alba forced her face into neutral and let her eyes drift up to the deepening crease in the superintendent's forehead to avoid a stare-off.

His face smoothed and a small smile appeared. "Relax, Inspector, I won't get in your way. Just let me comfort my old friend. Tomorrow you can...respectfully," he paused, his words as heavy as his gaze, "talk to her and the other family members."

The only photo on Superintendent Russell's desk was of his dog, a large cheerful animal with big ears. Alba thought him single until Stephens shared that the superintendent's husband had a reputation of putting in complaints and that if she got one she was to treat it the same as if from any other citizen. So what was it about the Williams family that got them more special treatment than his own husband?

"Sir, should we ask for help on this?"

Russell sat back in his chair and peered at her. "You think we can't handle it?"

"How many of the team have worked a homicide before, sir?"

"You have."

"Yes, but—"

"Inspector, if we asked for help, well, we would get someone exactly like you, so since we have you, we don't need to, do we?" He smiled at her.

She kept her eyes on his forehead. Actually they would have gotten a small team of specialised officers that could get in the field and lend a hand.

"Respectfully sir, I'm an inspector. Normally...normally I'd not be involved in the day-to-day investigation—"

He waved his hand dismissing her words. "We're too small a department for that kind of thinking. This is the first unlawful death investigation in twenty years. I expect you to share your skills and knowledge with the team, including leading and assisting with the investigation."

"Yes sir," said Alba, shifting her weight and stifling a sigh. "I'll start by following up on the witness who discovered the body and seeing if we can trace Michael's movements that morning."

"Excellent, I'll let you know how I get on with the family."

She was right. An absolute shitshow.

3

Greer

Greer jolted at the sound of the door clicking open and closed. The sun was now fully up, making the shop's windows sparkle and highlighting the shadow thrown by Inspector Mauzer's frame across the floor. The Inspector's shade was distorted by books randomly distributed across the floor, in various states of being unpacked. Greer had tried to roll around on a bed of books once. It had been incredibly uncomfortable, and she had bent a cover, so now she just contented herself with caressing and smelling them.

"Inspector Mauzer," said Greer, moving to the chair behind the counter. It made her feel comfortable, reminding her that this was her space. She doubted the inspector cared. Inspectors were probably like Miles, and all spaces were their spaces.

"What were you doing between midnight and seven this morning?"

The inspector looked around. Greer's gaze followed hers. The room itself was typical, with its white walls and office lights. But Greer had done her best to make it inviting. Mostly achieved through the generous distribution of chairs, rugs and lamps and complemented by every second fluorescent light not working, giving a sense of stepping into somewhere outside normal space and time.

"Of course, because murderers always call it in," said Greer.

The inspector walked further into the store and perched on one of the red velvet high-backed bar stools in front of the counter. "More often than you would think."

Greer's spine straightened, and the tension flooded back into her shoulders. "I'm afraid I can't offer much of an alibi. I was asleep with only a snoring cat as a witness. I can say that I left my house around six thirty."

"Do you always walk down the laneway?"

Greer took a breath and shuffled a few books around. "Yes."

"Do you have a routine? For example, do you often come in early on a Monday?"

"No, it just depends on what needs to be done. This morning there was some paperwork due to my accountant."

"Did you know the victim?" The inspector seemed to look past her most of the time, her gaze only landing when she fired off a question.

Greer studied the inspector and guessed she was close to her in age. Despite the deadpan expression, she could see a myriad of laugh lines at the corner of the inspector's eyes. Or maybe they were just from peering suspiciously at people.

"I don't even know who the victim is, I am afraid. Do you...know yet?"

Quiet descended as the inspector made notes.

The inspector's average height, shoulder-length dark hair and lack of distinctive features somehow combined to emphasise her intensity.

"His name was Michael Williams. He owned the Hidden Gem."

Greer controlled her next breath, forcing her shoulders to stay down. "Michael...oh how terrible for Fran. I didn't even recognise him...I mean, preoccupied with the hit on the back of the head and all that." She dropped her gaze to the fingertips that had touched Michael's body. "Though there wasn't as much blood as you would expect."

"Normally see a lot of blood, do you? On dead bodies?"

Something in the inspector's tone made Greer look up. "I don't know if I have ever thought about it." She blinked at finding the inspector's laser-like attention now firmly on her. "There always seems to be more blood in the movies, especially when fresh like that."

"Fresh..."

Greer watched as the inspector made another note.

The inspector cleared her throat and turned her gaze back to Greer. "I'd remind you this is not one of your books, Ms Roberts. We'll have to take your fingerprints, especially as you *checked* to see if he was alive."

Greer wanted to object and say she had only touched the wrist. However, experience with the police had taught her less was better.

"You'll need to come down to the station to complete your statement now." The inspector rose to her feet.

"Was that a request or an order?"

"Which will get you down to the station?"

Greer wasn't sure if the inspector was joking. But she supposed murder trumped a bookstore's opening hours. She flicked a quick text to her assistant before closing up and following the inspector. Hopefully Victoria was free to come in, though she wouldn't be happy about it.

"Patrol's busy, so we have to take my car." The inspector walked up to the passenger side of a car parked out in front of the shop and opened the door.

If someone had asked her what kind of car the inspector drove, Greer would have guessed something sensible, even dull. The inspector came across a bit of a thug, albeit an extremely pragmatic one.

The inspector's cheeks darkened under Greer's stare.

"It isn't far," she said before making her way around to the driver's side.

Greer wasn't sure what to think about the two-seater white Fiat 124 Spider with a red stripe down the side, the type of car she would expect to see in a movie, not being driven by a police inspector in a small town. Was it reinforcing the thug or showing a new facet?

A few minutes later, they pulled into the police station car park. A wave of exhaustion rolled over Greer, and she numbly followed the inspector into one of the interview rooms and slumped into the uncomfortable seat.

"Coffee?"

"Yes, that would be lovely," said Greer, not bothering to shift to find a good angle in the seat, or at least an angle that didn't have the edges digging into the back of her knees. She hadn't had coffee yet, or any food. Apparently finding a dead body was one way to decrease the appetite.

The inspector gave a bit of a grunt. "How do you take it?"

"Oat milk and two sugars."

"This is not a bloody café." The inspector's voice whipped across the room and Greer tried to hide her wince. The inspector raked her hand through her hair and added, "We have normal milk. Will you die if we use that?"

"No, I won't die." She might get gassy, but that would be the inspector's problem.

"Fine."

The superintendent entering the room inhibited the inspector's exit.

"Greer, I heard you discovered poor Michael. I'm so sorry you had to go through such an unfortunate experience. Is there anything we can do for you?"

"I'd like to go back to my bookshop, to be honest."

The superintendent frowned. "Yes, well, of course, unfortunately, we'll have to get your statement. Have they offered you a drink? Would you like some coffee?"

"The inspector just offered to get me one."

"Yes, yes, of course. How do you like it? I will get that sorted while the inspector gets your statement. That way, you are out of here as soon as possible."

Greer, flattered that the head of the local police thought she was important enough to organise a coffee for her, smiled. "Milk and two sugars," she said, not wanting to repeat her request for oat milk. The police probably all drank their coffee black.

Like their souls.

Greer swung from being pleased to hoping she could hide her dislike. The superintendent would only be friendly if she did what she was told, and her statement helped them close the case. She knew both would throw her under the bus if it meant they resolved this matter faster.

"Well, I know that Inspector Mauzer will be as fast as possible."

As the superintendent left, Greer had a moment of familiarity. So far, she had stayed out of the way of the local police, however, she was sure she had encountered the superintendent before. She couldn't quite place where—perhaps at one of the town events or maybe he had come into the bookstore. She knew he was a member of the book club. However, since she did not get to go, it could not have been there.

"Ms Roberts, can I call you Greer?" asked the inspector.

"No."

They stared at each other until the coffee arrived. Greer took a sip and surprised that it was not that bad she took a second.

"Okay, Ms Roberts," said the inspector, over-enunciating it. "I need you to tell me everything that occurred from the time you left your house this morning."

Greer took another sip while she promised herself to behave and not antagonise the police. But she couldn't help the resentment filling her knowing that if she had just ignored her alarm she would have been spared this entire ordeal.

The questioning ended up taking over three hours and by the time it was over, Greer regretted not having a lawyer with her. Naïve of her to think that just because she had no reason to kill Michael, there wouldn't be any risk.

The last of the winter sun did little to illuminate the way back to the store. When she entered, Victoria's heavy tread heralded her assistant's emergence from the back. Victoria had gotten her text and come in, and for a moment Greer could imagine that life had returned to normal. A rare smile crossed her face as she studied Victoria's dour countenance.

How Victoria had developed laugh lines, Greer did not know as she had only ever seen three expressions. Dour, with a slight hint of irritation. This was the most common one. Extremely dour, especially when she was about to predict some dire future for someone. And scorn, this one was rarer, as it took a lot for someone to surpass her already low opinion of them; however, when they did, Victoria's expression was a thing of beauty.

Right now, she had her extremely dour expression on.

"Hello, you're looking sprightly today," said Greer with a small smile.

Victoria was wearing her hat inside again. She seemed to think it made her look on-trend. Today's was a green hat to go with her green vest and trousers, topped off with a pink scarf. Not that Greer could talk. They were quite a pair, with her own outfit of loose teal trousers, a plaid jacket, and blue boots.

"Don't sprightly me, murderer!"

Tension flowed from Greer's body. If Victoria could be dramatic about it, everything was going to be okay.

"News travels fast, I see." Greer lent against the counter at the front of the shop.

Victoria's eyes narrowed. "At least you'd the sense to take out Michael Williams, a useless waste of space if I ever saw one. I don't know why anyone would waste their money on the crap sold in his store. That's the problem with today's society...too much stuff."

"First," Greer held up a finger. "I didn't kill him. I discovered his body. Second," she held up two fingers. "There's nothing wrong with wanting things that will make your place look and feel good."

"I've never needed them," said Victoria over her shoulder as she shuffled behind the front counter. She sat on the gas lift seat, which she used to place herself subtly higher than the customers.

"You've just used books and music." Greer shook her head and picked up one of the books stacked on the counter.

Victoria had been a tall woman when she was younger and while her body no longer had the same presence as

Greer had seen in some of her older pictures, she made up for it with her energy, and of course, the gas lift chair.

"Both of which enrich the world." Victoria reached forward and pulled the book out of Greer's hand returning it to the pile. "Unlike a picture with a pink stripe through it that someone calls art. If you hadn't taken out Michael Williams, I'm sure someone else would've. Besides being useless, he was an ass."

"You think everyone's an ass."

"It's a sad indictment of today that most people are."

Victoria turned away from the conversation and started reading messages on the screen in front of her.

"You understand I didn't kill him, right?"

"Sure, sure."

"At least give me credit that if I killed someone, no one would find the body," said Greer, the edges of her lips tilting upward.

Victoria's face moved from extremely dour to dour.

"I would hope not. Anyway, you aren't stupid enough to do it outside of your own store." She turned back to Greer. "Do the police have any idea who did?"

Greer thought about Inspector Mauzer. Was she competent? Or just motivated to close this as quickly as possible, and any suspect would do?

"I'm not sure." Greer's gaze wandered over shelves of books. "And in the absence of any suspects, they might..." she shook her head and glanced at Victoria. "Thanks for covering the store."

"I was beset by a horde of gossips." Victoria delivered this statement with disdain.

Though Greer suspected that the only reason Victoria had not enjoyed herself was that she had not known the details. Something it might take Victoria a while to forgive her for.

"Sorry," said Greer.

Victoria shot her a sharp look and turned back to the screen in front of her. "The newsletter should've been out last week."

"I tried to edit it this morning, but in light of recent events…do we need to change the theme, or would a murder mystery focus be in bad taste?" Greer ran her finger down the spine of a crime novel sitting on the counter.

"Don't be ridiculous, our public will expect it," said Victoria, shifting the screen around so Greer could see it as well.

Greer sat across from her in the same seat the inspector had sat in earlier and they got to work.

They would have presented a pretty scene to anyone walking in as they discussed fictional death surrounded by books and velvet upholstery.

"Too much to only have murders by blunt force trauma on the list?" asked Greer.

"It's a bit on the nose," Victoria said, scratching her chin, "Still, it is what the readers will want."

"Do you think it will upset Fran?" asked Greer.

They were both silent. Greer contemplated Fran's depth of grief over the death of a husband with whom she had what was, at best, a disinterested marriage.

"Nah," said Victoria, "I mean, she won't get a laugh or anything out of it. I don't think she will care either."

"I'm putting a Blunt Instrument in," said Greer.

"What? I was going to choose that one," said Victoria.

And for a moment the real world, the actual death was forgotten as she squabbled with Victoria about whose recommendations were whose.

They broke the newsletter up into three parts—Greer's recommendations, Victoria's and the Book Distillery united section. They aimed to find at least one book a month that they both liked. Since they had changed the focus to whodunnits, they had to put their initial brainstorming notes aside and start again.

"That's why we have the united section," said Greer dryly.

"Well, what am I going to put in mine then?" asked Victoria. "What other murder mysteries have a blow to the head?"

Greer drummed her fingers on the counter.

"There must be others," said Greer.

"Yes, but do you remember them?"

"Surely someone has created a list somewhere." Greer pointed to the screen. Victoria shot her a glare but started searching.

A few customers came in, disgruntled about the closure earlier that morning and curious about the murder. Greer left Victoria to the research and got on with the business of sharing her love of books. As predicted, it ended up being a good day for sales in the murder mystery section. Human beings can be gruesome creatures.

By the time they closed, Victoria, claiming she feared for her life, organised a lift home with one of her admirers. The fear didn't extend to Greer's welfare, whom Victoria left to lock up the store alone.

Greer closed the door behind her and looked out at the dark street. Normally, she would walk home along the esplanade near the edge of the lake. She enjoyed the water, crystal clear during the day and at night, dark with the moon throwing sprinkles of light along its surface. It was hard to feel anything other than calm in a place of such beauty.

Still, she started the day discovering a body, so she took the shortest way home at a brisk pace. Cool fingers of air reached up from the lake to stroke her cheek as she started up the cliff-side stairs. She shivered, walking faster.

With her imagination running in overdrive, she was grateful to close the front door of her home behind her. The sound of an elephant stampede drove all thoughts of cool fingers from her mind and relaxed her back muscles. She locked the door behind her and greeted her cat, Miles, with lots of pats and scratches as he stretched out on the floor in front of her. Once he was sick of pats, she changed into long, loose slacks with a soft wrap top and, with a huff, flopped onto her couch. She was only there for a few moments when she felt a claw tap the top of her head. With an embarrassing display of a lack of core strength, she scissored her legs to leverage herself up.

After feeding Miles, she poured herself a scotch and grabbed a bag of corn chips. The dinner of champions. She needed to reach out to her brother Dale to debrief about the day. Later.

Returning to the couch, she turned on the TV and tried to lose herself in the lives of people whose major problem seemed to be that they were too attractive. A heat-seeking missile landed on her, pushing the air out of her lungs. The last vet visit had him weighing close to ten kilos, which was not an insubstantial weight to have land on your sternum. Originally a local stray, it hadn't taken Miles long to realise Greer was a soft touch and move in. He now spent most of his days with his feet in sunspots and moving as little as possible unless she was home and there was the potential for food.

Too tired to watch the show, she turned on some music and let haunting strings float through the air. Greer buried her face in Miles' fur. Somehow, although he never went outside, he smelled like earth. She lay there, holding Miles until it was time to go to bed, hoping that tomorrow would be a better day.

Dale

What a day! Sorry, I didn't have time to email you this morning. I didn't have my coffee time. There is something about Monday mornings, or to be honest, any morning these days, that makes it so hard to get out of bed. It is not just winter approaching. I just feel listless, though it feels ungrateful to say that when I am living our childhood dream. Admittedly, I am still looking for the resident reading dragon we imagined! I leave a small *dragon wanted* sign up and it would certainly be useful to have one to provide heating as it gets colder. I have found a candle that gives a smoky scent; however, I can only burn it when Victoria isn't in as she says it makes her nose itch.

Unfortunately, a more metaphorical type of dragon has interrupted my life. I can't tell you how much I wish I had just ignored my alarm and slept in this morning. Or even just stopped and had my coffee and breakfast.

I don't want you to worry. I am handling it. However, I have somehow once more gotten caught up in a homicide police investigation. Now, before you freak out, I want you to know that I am doing everything in my power to avoid being dragged into it and have no desire to work for the police again. We both remember the last time.

I was walking along, minding my business, when I stumbled over a dead body, no love looking me in the eye here. This is me, after all. I get dead people.

It was the body of a local business owner called Michael Williams. I know his wife, whom I met a few times at the bookstore. Anyway, I didn't recognise him. I just knew someone was dead. The shape of the skull wasn't normal, which kind of gave it away. Still, I had to double-check. Touching dead skin is just terrible. I had to wash my hands repeatedly.

Maybe I should have called the police anonymously. I wouldn't have gotten away with it. You know what small towns are like, or maybe you don't, which is why you always preferred the bigger cities. You will just have to use your imagination and accept that not telling them would soon backfire. Rock and a hard place, really, as the police are interested in me and no doubt doing a background check.

I have been lucky. The last five years have been wonderful. Now, I feel like a sledgehammer has come in and smashed my fairy tale and I wasn't even supposed to be there! Fate is so unkind.

I meant it when I said the last thing I want is to be pulled into that world again. I am just worried that they might think it is me. Especially if they don't have any other suspects. I feel that the new inspector cares more about making a good impression than justice. It also doesn't fill me with confidence that the other police officers appear to be afraid of her.

Anyway, that is tomorrow's problem. Right now, it is sleep time.

Wish you were here.

Greer

4

Alba

Alba had spent the afternoon setting up the conference room as the base of operations, and now she was working her way through what seemed like a mountain of paperwork needed to get this investigation started. She hit submit on another form and another and another. Her eyes lost focus, and her keystrokes seemed to get rhythmically louder, almost piercing.

"I can finish it, Inspector."

She looked up at Stephens. He was never afraid of paperwork. Even if he mucked it up, it would be easier to check it in the morning than drag herself through it tonight.

"Great."

Alba handed over what she was working on, and it wasn't long before she was in her car and heading home.

At the outer edge of the town, there were rows of cramped houses on small lots with the windows all lined up. She assumed it was unfortunate planning or from an era where people wanted to see each other. Today, the fight for privacy between the houses had led to a lot of creativity and greenery.

It seemed a long way from the lights, glass and steel of her old apartment, a small shoebox with views over the city. She didn't regret selling it. No matter what happened, she wasn't going back.

They say you shouldn't make any big decisions for at least six months after a significant event. So, taking a new job, moving to a new town and buying a house a few weeks after her entire world crashed was probably the worst thing she could have done.

While it wasn't grand, every time Alba turned into her street with the glimmering lake at its end, she felt a flare of something she hadn't felt in a very long time—contentment. Maybe it wasn't all so bad.

She parked across the road from her small two-storey home, ignoring the twitch of the curtain and glare she inevitably received from her neighbour.

A murmur of relief escaped as she stepped through the front door.

She even liked that the floor plan had the laundry opening right near the front door, and next to it she had put a narrow second-hand wall stand used for umbrellas and coats. She grabbed the old warm tartan leggings and a thick, slack, long-sleeved shirt and robe that she had tossed over it that morning.

After changing into them, she threw her work clothes in the general direction of the washing machine and made some lemon and honey tea with a dash of whisky. It had been that kind of day.

In a few steps, she was outside on the patio.

It was a frosty night, so she slipped her feet into some woollen slippers and turned on the outdoor heater before settling into a comfortable chair. She enjoyed this outdoor space where the vines covering the fence created the illusion of a green haven.

Eyes closed, she sipped her tea and enjoyed the quiet.

"Alba."

It was almost idyllic.

"Alba, guess what?"

Just a pity the fence wasn't higher.

"Alba, I've created the most amazing risotto. You have to try it."

Alba opened her eyes and smiled at her neighbour Eli waving at her over the fence.

"A risotto?"

"Yes, I had Henri film it, and I was rather brilliant if I say so myself. Posted it online, and it already has thirty likes...thirty likes within an hour."

Houses so close to each other invariably came with neighbours, and she had been lucky to find some instant friends as well. Eli was rather charming, if somewhat over-enthusiastic about his cooking.

"A second career, Eli?"

"Probably fourth or fifth." He grinned. "Let me be an example to you that age isn't a barrier." His face lit up with excitement. "Famous after seventy can you believe it? But then not only do I look good while cooking...the food tastes amazing."

"Eli, leave Alba alone. She just wants a drink in peace." Henrietta, known as Henri to her friends, waved Eli off as she let herself into Alba's patio area. Alba wondered what the previous owners had been thinking to install a gate between the properties.

Henri sat down with a glass of wine in her hand and a bottle in the other. Eli disappeared.

"You look like you need a strong drink," said Henri.

Alba raised her mug.

"The tea has a kick to it."

The bang of the gate mixed with Henri's laugh, and Eli came through carrying a wooden tray with three large black bowls and spoons. It was risotto time.

"I hope it tastes better than your last one," said Henri. "It took me a couple of days to pass that rice."

Alba had only been here a few months and had already tried several of Eli's cooking attempts. She smiled at Eli and accepted her risotto gratefully, attempting to hide any hesitation.

It was a lovely evening, and despite Alba's desire for solitude, she was grateful for the friendship shown by Eli and Henri.

"Another risotto? Brave souls."

Alba was suddenly conscious of the worn-out parts of her tartan leggings and the hole in the shoulder of her robe.

"Clem," said Eli with a broad smile. "I'd like to remind you of my chicken casserole and its six hundred views."

Clem, also known as Dr Clement Yardley, let himself into Alba's courtyard through the other side gate. The original owners really had a lot to answer for. Clement's intrusion was easy to forgive though due to his warm hazel eyes and ready smile.

"Six hundred," said Clement with a smile. "You'll be a star before you know it."

He joined them, taking the spare seat next to Alba, right next to the shoulder with the hole in it.

"Need a drink, Clem?" asked Henri, gesturing to her bottle on the table.

"Love one, sorry should have brought something," Clem smiled at Alba. "I don't mean to be such a terrible guest, it just comes naturally."

She gave a half-smile back.

"Alba, do you have a spare glass?" asked Henri.

"Yes, of course," said Alba, standing. If they were all staying she might as well get one for herself and Eli as well.

A loud knock on the door made her groan. Did someone put out a flyer? Was it visit Alba night? She moved through the house and opened the front door to discover Julius Brogley, her neighbour from across the street.

"You parked your car in front of my house."

His long black hair hung around his face, highlighting his cheekbones and jawline. A jawline that seemed unnaturally tight. Alba wondered how much his dental bill would be if he kept grinding his teeth like that.

"Is it blocking anything?" asked Alba. She couldn't believe he was making such a big deal about this again.

Julius' frown deepened.

She didn't subscribe to stereotypes, such as accountants being boring. She genuinely believed that several accountants out there who were fascinating people. Julius just didn't seem to be one of them.

"That's not the point. Park in front of your own house."

Alba could hear *let it go* playing in her mind.

"Henri, Eli and Clement are here. Would you like to join us for wine and risotto?" It stuck in her throat to offer the invitation. But, if she was going to stay in this town, she should try to be friendly. And she didn't want to fight with him. Not today anyway.

"Is it Eli's risotto?"

"Yep."

"Better not risk it. I've got a client coming around soon. A client who will now have to park down the road because of you." With that parting—but not very cutting shot—he left.

Alba collected the wine glasses and headed out to the patio to join the others.

"Thanks." Clement smiled warmly up at her taking a glass. "Was that Julius?"

"Probably complaining about your parking again," said Henri as she poured the wine. "We'll need another bottle."

The last thing they needed was more wine. Alba, sure the entire street could hear Henri's voice, only hoped that no one else took it as an invitation to turn up. Eli had disappeared, presumably to get more risotto.

"We need to talk about the murder," said Henri.

Of course.

"I can't share the details of an ongoing police investigation," said Alba, frowning at Henri.

"Don't expect you to. *We're* going to share all the gossip with you." She flashed Alba a smile. "How else are you going to know what's going on?"

"By carrying out an investigation and using forensic evidence?" asked Alba.

"Ah, Eli, well done," said Henri.

Eli returned, carrying a wine bottle under one arm, a laptop under the other, and a bowl and spoon for Clement. Henri took the wine, Clement his bowl and once settled, Eli opened his laptop. Alba suspected he was checking the viewing numbers on his latest video.

He glanced up at Alba and wiggled his eyebrows. "I'm sure you'll find the local gossip much more useful."

Once a carpenter, Eli had officially retired about three years ago and, according to Henri, watched shows and clips for a year before deciding to be an online video star. Henri, his in-house tech support, had agreed to do the filming and away he went. To date, he had over a thousand subscribers and was hoping to hit five thousand that year.

"*I* heard," said Henri, topping up Alba's wine, "Michael was having an affair."

"An affair? He was hardly a ladies' man," dismissed Clement.

"I checked Michael out online." Henri sat back and took a healthy swig from her glass. "Did you know he had a social media account? Not just one for his store, but a personal one? And...Fran is not on his list of friends."

"I just can't see why Fran would murder Michael," said Eli. "Why now?"

Alba glanced at his laptop screen and saw he was refreshing it, but the viewing statistics didn't change.

"Alba, what do you think?" asked Henri.

"I can neither confirm nor deny anything about an ongoing investigation," said Alba. Despite her best efforts to keep her face severe and impartial, she could feel her body relaxing and her mouth curving upward. Which of course would only encourage them.

"I can see it," said Henri, "the building up and up of everything, and one day he leaves the lid off the peanut butter jar and, bop."

Eli stopped playing with his laptop and looked at her. His eyebrows rose, and the colour faded from his cheeks.

"I said I was sorry. I didn't realise it was a thing."

"Bullshit." Henri ate another spoonful of risotto. "Anyway, I'm telling you there's only one reason for a husband to have a social media account not connected to his wife's. So, he can fish for women."

"We're talking Michael Williams here, right?" enquired Clement, putting down the risotto bowl, which he had just shovelled down. "Middle-aged man with a bit of a paunch and very little in the way of a sense of humour?"

Everyone sipped their wine.

"Okay, I'll give you it's unlikely," said Henri. "But the pool gets smaller as you get older, and he wasn't repellent."

"What?" asked Eli. "Is there something I should know about?" He closed his laptop. "Besides, he cared more about money than sex."

As Eli and Henri looked like they were about to square off, Alba took it as an opportunity to top up everyone's wine. Compliments on the grenache and a few comments on how nice it was to sit outside even if it was cold, drifted the conversation back to more pleasant topics. However, Henri was not to be distracted so easily.

"If you don't think it was an affair, why is he dead?" she asked.

"Money," Eli responded.

"Clement?" Henri prompted him when he didn't immediately offer an opinion.

"In my experience—"

"You have experience in murder?" asked Henri.

"In my experience," Clement said, mock glowering at Henri, "it's usually an accident. But maybe this time it was a random person passing through. This place is not exactly a hotbed of crime."

They all thought about it and, like synchronised swimmers, turned toward Alba.

"Well?" asked Henri. She leant forward to top up Alba's wine, but Alba covered her glass with her hand. Henri looked disappointed but filled the others instead.

"Statistically..." Alba wondered how she could word this so it didn't end up as a quote on the gossip network in the morning. "The most common reasons for murder are when committing other crimes or domestic violence. Either way, random killings happen a lot less than you think."

Everyone focused on their wine and what was left of their risotto. Alba wanted to give herself a pat on the back for her ability to kill a conversation.

"Eli, I have to give it to you. This risotto is edible," said Henri.

Eli beamed at what was high praise from his wife.

From what Alba could gather the two, married for almost fifty years, had changed their roles in the relationship several times. Henri had never been much of a cook but had done her part while Eli had been doing long hours as an apprentice and later setting up his own business. When she got promoted to head of technology at the local council, they moved to a world of eating out and with Eli doing bulk cooking on the weekends. Now Eli was the aspiring chef and Henri his sommelier, a true power couple at parties.

"A body left on a public road is rather messy though," said Clements. He swirled the wine in his glass. "I mean...if you were going to kill someone how would you do it?"

"Oh, I love this game," said Henri, she straightened and leaned forward. "I think it must be Eli. Sorry, Eli." She patted his face. "It's usually the spouse, isn't it? I mean, they're the ones that have years and years of pent-up annoyance at the other person."

Eli looked over at Alba, his eyes wide. "Can I sleep here tonight?"

"Don't be silly," said Henri. "If I were going to kill you, I certainly wouldn't share it here." She drummed her fingertips on the side of her glass. "A cast-iron pan. Put a bit of force into it and I'm sure it would do the job. It's the disposal of the body that's the tricky bit. I hardly want to go about cutting you up."

"Pigs are good," said Eli. "If the body got eaten by pigs, there wouldn't be much left, or if you can't find pigs, maybe a new garden feature? You could cover the body with lime to hide the smell. I would like to give life to flowers."

"Risky keeping the body though," said Henri. "The most effective would be the acid thing, but I always retch when I see the bathtub with liquefied remains on TV."

Clement shook his head. "I agree, use the acid, no body, no crime. If you had it in your backyard, you'd constantly be worried about people finding out. Too much stress, best to get it over with."

"You'd be the best person to commit murder, wouldn't you?" said Henri with a smile. "You'd have all the drugs for taking someone out. Who would you kill?"

"I think if I was going to go all murdery I would want to go full-on Dexter," said Clement. "Make a bit of a splash on the serial killer scene, but only killing people who were bad, no young blonde women for me."

Henri laughed. "Surprising everyone didn't dye their hair black the way they were taking out the blondes in those TV shows."

"Should I get my notepad?" asked Alba. "So I can make notes for when I discover bodies?"

Laughter, and more edifying conversation about getting away with murder ended when the temperature dropped below what even outdoor heating could handle, and everyone left for the warmth of their homes.

Alba smiled to herself as she went about her ritual of locking up and tidying the kitchen ready for the morning. Even though she had thought she wanted to be alone, it had been good to talk to someone other than police officers and witnesses. As an added bonus, Eli had taken everything home again so she didn't have to worry about washing up either.

She turned off the downstairs lights before remembering her phone next to the kettle and shuffled over to pick it up, instinctively checking it.

A message from her father. Her throat tightened painfully. With her fingers curled around the edge of the phone, all she had to do was move her thumb one centimetre to open it.

Alba stood there, letting the cool darkness wrap around her. The sound of her phone locking released her body, and she walked up the stairs. What was the point of rebuilding your life if you brought your old baggage with you? She set her alarm and put the phone aside.

As she crawled into her bed, the mattress took her weight and her body sighed with relief. The flannel sheets were soft and warmed her muscles. She did her breathing exercises and felt each one of her muscles relax. Her brain wasn't as easy to tame and after lying there for what felt like hours, she reached for her phone. With its light bathing her face, she opened the message.

Alba, my daughter

I just want you to know that I would change everything if I could go back in time.

I am a fool. What else can I say? I thought it was a harmless choice. A morally ambiguous choice, yes, but not a choice that hurt anyone. I know that is wrong now.

I value you and our relationship more than anything, more than being one of the boys, more than my loyalty to the department. I didn't see those things in conflict until I realised how much my choices hurt you. How much it hurt us.

You are my only family, my daughter.

I love you.

Alba locked the phone screen again and placed it face down, stifling the light.

Prick. Martese might have been sincere, or he knew precisely what to say. She refused to give him the satisfaction of a response, but her brain spent the rest of the night working out what she would tell him next time she saw him.

Once upon a time, she wouldn't have needed an alarm to wake her. Her life had been governed by good choices and routines, at the gym by five thirty, and a diet of sixty per cent vegetables without even thinking about it. Now her routine was sleeping in and eating the heaviest food she could find. But the image of criminals outrunning her made it possible to do the occasional jog. With a groan, she sat up, swinging her legs over the side of the bed and pulling on a, meant to be loose, tracksuit.

Before her brain had time to kick in she was outside. She headed down to the lake and soon the crunch from the tarmac disappeared as she moved onto the smooth stones of the esplanade. The lake's waters were silver in the early morning light and the clean scent of the lake made the air lighter and sweeter. She liked these moments. The only noise was the air rushing off the lake mingling with the sounds of her puffing until the footsteps of other jogging enthusiasts made her turn to her right.

Joggers...there were always at least three or four joggers out and about, no matter how early it was. Had Ms Roberts said anything about seeing joggers? Even if she hadn't, it doesn't mean that they weren't there. Alba's breath dragged at her throat. Being sensible, she went back for her car, grabbed her coat and headed towards Merchants Lane. Parking, she walked down to the esplanade from where Michael had died, trying to keep a glimpse of the entrance of Merchants Lane in view. A tall fit man in expensive exercise gear ran towards her with the seasoned stride of an experienced runner.

"Excuse me, sir."

He stopped but kept jogging on the spot.

"I'm Inspector Mauzer." She opened her wallet showing her ID. "Were you here yesterday morning?"

The man stopped jogging. "Inspector." He examined her but Alba could not tell what conclusions he drew. "I assume this is about poor Michael's death?"

Small towns were the worst.

"Yes, can I start with your name?" Alba tried not to think about what she looked like in an ill-fitting tracksuit, hastily covered by a coat and with sleep crusts still in the corner of her eyes.

"Yes, of course, sorry. It's Jayden Merritt."

He flashed a smile at her. She suspected he thought it was charming.

"Were you jogging here at this time yesterday?"

He certainly looked as if he jogged every day.

Jayden nodded. "Yes my usual route."

"Did you see anyone else around?"

He rubbed his hands together and tucked them under his arms. Alba adjusted her own warm coat and was about to take pity on him when he spoke.

"I saw her. Not unusual. She's sometimes around here in the early morning."

Alba forced her lips to stay closed and just stared at him letting the silence and the cold do the work. It didn't take long.

"Fran," said Jayden, his tone reluctant. "But don't jump to conclusions."

Alba forced her face not to show the frustration that rolled through her. "Why didn't you come forward when you heard about Mr Williams?"

"What if it was just a coincidence?"

Alba tracked Jayden's gaze out to the lake before it returned to her. The expression in his eyes pleading.

"Where and when did you see her?" asked Alba, her tone cool as the morning air even to her own ears.

She made him outline what he had seen and recorded his contact details on her phone. The sun was failing to warm the air this close to the lake, so once he gave his commitment to come down to the police station to complete a formal statement Alba allowed him to shuffle off.

She interrupted a few other joggers. None admitted to seeing anything but she took their names and contact details for the constables to follow up anyway.

Walking back to her car, she sent Stephens a message. They had a witness.

In a rare moment of brilliance the Lakes End Police Department had invested in an excellent espresso machine and Alba liked to leave enough time to savour a coffee at her desk before commencing the paperwork of the day.

She ran her hand over the wooden desk's worn edge. At least it was actual wood, a novelty after years of grey synthetic furniture. Seated near the superintendent's office, she looked out over the disordered crowd of desks. She was okay with the lack of view, preferring to watch the hustle and bustle or because it was Lakes End, the slow-moving quiet of the police department.

A sound made her turn toward the window behind her. Outside, one officer was helping an elderly man carry groceries to his car. She wondered if that was really the best use of their time, but a ringing phone pulled her attention back to the office. Setting down her coffee, she leaned forward ready to assist, only to hear what sounded like yet another complaint about a neighbour's barking dog.

The chair groaned under her weight as she leaned back and wrapped her fingers around the warm coffee cup. No talk of quotas here. No backroom deals or favours bartered between badges.

The first sip was always the best, and she took a moment to breathe in the aroma of the undiluted single-origin bean. The warmth of the coffee cup was a pleasant pain against her frozen fingers. She lifted the cup.

"Morning, Inspector."

The coffee ran like a life-giving elixir down her throat and into her body.

"Bloody freezing this morning."

Just knowing that it was in her body seemed to bring her brain to life. This was her second favourite part of the day.

"Not sure I'll survive this winter, probably be my last, not that anyone cares."

For fuck's sake, the hand holding her coffee cup wobbled before she placed it back on the desk and gave Stephens her attention.

"Stephens. What brings you in this early?"

He collapsed into his chair, like a cat who had found his spot. And considering how long he had been sitting in it that was not surprising. Years ago, when presumably he had been young and ambitious, he had been a member of the fraud squad in one of the big cities and from what she could see he had left that ambition back there. For the last couple of decades, he had been happily sitting behind a desk at Lakes End and making sure the paperwork was up to date. It hadn't taken her long to realise that Stephens didn't enjoy interviewing people, talking to people, and anything outside, especially during winter.

Still, he wasn't as untested as the others.

"This bloody murder." He heaved a sigh and stared at his desk, with an almost wistful expression on his face. "I suppose we'll have to be out and about today?"

He hadn't yet taken off his layers of coats and scarves, and experience had taught her it would take him a few minutes before he would brave divesting himself of his outdoor wear. She thought that continuing to feel cold despite his layers of clothes and central heating showed a powerful presence of mind.

"Yes." Alba cradled her cup of coffee and breathed in its perfume. "Background checks first, then we'll head out to question the family."

It had been almost a decade since she had first investigated death. Now it had smashed her tranquil small-town bubble, which she had high hopes of just being traffic control and some minor drug possession charges. The sooner she could complete this case, the quicker she could get back to quiet mornings with her coffee.

"Do you think the superintendent will want to come? Maybe you could take him...," said Stephens.

Alba took in the despair on his face and another sip of her coffee. She could understand not wanting to have anything to do with a murder, though he seemed more concerned about the weather.

"No," said Alba. She imagined trying to interview Michael Williams' family with the superintendent hovering over her. "He visited yesterday." Breathing in through her nose helped her to calm down, and she turned on her computer.

The background checks had come through. Curiosity led her to open Greer's first. Or should she say *Ms Roberts*?

She read through the usual address changes, noting that Ms Roberts had only moved to Lakes End five years or so ago. Interestingly, it showed that she had been a psychologist who had once consulted with the police. That might explain where some of the disdain came from. Alba put in a request for further information.

Greer

The sun sneaked in around her eye mask and Miles snuffled deep in her ear—one of the worst noises and sensations anyone should have to suffer on waking. Not quite ready to give up on sleep she snuggled in deeper under the covers. A robust tap of a paw followed. She shifted the mask to find Miles staring down at her, his paw—claw extended—stretching towards her. Once she made eye contact with him, he jumped off the bed, stopping in the doorway and giving her the look.

She laughed as she got up and obediently followed him. With her dusty kitchen cabinets overflowing with rarely used kitchen appliances, the coffee maker was her pièce de résistance, fully integrated with the fridge and the same cost as a second-hand car. She hit start and the smell of freshly ground coffee filled the air, beginning her morning routine.

This morning that meant putting out some warm, tasty meat for Miles and sitting in her spot looking out over the lake. She sipped her coffee and with it came memories of Michael's body and the police. Her fingers tightened around the cup. Why did the cost of procrastination have to be so high? She meant what she had said to Dale, that she didn't want to get involved. But could she trust the police?

It couldn't hurt to make sure Fran was okay, and if she found some information that protected herself, all the better. A quick message to Victoria about being late and she found herself at Fran Williams' house with a box of doughnuts in hand. Greer used the doorbell despite the open entrance and Fran, with a wan face and glazed eyes, appeared.

"Fran, I'm so sorry for your loss."

"It's all been a terrible shock." Fran looked down at the box in Greer's hands. "Are those Elvira's doughnuts?"

"If there was ever a time for guilt-free doughnuts," Greer's lips curved upwards. "I thought this was it."

Fran attempted a small smile in return but with limited success. "Please come in," she said before lowering her voice and adding, "I need a break from the rest of them."

Greer winced. Of course, her daughter Sam and son Alex would be here. Not that they were unpleasant, not directly. And then probably Michael's cousin, Gregory Williams and his wife, Hillary. Gregory was okay, but Hilary and her brother Alfie Jones who would probably just tag along for the gossip, were another matter. Greer hung up her coat but hid the box of doughnuts in her carry bag.

They walked into a living room filled with people. Fran looked around like she didn't know where to start but she took a breath and addressed the room.

"Everyone, this is Greer. Most of you would know her from the bookstore."

All conversation ceased as their gazes settled on her. The fact she had guessed who would be here correctly was of little comfort now. Greer's stomach clenched. She barely knew them and she had just inserted herself into their grief. For what? This was a mistake.

But before she could spiral further, Hilary interrupted. "What are you doing here? Come to *discover* more bodies?"

Fran jolted.

"I just came to...reach out? Offer any help I could? I'm sorry for intruding." The last addressed to Fran.

"Nonsense Greer," Fran shifted her body towards Greer, away from Hilary. "Why don't you come and help me make tea?"

Greer followed her into a small bright kitchen full of windows illuminating a clean white bench space, a spotless sink and not a crumb in sight. Was it because no one had it in them to cook, or because Fran found cleaning therapeutic?

Fran pulled out a teapot and set the kettle to boil, her eyes unfocused and seeming to rely on muscle memory of moves made a thousand times before. Greer pushed the box of doughnuts towards her.

"I'm surprised Elvira let you buy that many," said Fran, with a small smile at the box. "You must have cleaned her out."

"I had to tell her they were for you." Greer smoothed back her hair. "She's not my biggest fan."

It was Fran's turn to look at her sympathetically. "She thinks you're going to open up a café and become her competition."

Greer didn't stress about Elvira's dislike of her. It reduced the amount of small talk she had to pay for a coffee.

Fran examined the doughnuts closely while the kettle came to a boil. She chose a dark chocolate and raspberry one while Greer chose lemon. For a moment, they were quiet, enjoying their doughnuts and a well-made cup of tea.

"How have you been holding up?" asked Greer.

"I took some sedatives last night, so slept hard." She sipped her tea. "I don't know if that was helpful, as I am a bit out of it today." She glanced at Greer. "It doesn't feel real, to be honest. Like he's away on a business trip or playing golf and will be back after lunch."

Fran took another bite of her doughnut and fiddled with her cup before she turned and asked the question Greer had been dreading.

"Did he suffer?"

"I'm sorry Fran." Greer put her own cup down. "I don't know." She swallowed, her throat tight. "I checked Fran. There was nothing anyone could have done."

Fran's shoulders slumped. "I'd gone to check on him that morning and he was gone, I just assumed he'd gone out early." She looked at Greer almost pleadingly. "What was he doing there?"

"I don't know Fran, I really don't."

They both sighed and focused on finishing their sugar-filled dough. Fran hid the rest while Greer topped up the teapot and, taking out tea and cups, they re-joined the others.

"Still here then?" asked Hilary, her lips thin and tight.

She was an elegant woman with long legs and impeccable taste in clothing, but the heavy use of eyeliner made her eyes small and beady.

"What I want to know is how we can be sure you weren't the one to kill Michael?" asked Alfie.

Greer tried not to let her distaste show as his voice boomed across the room.

"Alfie..." said Fran, her tone heavy with the resignation of someone who knew her words would fall on deaf ears.

"I'm just saying," said Alfie, his voice no softer, "no one else was around—"

"Uncle Alfie, stop it," said Alex and Sam simultaneously.

He grunted but at least stopped talking.

Greer gave them a smile of thanks and sat down next to Fran. Sam was a local dentist and Alex, a pharmacist. Both seem to have taken after their mother and had a pleasant mix of pragmatism and affability, if a little bit self-focused like their father.

The family shared stories of Michael—his likes, dislikes, strengths, and weaknesses. Though Greer's discomfort grew as the morning wore on, she gained a clearer picture of how his family saw him. Her initial awkwardness seemed to fade too and they appeared to accept her tenuous right to be there. When Inspector Mauzer entered the room however the atmosphere shifted. It didn't take a psychologist to see that the inspector was not happy to find Greer there.

Exhausted by the time she left, Greer still had no answer to the question of who had a motive to kill Michael. Gregory had spent what felt like hours discussing Michael's business plans to sell online—hardly relevant now. Hilary and her brother Alfie seemed more interested in the contents of the will than in helping Fran, while Sam and Alex, though obviously grieving their father's death, offered little insight into the complexities of his life.

Glad she had walked, Greer slowed her pace as she approached the lake. The beauty of the day felt almost inappropriate—her dark thoughts at odds with the brilliant water, bright winter sun, and gently swaying branches above.

She pulled her oversized coat closer around her shoulders, not to shield herself from the breeze, but to settle in and savour its cool caress against her face. Others might describe it as icy, but it swept away the fog of her thoughts. She lingered at the water's edge, watching ripples dance across the surface, but with each passing minute her responsibilities at the Book Distillery called to her. After a deep breath, she forced her reluctant feet to turn, each step away from the lake heavier than the last.

When she arrived, Victoria, perched behind the counter, greeted her with a pointed glare—the kind meant to inspire guilt and apology. On any other day, it might have worked. But today, with Michael's death weighing on her mind, her indifference must have shown on her face because Victoria's glare intensified.

"So..." said Victoria.

"So..." Greer looked around and couldn't see any customers. She headed towards the back of the store to hang up her coat.

"Had a good morning?" asked Victoria, her tone snide.

"I don't know if you would call it good," said Greer over her shoulder. "The family was there."

She turned to find Victoria swivelling toward her, eyes bright with interest.

"My vote is one of them did it."

"Oh?" said Greer, moving back towards the front of the store. "And how did you come to that conclusion?"

She leaned against the chair near the counter. Of course Victoria had an opinion.

"It's always family. No one else hates you enough to kill you." Victoria paused. "Except those disturbed in the head like Dexter and Spector."

The door opened, and an elegant older gentleman entered the store. Victoria straightened and focused on the screen in front of her.

"Kendall, how wonderful to see you," said Greer.

"Good morning to you Greer, Victoria. It's a beautiful day today." He smiled warmly at both of them. "But sadly, I appear to be bookless."

"A tragedy," said Greer with a smile.

She liked Kendall. He was approaching eighty, though that wasn't uncommon in this town with its significant over-fifty population. After all Victoria was seventy herself, or close to it. Not that there was anything wrong with being old.

What she appreciated most was how he seemed to enjoy life even when things didn't go his way. He was slim now, a little too lean, really. Kendall had once told her he'd been quite plump in his fifties and missed the sense of security that a bit of padding had given him before age and stomach troubles had worn it away.

"Do you have any you recommend?" Kendall did a quick scan of the store however, as always, turned to Victoria for his recommendations.

Victoria shot him a sideways glance but returned her gaze to the screen in front of her. "What are you looking for?" she asked, her tone disinterested.

Greer would have found Victoria's disinterest more believable if she hadn't perked up—well, as much as it was possible for Victoria to perk. As Kendall moved towards the shelf of latest releases, Victoria pretended to ignore him, focusing intently on whatever was in front of her while making only the occasional shift to keep him in her peripheral vision.

"Oh, you know, a bit of death, a bit of mayhem and a bit of romance." He flashed Victoria a smile.

"How about a little magic?" Victoria looked at him fully for the first time. If she had delivered it with a wink, it could almost have been a pickup line.

"Well..." Kendall blinked and focused on Victoria. "I've never gotten into fantasy. It just seems to be people wandering around the countryside looking for something that was at home all along."

Greer retreated between the tall bookshelves, but the bookstore's intimate dimensions betrayed her. The fact that the store was designed to be cozy and intimate, something she usually prided herself on, now felt like a punishment. Nowhere to hide and nothing to do but listen to the awkward flirting, or whatever it was that was unfolding.

Victoria's fingers tapped on the counter. "There are other types. I'm thinking of one called urban fantasy. They set it in today's world where magic also exists, but it is a bit more murder mysteryish. Has a kind of film noir vibe. It definitely has a bit of death, mayhem and romance in it."

"Which one should I start with?" asked Kendall.

"One high on mayhem," drawled Victoria.

And with that, they sold their first book of the day.

It was a good thing Greer wasn't relying on the Book Distillery to pay the rent. She was just glad that she could choose to spend her time here.

"Is Dexter disturbed?" asked Greer after Kendall had left and she had braved coming out from her hiding spot amongst the shelves.

"Dexter literally disturbed himself," said Victoria.

"Fair point." Greer shuffled some books around on the shelf. Victoria's willingness to alphabetise had its limits. "I didn't get any evil-killer vibes from the family though."

"Did you know..."

It was Victoria's favourite way of starting a sentence. It usually meant she was about to spout some fact that only a random scholar would know.

"That in ancient times in Scotland it wasn't murder unless it happened to a stranger? If it was family, it was up to the local clan to sort out." Her voice had an edge that tempted her listeners to disagree.

"Are you saying we should allow families to kill each other?" Greer laughed. "Are you really okay with your nephew and niece being able to kill you with no police or government to intervene?"

"I'm just saying..." Victoria glared at her. "I'm just saying that family killing family is understandable."

"It's all speculation." Greer waved a book in the air. "And we need to prep the order for the book club and finish the newsletter."

"Oh, now you want to work?"

Greer chuckled as she took over the computer and pulled up the latest book club order. The club had taken up her somewhat inappropriate suggestion of Georgette Heyer's Blunt Instrument, so she needed to source some quickly. They both went about their tasks silently until Victoria declared she needed a break and headed out. Greer lost herself in shelving books while listening to classical music weave through the shop.

Bang

Greer jerked towards the front door as it was thrown open.

"Michael was a crook," declared Victoria as she stormed back in.

Greer stared at her.

Victoria strode to the counter, fiddling with the sleeves of her shirt and fussing with her hat.

"I met Kendall for a glass of prosecco at that new wine bar, and well—"

Greer held up her hand.

"So that *break*, which lasted over an hour I might add, was...you and Kendall having some sparkling?"

"Yes, yes...but that's not the point."

"How long has this been going on? Do I need to call him up and ask him what his intentions are? Why is he hiding his relationship with you? You deserve better, Victoria."

Victoria's face flashed with scorn. "Are you done?" she asked.

"Just getting start—"

"I have information, you ridiculous human being."

Greer's smile bloomed wide, and she raised her hands in mock surrender. "I'm sorry, please continue."

Victoria's jaw tightened, her body half-turning toward the door. Instead, she stepped closer and thumped the counter. "Michael was a crook."

"Okay," said Greer.

"He bought all of Kendall's stuff for nothing."

"What stuff—"

"Kendall had a whole garage full of furniture and knick-knacks. Michael offered to look at it and see if it was worth anything. He gave Kendall two thousand dollars and took it all away for him. Kendall, of course, was glad to have someone else taking care of it. Then he was visiting a friend and saw one of his figurines, which the friend paid over a thousand for." Victoria's hands were windmilling by this point and Greer winced as Victoria used her outside voice at full volume.

It was morally wrong, yes, however—fraud? Maybe. That was something for the police to determine.

"I suggest you tell Inspector Mauzer," said Greer.

"Why me?" Victoria took a step back and crossed her arms.

Greer tried not to roll her eyes. "You're the one who found the clue, Sherlock."

"You're the one who needs to be presenting viable alternatives to the police," said Victoria.

"The first thing they will want to do is talk to Kendall. I would only be passing on hearsay."

Victoria's dour face flashed with scorn again. "Kendall hasn't done anything."

Greer turned back to a stack of books that seemed to multiply when she wasn't looking. "Seriously Victoria, if you have the information, go to the police or get Kendall to."

"I don't want to talk to those ignorant dipshits," said Victoria.

"And I do?" Greer shot her a glance and Victoria left the store in what could only be described as a huff.

Greer shook her head in confusion, dismissed it as not her problem, turned up the music and got back to work.

Despite concentrating on the comforting weight of books and the smell of their pages, her frown lingered. This bookstore was her sanctuary, however despite its walls of tomes, death had found her again. Perhaps it was a sign that it was time to move on.

She walked over to the true-crime section and looked for crimes where the victim had died from blunt force trauma. Most seemed to be stabbings and poisonings, with only a few featuring bats and crowbars. The shape of Michael's skull seemed to imply something bigger. But what did she know?

Greer patted her hair, putting nonexistent tufts back in place. Coffee. She needed coffee if she was going to get through the rest of the day. Making an executive decision to break her one coffee a day rule, she hung the "someone would be back at some point" sign on the door and headed out. She exited through the front of the store, but other than a quick glance down the road aptly named Lakes Way, she ignored the cafés down on the waterfront and headed in the other direction. In Lakes End there was only one café worth going to.

She joined the queue that spilled onto the footpath despite the post-lunch hour. Even with locals lined up for their coffee fix, Lakes End felt relatively quiet this time of year. Only an occasional car drifted past—no traffic jams, no jostling crowds. Everyone seemed content to chat and soak up the rare winter sunshine. A whip of chill across the back of her neck had her regretting the absence of a scarf, but a deep, yet somehow still abrasive, voice grating in her ear caused her internal temperature to rise.

"Slacking off again I see. Not going to stay in business long if you keep closing the door."

And there stood Amos, all weathered scowls, with a thick beard and a Captain Hook moustache, looking like a Bond villain who'd wandered into the wrong century. The book club ladies adored him. Greer had been feuding with him for three years running—which would be fine if he didn't happen to own her building *and* run the book club.

"Indeed." Greer gave him a small smile. "I have to thank you for your concern. I must admit I didn't realise you were so invested in my success."

A sneer rippled across his face.

"No skin off my nose if you go," said Amos. "I'm sure I can get another bookstore interested in the space, one who can get orders in faster as well."

Greer widened her eyes and tilted her head. "But if I'm not around, who will suggest books for the book club?"

She was amazed someone could flush that deeply behind a beard that thick. For a second, she actually worried about his health. All this drama because the book club preferred her book recommendations over his. How was she supposed to know he'd take it so personally? The arrival of other members saved them both, as they greeted her relatively warmly and distracted Amos with meeting logistics.

She escaped into the café, ready to grab her coffee and flee back to the bookstore. The space was tiny but efficient, with four stools that served more as waiting spots than actual seating. Elvira stood behind the counter—tall, no-nonsense, hair pulled back—wearing her usual generous smile until she noticed Greer. The smile vanished. Most people found Elvira delightful, but Greer seemed to bring out her worst side.

"Oat Latte, two sugars?"

"Yes, thank you."

Usually, that was the extent of their conversation but it turned out that the discovery of a dead body was more than even Elvira could ignore.

"Killed anyone lately?" asked Elvira, her focus on the coffee machine in front of her. "Just asking for a friend."

If she had been joking, it might have been funny.

"No, however I'm sure you'll be the first to know if I do." Greer showed too many teeth.

Elvira sniffed and quickly finished the coffee.

"You can go now."

She paid and slipped past Amos without incident, leaving him to his impromptu meeting as she headed back to the Book Distillery.

Dale,

I hate them all. Seriously, I live in this idyllic community with a bookstore, and somehow they have ruined it! The book club is the worst. I know. I know the whole point of the bookstore is for people to read books, and book clubs are part of that...

I can literally hear you saying that if it weren't for Amos, the book club wouldn't exist and be such an active group and remind me he refused to rent out the space to anyone other than a bookstore. You would have thought he would have been glad that I came here. I am not saying he has no value. Everyone has value. He just ruins it with his ego! For years, I have had to put up with his bitching and complaining. All because I suggested a space opera series, and he took having a different point of view as besmirching him!

Sorry, you are tired of hearing this. I am complaining about it because Amos was less than pleasant at the café today.

Deep down you like Amos don't you? Wanting to hang with him? Swapping beard care tips? You always looked so suave when you styled your hair with your vest and pocket watch. You would like my outfit today, mustard yellow boots. I just wouldn't be me if there wasn't something!

It is cold now, though we have been lucky with the weather in the last couple of days. It might be an excuse to buy a different coat. I am wearing the one you lent me. It is comfortable and stops the wind, so it is hard to do better than that, except it isn't bright yellow or blue.

You are wondering what is happening with the murder, though, right? Well...

I visited Fran, Michael's wife. I know I said I wouldn't get involved. However, it seemed like the smart thing to do. It was awkward. Victoria thinks she has solved it. I told her to take it to the police, which somehow resulted in her not talking to me. You know people are weird, right?

Victoria thinks the police here are, and I quote, "ignorant dipshits".

Here's to her being wrong.

I miss you. I wish you were here.

Greer

6

Alba

Alba observed the arrival of her fellow officers and conducted a preliminary assessment: fuckstick status pending further evaluation, investigative competency hovering somewhere between questionable and she was doomed.

Her keyboard strokes became louder and she forced her fingers to relax, focusing on finishing the report for the superintendent and working through the mountain of paperwork that death brought.

Alba rubbed her eyes for what felt like the hundredth time when the reduction in background noise alerted her to Russell's arrival. His gaze sought her out, and she followed the superintendent into his office. The wooden door made an echoing thump despite her efforts to close it gently.

Russell sat down and swivelled his chair to gaze out his window. Alba took a seat in the visitor's chair but didn't let herself sit back in it.

"A sad business," Russell murmured.

Russell's office looked out over the park toward the lake—a stark contrast to her carpark view. Between the bare branches of the trees, Alba caught flashes of water sparkling in the sunlight

"A sad business indeed." Russell heaved a sigh. "I've known Michael and Fran for over thirty years." He turned from the window back to her. "Any initial thoughts?"

"No sir."

The superintendent rapped his fingers against the desk, staring at Alba, waiting for the information she didn't have.

"I know you are just getting settled in. However, I hope I don't need to remind you how important it is that you act with all due diligence on this case, Inspector?"

Alba closed her lips to prevent a mutter that wanted to escape. What could she say? The superintendent hadn't even allowed her to interview the family yet. She wanted to shift in her seat, stretch her back, but she refused to give Russell the satisfaction of thinking she was nervous.

"No sir."

Russell huffed. "Well, what are you sitting here for? Go find out what happened."

You couldn't win.

She stood, gave Russell a nod, and carefully stepped around the chair and through the doorway to avoid any embarrassing stumbles. She made it to her desk and stretched her hands above her head. A few cracks of the neck, and she was ready to go again.

Stephens had returned, and he looked about as eager to get to it as a cat getting out of a warm bed. But get to it they did.

She took her car and they arrived at the Williams' residence to find a fleet of cars parked along the street. Alba left hers across the front driveway, making sure her police car sign was on the dashboard visible for any enthusiastic traffic police or, as she called him, Jeffrey.

She already had three parking tickets. The part that got her was he knew her licence plate, and that she had been on police business. Still, he insisted that the sign had to be displayed, or how else was he to know she wasn't abusing her powers? The superintendent had made them go away and politely asked her to make sure she displayed the sign in the future. Ridiculous. Surely there had to be some advantages to living in a small town.

The front door was open, so they entered and walked through to a room full of people, including Greer Roberts. Who sat with a tea service in front of her like she was hosting a party or something.

What the fuck was she doing here?

Alba just bet *Ms Roberts* had been more than happy to share details about the crime scene to keep them entertained. Between Russell and Ms Roberts, it was an excellent thing that she had learnt to accept the world as it was, rather than as she wished it could be.

"Good morning." She waited until she had the room's attention. "I'm Inspector Alba Mauzer. I understand Superintendent Russell let you know I'd be here today?"

"Yes, Bana, the Superintendent, was very kind and explained the process," said one man. He looked like a beige sort of person, and it surprised her it was him and not the big, blustery fellow glaring at her who spoke.

"I appreciate your cooperation during such a difficult time." Who was he and which was Fran? She turned to Stephens next to her. "Senior Constable Stephens, if you could kindly escort Mrs Williams to a room where we could talk?"

"She has the right to a lawyer," said the larger man with a voice that should have come with volume control.

Two women stood up. One was tall, perfectly made up, while the other looked exhausted, wan and unsure of what was going on. Still, this was not the time to guess. Fortunately, the beige man helped by reaching up to the tall woman's arm to pull her back down to her chair.

"Hilary, she means Fran," he said.

"Right," Hilary's face reddened, but she turned to Fran. "Fran, I don't think you should talk to them without a lawyer present. Maybe I should go with you."

"Hilary's right Fran," said the larger man, his voice still unnecessarily booming. "You can't trust them. Best to take either me or Hilary."

Fucking great. Two lawyers in the room.

"No, no, I want to talk to them. I'll call you if I need you," said Fran.

Stephens led the way and Fran followed him. Alba tried not to glare openly at *Ms Roberts* as she left to join them. They had moved to another room filled with bookshelves framing a bay window with a couple of armchairs, a desk and a gaming chair.

Fran took one of the armchairs near the window and Alba joined her, sitting in the one across. Stephens headed towards the desk, happy in his role as note-taker. Alba didn't talk straight away, allowing Fran to set the pace of the conversation.

"It still doesn't feel real." Fran glanced out the window. "I feel sorry for Greer, discovering him...that way."

"How well do you know Ms Roberts?" Maybe Greer was more involved than she originally let on?

"Just through the bookstore." Fran peered at Alba. "Bana said he didn't think she had anything to do with it. I can't imagine why she would."

Of course he bloody did.

Still, why did Fran care about the innocence of an acquaintance?

"Can you tell me about Michael and his movements yesterday morning?"

Fran chewed on her right index fingernail while her left arm looked like it didn't know where to go.

"I've been trying to think...think if anything differed from normal. I don't know if this makes me a poor partner...but I find myself unsure if my memories are from this week or a week before."

The smell of deodorant or cologne made Alba's nose itch, but she resisted rubbing it. The cheap scent reminded her of those TV commercials promising that women would throw themselves at any man who wore it—and she didn't need the drive over to confirm the scent didn't belong to Stephens.

"I'll ask you a few questions. If you don't remember just say so." Alba paused and waited for Fran to nod before continuing. "Do you know anyone who might have been angry with Michael? Any threats?"

Alba took in the surrounding room. It had a masculine vibe. Likely Michael's space. Extra care would be needed when they searched through it.

"Threats?" said Fran.

"Letters, phone calls where someone hangs up, text messages, social media posts, things like that."

"No, nothing that I am aware of."

"Who do you think could have done this?"

"I honestly don't know. Michael's greatest joy was making the store successful...hardly what creates enemies."

Alba agreed it seemed unlikely, but still she hoped Stephens was noting it down.

"What would bring Michael to that area of town so early in the morning?"

"I...I don't know... I can't think. I woke up that morning, and he wasn't there."

"Was that normal?"

"I wouldn't say it was normal, but it happened. He was busy with the store, coming home late, leaving early. It's hard to run a small business these days."

Alba kept her face neutral. Michael's movements were already under investigation, and the superintendent would not thank her for pushing on that right now. Better to come back when she had something more concrete.

Fran heaved out an enormous sigh. "I just can't think what he was doing there. None of his suppliers are in that area of town. I suppose he could have had an order. It seems unlikely because of the time of day. Do you...do you think Michael was coming back from seeing someone..."

Okay, they were going there. Alba guessed the superintendent would not be happy with this line of inquiry. She just hoped Stephens recorded Fran started it.

"Do you have any reason to think that he was having an affair?"

"He valued our family." Fran's laugh stuttered. "I'm sure you've heard countless spouses say the same." She picked at one of her nails. "Will you let me know?"

Alba looked at her pale face. Even if she didn't the superintendent probably would. "We'll let you know everything we can."

"An answer that's no answer."

Alba opened her mouth, but before she could say anything, Fran waved her hand, swatting the words away. They examined each other for a moment.

Alba took a breath. She had a job to do.

"Did Michael have any vices...gambling, drinking?"

"He was a happy drinker, but nothing excessive. He didn't gamble, except maybe to play the lottery. He made those impossible bottles. I just can't imagine him...."

Alba could see a few ships in bottles scattered around the room. They actually looked kind of cool. Maybe that is what she needed, a hobby.

Alba attempted to moisten her mouth and push the image of the superintendent looming over her out of her mind. "Can you tell me where you were that morning?"

Fran suddenly seemed to have a blood flow and breathing issue. Alba was considering organising help when Fran took a breath, and some colour came back into her face.

"In bed." Fran dropped the nail she had ripped off and moved on to the next fingertip.

"What time did you wake up?"

"I'm not sure, sorry. I didn't think to look at the clock."

Alba was glad Stephens was taking this down. Well, she assumed he was. Unless he was writing poetry to himself. Who knew?

Focus, Alba.

"You didn't check the clock on a Monday morning?" Alba kept her voice calm and professional.

Fran stared at her. "If I did, I don't remember."

"Okay, what did you do after waking up?"

"I had coffee."

"And after coffee?" Alba tried to swallow back a sharp retort. She wasn't sure if Fran was being obstructive or actually struggling. Though she wasn't exactly giving off the vibes of a grieving widow.

"I made coffee, I checked some emails and made some breakfast until someone came to tell me that my husband was dead and interrupted my morning. Is that enough detail for you?"

Lie.

Alba decided to leave it for now—better to return with more specific questions. She stood and walked with Fran back to rejoin the group. Stephens didn't bother rising, simply remaining in his chair as he scribbled notes to himself. Back in the living room, Alba noticed Ms. Roberts had gone. No doubt she'd left satisfied with whatever damage she'd inflicted.

She looked at the two younger members of the group but they looked about as useful as decaf. The man who spoke when she came in, if her guess was right, was the cousin Gregory. Her brain had kicked in and she remembered his wife was the tall woman Hilary, a lawyer, and that meant the big man was probably her brother Alfie, the other lawyer. She wouldn't get anything useful out of them.

"Gregory, would you mind if we spoke next?"

Her guess was correct and the smaller man pushed himself off the couch, checked his hair and tugged his jacket as he walked towards her. It surprised her that Hilary and Alfie didn't object, but they seemed more focused on Fran.

Once they were in the home office, Gregory sat down. His face settled into an expression mixed with concern and knowing.

"Gregory, I've a few questions about Michael."

"I'm sure you do." Gregory sat forward in his seat and started talking.

Alba had always admired some people's remarkable talent for turning half an hour into absolutely nothing—a skill Gregory had clearly mastered. Despite his verbal marathon, one thing became crystal clear—Gregory thought he was the most important person in Michael's life. But there was no hint of an affair in his epic monologue.

She met with Sam and Alex, who obviously held their parents in affection but had little to do with their lives beyond the occasional Sunday family catchup.

Hilary Jones and Alfie Jones, unsurprisingly, refused to say anything and apparently represented Michael and his business. A severe conflict of interest. Still, everyone seemed to just accept it as routine.

Fucking small towns.

She wondered if Ms Roberts had more luck.

The sun might have been out, but the wind was biting. They returned to the police station and she hoped everyone, including Stephens, was ready to get out into the cold and talk to potential witnesses.

She now had Stephens and four constables, whom he introduced in something of a blur as Clair Grimaud, Kabir Ceesay, Irena Kotowska and Zarab Beitean. Maybe she could bribe Stephens to keep using their full names until she remembered them.

They went through what the constables had collected so far, which wasn't much. Apparently, a Monday winter morning wasn't a time for people to be out and about. Most of the locals didn't even open their shops until lunchtime if they weren't hibernating for the winter.

"Constable Ceesay, are you seriously fucking telling me that after five hours of canvassing yesterday," Alba started pacing the room they had commandeered for the investigation, "We don't even have a list of everyone in the area." She spun around and stared at her senior constable who was meant to be supervising them. "Stephens, what were you doing? Sucking on your thumb?"

Stephens looked at her over his reading glasses, channelling librarians through the centuries. "We just aren't sure if we have everyone. Some places are closed. Makes it difficult to identify owners...let alone potential employees."

Constable Ceesay threw a grateful look towards Stephens, then immediately turned back to her, practically vibrating with energy. He kept shifting his weight from foot to foot, his pen tapping against his notepad. At barely five-foot-six, he had to crane his neck to see over the taller officers, but his eagerness was unmistakable. She'd seen that hungry look before—ambitious constables who thought a high-profile case would fast-track their careers. Right now, his overenthusiasm wasn't earning him any recommendations from her.

His partner, Claire Grimaud, presented a stark contrast. Where Ceesay buzzed with nervous energy, Claire had withdrawn into herself. She stood with her shoulders curved inward, trying to make her tall form smaller.

The other two were handling the situation more appropriately. Irene Kotowska moved methodically through her interview notes, her pale hair catching what little winter sun made it through the window as she leaned against the wall. Next to her, Zarab Beitean's bright eyes tracked every movement in the room, his colourful mohawk somehow not diminishing his professional appearance. Between them, they'd gathered twice as many statements as the other pair, their notebooks filled with careful observations rather than scattered excitement.

Alba stretched her neck and tried to focus. She would just have to double-check everything. She hated being new, relying on a bunch of inexperienced constables and a senior who wanted to stay behind his desk. She didn't know if finding the owners was actually hard, or if they just didn't give a shit. Or worse, they were working to cover this whole thing up and protect a local like Fran. She tried to push the thought out of her mind, but it hung on and niggled at her.

Fuck.

So, they had a list of people who were nowhere near the area at the time of the attack and had seen nothing. You had to start somewhere, right?

She led them through mapping out the area on the board they had set up and identified ten shops and four offices that they hadn't yet been able to talk to. It was getting close to closing time, so Alba made them all, including Stephens, head out to Merchant's Lane to see if they could capture a witness.

Alba had taken all the shops that opened onto or backed onto Merchant's Lane. She looked at the list and realised that the store next to the Book Distillery was the Mad Cutter, the local barbershop owned by the superintendent's husband.

She stifled a groan and climbed out of the car. The others had split off to different stores—conveniently. Alba looked over at Stephens, wrapped up and shivering like he would die of the cold and obviously incapable of purchasing appropriate clothing for the town he had lived in for over a decade.

The Mad Cutter was open, so she decided to get it over and done with. Stephens shuffled along behind her and she was pretty sure he was using her as a windshield.

The door jangled as she pushed it open, and she looked up to see a string of bells used by shop owners worldwide.

"Mr Amos Beeching?"

A man who appeared to be in the middle of cleaning up, with a perfectly manicured grey beard and moustache looked over at them. His thick eyebrows lowered over his eyes as he took them in. "About time."

They examined each other and she found herself suppressing the urge to straighten her clothes.

"Mr Beeching—"

"It could've been me." His breathing sped up. "I'd planned to come in early that morning, did you know that?"

She wasn't sold on the random killing idea, and the attack had occurred at the other end of the laneway. If they had wanted to kill him surely they would have been closer to his shop?

"What time did you arrive?" she asked, trying to keep her voice soothing.

"About eight." Amos peered out his door into the laneway as if expecting the murderer to reappear.

"Did you see any strange cars or people around?"

She watched him note the other officers on the street. A pity it wasn't him who discovered the body. He seemed like someone who noticed things certainly more so than Ms Roberts, though that wasn't hard.

"A lot of police." His lips stretched thin in what Alba hoped was an attempt at a smile. "Are they strange enough for you?"

She gave him one of her new cards with her name, rank and phone number on it. "If you think of anything let me know."

"Humph." Amos slammed down the plastic container he was holding. "So you want me to do your job for you. How refreshingly honest of you."

He took the card and what looked like glee lit up his face. Her stomach dropped. Out of the corner of her eye she saw Stephens shake his head for a second before coughing and playing with his notebook.

"I'll call you, don't you worry about that." Amos looked down at the card and smiled.

At least she hadn't given him her mobile number.

After a few more questions that clarified that Amos had seen nothing, Stephens and Alba left.

"You're going to regret that," said Stephens.

Alba preferred to pretend it hadn't happened.

They visited a jewellery shop, a couple of art galleries, a milliner's, a music store and a handful of clothing boutiques. And all they established was that everyone slept in on cold winter mornings.

Stephens was going to follow up on the closed ones. Alba tried not to feel frustrated that this hadn't already been done. What had they been doing with their time? But it wouldn't help to go hard on them. Not yet anyway.

By the time it was six o'clock, Alba realised she was getting nowhere and hadn't eaten all day. She gazed up at the sky. Darkness gazed back at her.

Maybe she just didn't have it in her anymore. If she'd arrived brimming with enthusiasm, she might have inspired them, lifted them up. Instead, they were leeches draining her dry. They all stood around while staring glumly at their notepads. When they looked up, she could feel them ready to shift any blame to her shoulders.

7

Greer

The evening rush finished and Greer moved on to her least favourite job, packing away books that weren't selling.

"The police are back," said Victoria. "Probably here to arrest you."

Greer sighed as she glimpsed Inspector Mauzer and Senior Constable Stephens walking down Park Passage, heading for the Book Distillery's front door.

"Thank you for your vote of confidence," said Greer.

"Only a matter of time before you showed your stripes." Victoria gave a loud sniff. "Must admit, I thought you would commit fraud or something, not murder. Just goes to show it can always be worse."

Greer gave an exasperated growl and glared at her. "I didn't kill anyone."

"Glad to hear it," said the inspector.

Greer looked up to find her and Stephens standing in front of them.

"Ms Roberts, would you mind if we talked?" The inspector glanced around at the empty shop and then back at her, the expectation of Greer making herself available clear on her face.

"You aren't here to arrest her?" asked Victoria, peering at the inspector.

"No, Ms...?"

"Victoria and you don't need to know more than that."

"Good evening, Ms Howard," said Stephens, his face in its usual mournful arrangement.

"Oh Hugh, why did you do that?" said Victoria with something of a grin. "Now the fuzz knows my name."

Greer looked at Victoria and Stephens, whose expression wavered to allow a small smile to appear.

For all that was good, please no.

While Stephens was an older man, Greer calculated he was still ten years younger than Victoria. He stepped up to the counter and leaned against it.

"So, you don't think she's good for it?" asked Victoria.

Stephens shook his head. The inspector's frown deepened.

"Ms Roberts is being treated as a witness," said the inspector.

"She's guilty of something," said Victoria.

"Most people are." Stephens exhaled loudly. "Most people are."

Impatience flashed across the inspector's face. "I want to talk to—"

"She's not the only possibility, mind," said Victoria. "Did she tell you about how Michael ripped off Kendall Styles?"

Greer wanted to roll her eyes and tell them all to get out of her shop, but she forced herself to carefully place the book in her hand in the box in front of her. She reached in to check they were all aligned properly—spines flush, covers straight.

"Kendall Styles?" asked the inspector, veering to look over at Greer. "No, she didn't mention it."

"What's Kendall got to do with it?" asked Stephens. He crossed his arms and his face once more moved out of neutral. Though this time it wasn't to smile.

Victoria dropped her eyes and fiddled with a pen at the counter. "Well, we were out for a drink the other day."

Stephens was practically a statue now. Depressing to realise that her seventy-something shop assistant was getting more action than she was.

"Did you?" said Stephens. Victoria straightened and looked Stephens right in the eye.

"Yes, I did, and it was lovely. We had prosecco, a pleasant change from beer."

"Prosecco's very nice," said the inspector. "But if you could skip to how this applies to the case."

Victoria, an advocate for straight-talking, nodded. "Michael cleaned out Kendall's garage for a couple of thousand—had pieces valued at only a few hundred each." She leaned forward and stabbed the counter with her finger.

"Week later, Kendall saw one of his pieces at a friend's house. The friend paid over a thousand for just that one."

The inspector's gaze tracked Victoria's finger. "We'll look into it, see if it's anything."

"If?" Victoria stood up, her eyes wide.

"Ms Roberts, if we could talk?" The inspector's gaze flicked towards Victoria. "Privately?"

Greer glanced outside into the dark and the long day dragged down on her. "Can this wait until tomorrow?"

"It'd be better now." The inspector tapped her fingers against her thigh.

"I'd feel uncomfortable leaving Victoria here alone."

A weak excuse, especially considering Victoria often opened and closed the store—one of Greer's favourite things about her.

"Stephens will get her home safely." The inspector stood there like an immovable wall. "I'll take you to the station."

"I'm not going to the station tonight." Greer stood there, arms crossed, pretty sure that the inspector couldn't force her unless she made it formal.

"Greer...this is a murder investigation." Stephens gazed at her with mild rebuke.

Greer's cheekbones heated. She knew that, however didn't see why she should be the one to suffer.

"How about the Trattoria?" He turned towards the inspector. "It's Tuesday night and quiet. If you sit near the back, no one will overhear you."

The inspector shot a look at him. "Do you usually go to dinner with suspects in Lakes End Senior Constable?"

"I don't think the superintendent would mind, Inspector. In fact, I think he would consider it an excellent compromise."

The inspector gave a grunt.

"So, what is it to be, Ms Roberts? Italian or the station?"

If she had to talk to the police, food would undoubtedly dull the pain.

"The Trattoria," said Greer. Added bonus—a full mouth meant no talking

As Stephens had predicted, the restaurant sat largely empty. The only diners clustered at the front, gazing out over the darkening waters as the sun slipped behind the mountains. They chose a back booth giving them a clear view of the whole restaurant without putting themselves on display.

"Good evening, my name's Drew," said a young man in a server's uniform who placed a basket of bread and small bowls of balsamic vinegar and olive oil on the table. "Would you like to start with some wine?"

Greer's stomach gave a hollow twist. When had she last eaten? Had she had anything other than coffee, tea and doughnuts? The scent of garlic and herbs wafting through the restaurant made her mouth water.

"Good evening, Drew. I'd like a small insalata di rinforzo and the fish." Greer turned to Alba, who was looking at her like she was some sort of alien. "The fish's always fresh, and they make the rinforzo salad up of—"

"I know what a rinforzo salad is," said the inspector. She turned to Drew. "I'll have a glass of Sangiovese and a main course lasagne."

Greer heard herself saying, "They make large portions here. Perhaps you would be better to get the entrée."

"I'm familiar with the difference between an entrée and a main."

Even though Greer could feel it happening, she couldn't stop it. Her eyes dropped to the inspector's slightly overweight body. Greer's cheeks burned, and she pulled her eyes back up to the inspector's face, hoping it had gone unnoticed.

Not taking her eyes off Greer, the inspector reached for the bread and tore off a piece, dipping it into olive oil and balsamic vinegar before ripping into it with her teeth.

Greer added a glass of Vermentino to her order as well.

Her fingers turned her own piece of bread into breadcrumbs. The unwavering stare was a bit off-putting, though Greer knew she only had herself to blame. The wine arrived. Picking up her glass, Greer tasted it and waited for the inspector to speak.

"So," said the inspector, picking up her glass. "What made you go to Fran's?"

Greer wondered why she had ordered two courses. Could she let Drew know she wanted it all brought out together without it being even more awkward?

"I know Fran. I suppose I felt a duty to check on her," said Greer, taking a large mouthful of wine.

"Is it too much to hope that you didn't give them a detailed account?"

"I was discrete," said Greer, using the glass to cover her face as she drank some more wine. "Broad facts only, going to work...found the body, Michael...called police."

"Remember, you're the only person we can put in the lane...not to mention your fingerprints on the body."

Greer realised she had almost finished her wine and looked for Drew. He was leaning against the bar, texting on his phone. With the sixth sense of servers, he looked up and, seeing her almost empty glass, pulled a bottle out of the fridge and headed her way. Maybe this was her chance. She just didn't know how to do it without being obvious.

"More, my lady?" He gave a broad smile and a slight bow, holding out the bottle.

"Yes, thanks," Greer smiled at him and was just working out what to say when the inspector solved her problem.

"Just bring all the food out at once."

There was something to be said for getting straight to the point.

"So before drinking the entire bottle," the inspector eyed her glass, which was already lower than the level Drew had poured. "I need you to tell me what Fran told you or anything else the family might have said."

"Is this an official statement?" asked Greer, gulping more of her wine. Would she be throwing Fran under the bus by revealing what she had observed? What if Fran had in fact murdered Michael?

"This is sharing information. If I need you to make an official statement, you can come into the station..." The inspector's eyes tracked Greer's wine glass as it lifted. "Tomorrow."

Perhaps the second glass was a mistake.

"I would say that Fran and Michael hadn't been close for a while. I would also say that they were sleeping in separate beds and that she knew he hadn't come home that morning. Something she was used to."

"Why do you say that?"

Greer almost put her wineglass down in the pile of crumbs she had created.

"She was sad, not surprised."

Putting the glass to the side, she tried to gather up the crumbs but gave up and dusted off her hands over the floor. Drew, after a look at the mess Greer had made, brought out a small dustpan to take the crumbs away. Once the table was cleaned up, he laid out their food. They were silent as they ate.

She finished her salad and ate some of the fish before picking up her wineglass again. She watched the inspector put away a significant amount of lasagne, pausing only to eat some more bread. By the time the inspector had stopped eating, Greer was onto her third glass of wine. She really should have just gotten the bottle.

"What makes you think they were sleeping in separate beds?" asked the inspector, sitting back and resting her hand on her stomach. "It looked like they were both in the main bedroom to me."

The last time she had seen anyone eat that volume of cheese, meat, and processed carbs, she had been with her brother.

"She said she checked on him in the morning, but he wasn't there," said Greer. "Why would she check in on him if they were in the same bed?"

"More something a parent would say," said the inspector.

"Exactly."

"Do you think Michael was having an affair?" The inspector took another small sip of her wine.

"If you mean a sexual relationship with another woman, I'm not sure." Greer pushed some of the fish around on her plate. "If you mean fully committing his time and energy to something other than his marriage, then yes."

"What could do that, other than sex?"

"Power, money, ambition. For some, it is even a need to help others."

"Sex is more common." The inspector tapped the side of her glass but didn't drink any more of it.

"It isn't sex itself," said Greer, giving up on her fish and settling back in her chair holding her wine. "It's how it makes you feel. Connected, powerful or accepted."

'So, which was it?'

"If I had to guess…" Greer examined the inspector across from her and what appeared to be the genuine interest in her expression. "I'd say power."

"Power?" The inspector's gaze shifted over the empty tables in the restaurant to the lake beyond. "Why would he run a gift shop in a small town if he wanted power?" She turned back to Greer, her expression expectant.

"Maybe he had dreams that got lost along the way. The kids have been independent for years now...could have been the trigger."

"An affair is more likely."

Greer shrugged and polished off her wine while the inspector finished her meal. All the better if the inspector didn't value her opinion

"Anything else?" asked the inspector.

Greer, ready for this evening to be over, felt she had done enough damage.

"No."

The inspector drained her glass. "Stay away from Fran and the family." She stood and left.

At least she paid her half.

Stars pricked the sky above the mountain ridgeline. The shops sat dark and shuttered for the night. Streetlight carved harsh shadows against the sandstone buildings, turning familiar doorways strange. Walking alone probably wasn't brilliant, but the cold air felt good against her wine-flushed skin.

Greer stopped to check the bookstore was locked up and found Victoria still there sans Stephens.

"So, what did she want?" asked Victoria.

"Just to know why I was at Fran's," said Greer. "I thought you were going home or that Stephens was going to stay here."

"He was annoying. I sent him away." Victoria stopped whatever she was doing and examined Greer. "I'm surprised she didn't ask for your help."

"Well, she didn't, and even if she did, I wouldn't." Greer tried to suppress the memory of having already said too much. In hindsight, she probably would have been better off just going to the station.

"So what?" Victoria threw her hands in the air. "You're just going to hide here?"

"I don't think running this bookstore and hanging out with you is hiding." Greer couldn't help the smile that broke across her face. "It's the best part."

"It's alright." A flicker of affection crossed Victoria's face. She shook her head. "I'm just not sure it is enough for you."

Greer raised an eyebrow. "Right. Have you been into the wine? You're getting awfully deep."

"Since I heard you making the wrong decision." Victoria turned away from Greer and got back to typing on the computer in front of her.

Greer tried to channel Yoda and look wise, measuring out her next words. "There are no wrong decisions, only different paths."

Victoria kept typing. Her humour really was wasted here. Still, Victoria had her opinions—she always did. However Greer was choosing the life she wanted, not the life others thought she should have.

"What are you working on?" asked Greer.

"Finishing the newsletter." Victoria flicked her a glance. "You remember we work here, right?"

"Let's close up and head home." Greer looked around the empty store, taking in the velvet chairs tucked into their familiar nooks between the wooden shelves, each one waiting under its own pool of lamplight. Even without customers, the place somehow still had a warmth to it. "The world won't end if we send it out tomorrow." There were some advantages of being the boss.

Greer turned down Victoria's offer of a lift. She needed her walk home. Greer lengthened her stride and let her arms swing freely. The only difference from last week was that she kept to the lit streets and took a shorter route.

Even the evening walkers were gone by the time she closed her front door behind her. Another long day. Greer smiled as Miles thundered towards her. There was something healing about being welcomed home with such enthusiasm. She sat on the floor and cuddled him while he head-butted her chin and smooched the side of his mouth across it, leaving a trail of drool behind. As gross as it was, Greer's body lightened.

She put food out for Miles and headed into her book room. A freestanding antique bar decorated with a whisky decanter and crystal glasses stood next to the couch. She poured herself a generous glass and softened it with a splash of water.

After she stretched out on the couch, Miles joined her, settling against her legs like a warm, breathing anchor. He only shifted when her hand stilled, tapping her wrist with one demanding paw until the pats resumed. With her free hand she picked up a book, however the words swam on the page refusing to stick. She gave up, letting the book slip to the floor, and just lay there in the lamplight, her fingers moving through Miles' coat while her mind churned over the last two days.

What had Michael been doing in the laneway? He must have been meeting someone. An affair? It didn't fit what she knew of him, though maybe he'd found someone who shared his ambitions more than Fran did. He might have craved connection beyond Gregory.

Greer tried picturing Fran smashing Michael in the head. Similar height, she could reach. But an over the hill woman who hadn't seen a gym in decades? It would take serious adrenaline to do that kind of damage.

She closed her eyes and visualised the town, moving the people around like little chess pieces, until eventually she dragged herself to bed in the wee hours.

The next morning she rushed her coffee and made it to the bookstore with no detours, arriving even before Victoria. Not that Victoria had cared. Sometimes Greer wondered if Victoria would just keep turning up and running the place if she weren't there at all.

"Would you stop?"

Greer looked over at Victoria in surprise. "Stop what?"

"You've been acting like you have ants in your pants all morning. Either go for a run," Victoria snorted at Greer's flinch, "or something, anything to get you out of here."

Greer could feel the adrenaline, almost like little pops of light pumping through her, making it hard to concentrate.

"I can't. We've deliveries coming in," said Greer.

"I don't—"

The door opened, and they looked up to see Fran Williams entering the Book Distillery.

"Fran," said Greer, "what...brings you here?" The inspector would not be happy.

"I wanted to thank you for coming around yesterday. It's all been a bit of a shock, and I wanted...I want...can we talk?"

Fran stopped to take a deep, if ragged, breath.

Greer pushed the face of the grumpy inspector from her mind and focused on the distressed person in front of her. "How about a cup of tea?"

Fran adjusted her coat, pulling it tighter around her. "Yes, thank you, that would be nice."

Greer looked around the bookstore and realised that there was nowhere appropriate to sit. They set the bookstore up for reading, not conversation.

A few minutes later Greer found herself once more sitting at a booth at the Trattoria, which was in the middle of its breakfast rush. The coffee and tea weren't as good as Elvira's, but at least the booth's high back blocked most of the morning chaos—clatter of cutlery, the hiss of the coffee machine, someone's toddler having what appeared to be an existential crisis over pancakes. She pressed her back into the worn leather, grateful for anything that might absorb some of the tension from the last few days.

Greer ordered coffee, her one-a-day limit a thing of the past, while Fran asked for tea. The young waitress greeted them with kind but scattered attention, and Greer hoped she'd actually bring their order—she needed the caffeine to get through whatever this conversation would bring.

"I feel..." Fran frowned down at her hands. "Out of control...like everything is happening around me."

"What do you feel is out of your control?" It was one of those questions designed to make someone open up. Asking it had been instinctual—as was the regret that immediately followed for letting herself get drawn in.

"Everything...my family...the neighbourhood gossip...the investigation...all of it."

The circles under Fran's eyes were deeper than yesterday. But no matter how much Greer was moved by her grief she was already too involved.

"I'm afraid I am not necessarily the best person to assist you."

She glanced around for the server, but no coffee was in sight. You would think she had learnt by now. Order to go.

Fran took a deep breath and raised her eyes. "I heard they invited you to join the police investigation," she said in a rush.

"The gossip network in Lakes End got it the wrong way round." Greer exhaled through stiff lips. "The police have asked me to keep out of it."

The server finally came back and put the coffee and tea down in front of them.

Fran picked up her teacup and looked at it. "I'm sure you can imagine what people are saying about Michael."

"I don't think anyone, including the police, knows what happened to Michael."

"Which is worse." Fran's gaze appeared to be fused to her tea. "It means people are free to make up all kinds of sordid stories."

Greer contemplated how far her sense of obligation from the coincidence of discovering Michael's body stretched. "What about the superintendent?" she asked. "I thought the two of you were close?"

Fran's lips thinned further, and she placed the teacup back on the table, raising her gaze. "All he does is pat my hand and tell me not to worry about a thing. I don't trust him to control the new inspector he has hired."

"I'm sure—"

"Sam and Alex just want me to leave it to the police and play the grieving widow. But I feel more angry than sad. Angry that he did something that got him killed."

"What makes you think he did something?"

"People don't get killed the way he did without reason." Fran picked up her cup of tea again. "It wasn't like a car accident."

"I didn't know him well." Greer drank her coffee and regretted it as her empty stomach churned. She should buy breakfast. But the last thing she wanted was to get trapped here any longer. "What do you think motivated him?"

Fran took a sip of her tea. "Respect, money." Fran peered over the rim of her teacup. "He wanted to make a name for himself. To be known as successful. I just...lived life and forgot about the world outside Lakes End, but I don't think he did."

She sat there drinking her tea, looking out over the lake.

"Do you have anyone to help you...with everything?" Greer tried to keep her tone disinterested.

"Yes, Elvira, Gregory, Hilary, Sam, Alex, everyone's chipping in."

"I'm glad to hear."

At least she was not alone. Something she would not appreciate until later.

Fran turned her attention to Greer. "Will you, will you share with me anything you know?"

Greer's comments from the night before coated the inside of her mouth. "Yes...of course." One day she would learn just not to speak.

"Thank you."

"Please don't thank me." In fact, so far she had been the opposite. "I fear I'll not be helpful at all." Like making her a suspect to the police.

They said little after that. When they finished, they gave each other half hugs, and Fran headed down to the esplanade. Despite her churning stomach Greer ordered another coffee to take away. She needed something to wash away the taste.

The winter sun hit the town at an angle, leaving most of it in shadow while the lake caught the light. The familiar calm of the place settled into her as she walked. Most of the shops hadn't opened yet—they rarely opened before ten in summer, let alone winter. With no foot traffic, the only sound was wind off the lake and her own footsteps on the brick pavement. The dormant window boxes and closed shopfronts made everything seem smaller, quieter.

Her third coffee of the day went down too easily, guilt and caffeine mixing in her stomach. The disposable cup was nearly empty by the time she reached the bin at the laneway entrance. She should have brought her reusable cup, but here she was. The bin had one of those annoying narrow slots that made you lean in awkwardly. As she angled forward an incredible weight came crashing down on her shoulder.

Greer hit the ground hard, rolling instinctively onto her good side as she tried to protect her head and catch sight of her attacker. Through the haze of pain shooting through her shoulder, she glimpsed a dark figure vanishing around the corner. Was this punishment for not using her reusable cup?

With her legs too wobbly to stand, she stayed on the ground, not quite in the gutter, but close. She used her wristwatch to call an ambulance. Exhausted by that herculean effort, she focused on not moving. She focused on staying still and lost track of time until a voice cut through her shock.

"Ms Roberts."

She tilted her head up. Despite what she thought of her, relief rolled through her at the sight of the inspector's visage.

"Inspector," said Greer. Her voice rasped as fatigue and pain ran alongside the adrenaline and coffee in her veins. Greer shifted and gritted her teeth. Where was that ambulance?

"Can you tell me what happened?"

"Someone hit me from behind.," said Greer, wishing she had something to lean her head against.

"Ms Roberts," the inspector tsked. "You've reasonable powers of observation."

Was that a compliment? Good thing she was already sitting down.

"Even I don't have eyes in the back of my head."

The inspector gave a grunt which might have been a laugh.

"Tell me what you remember. I'll work out what's useful."

"I'd bought a coffee at the Trattoria. I hadn't planned to, so I purchased a coffee in a disposable cup."

The inspector just nodded and started taking notes.

"I went to throw my coffee cup in that bin." Greer moved a finger on her right hand. "Those small openings mean you have to lean in a bit to do it. That's when I felt something strike me on the shoulder. I collapsed to the ground and rolled, trying to see who was attacking." Greer was pretty sure it was more a flip-flop, however if this was going in a public record roll sounded much better. "I saw a figure in shadow before they disappeared. I couldn't even tell you whether it was a man or a woman."

"Just one person, though?"

"Yes, that I saw anyway. The only thing I can tell you is they were wearing dark pants and a long jacket, and their height was about twenty bricks up in that building. It could be plus or minus a brick. It's all fuzzy."

The inspector's lips twitched. "Your fuzzy isn't half bad."

An ambulance appeared, coming in at speed around the corner and pulled up next to them. Lucinda and Isaac jumped out.

"Well, well, if it isn't our very own book pusher." Lucinda crouched down next to her. "Is this where I ask what the other guy looks like?" She glanced briefly around as if looking for someone.

Greer winced. "Please, Lucinda, have pity on me. Bad things have happened to my shoulder."

"Book pusher." Isaac shoved his sister out of the way and started the examination. "Why am I constantly being called to a scene with you in this lane? You belong in the bookstore surrounded by velvet"—Greer smiled—"and soft furnishings, with all the edges padded."

He always had to ruin it.

The inspector's face almost made Greer laugh.

"Now Greer," said Lucinda. "I thought we had discussed this. It is important to check your shelf before you wreck your shelf."

Isaac laughed and high-fived her.

"No, no book puns. I'm in a fragile state," said Greer.

"Of course, of course, my sweet," Isaac cooed and continued to work at pulling off her coat.

Lucinda squatted next to Greer with her pack open at her feet. "Do you know why books are so annoying to be around?"

"No, and I don't want to," said Greer.

"They don't have any shelf awareness," said Isaac. He and Lucinda giggled. She wondered how many times they had told that joke.

"Inspector. Do you have a gun?" asked Greer.

"Please don't shoot him, Inspector," said Lucinda. "I need him. He is the only one who laughs at my jokes."

"Isn't that saying something?" Greer frowned at Isaac, who was now poking around at her shoulder. Whatever numbness the shock had provided was wearing off, and her stomach churned.

"Now, Greer, remember I have this super nice painkiller here," said Lucinda, holding up a pack of tablets.

Greer stared at the painkillers with longing.

"A pretty bad dislocation," said Isaac and Greer groaned.

"Right, back to the hospital before you swell up like a balloon," Lucinda jumped up and pointed her hand in the air. "With haste."

"Did you know..." asked Isaac as he helped Greer stand. "They say dragons sleep during the day so they can fight knights?"

Greer moaned this time, and not just from physical pain. She thought she heard the inspector laugh at that one.

"Why did the book go to the hospital?" Isaac's gaze flicked between Greer and the inspector as he and Lucinda helped Greer into the ambulance. "It had to get its appendix removed."

"No," Greer and the inspector responded at the same time.

Isaac grinned and patted Greer's hair. It was comforting, even if he was a punning dufus.

"We're good to go." Lucinda closed the doors.

Isaac held her other arm and monitored her heart rate and breathing while Lucinda got the ambulance on the road again. They didn't put the sirens on, greatly reducing their chances of getting a laugh out of her.

8

Alba

The attack on Ms Roberts showed an unwarranted level of desperation. Just the wrong place at the wrong time? Or something more?

She was missing something. A few more hours of questioning spectacularly unobservant shop owners and analysing CCTV footage that showed nothing but an indistinct flicker—possibly human, probably useless—had gotten her nowhere.

All they'd done was ramp up the fear among the locals. The superintendent was not happy. Alba ran her fingers through her hair for what felt like the millionth time and took a deep breath.

Her phone rang, and the system identified the number as the business contact for the Mad Cutter. She sent it to voicemail to join three other missed calls.

"You're going to hyperventilate if you keep sighing like that," said Stephens.

"And...to be honest...you're stressing me out."

Alba glared at her computer. "Fuck this case."

"It sucks all right," said Stephens, lounging back in his chair and swinging side to side. "Much easier when they're still holding the murder weapon."

Alba transferred the glare to him.

He shrugged. "And I don't think rereading the same reports is helping."

It almost hurt that she agreed with him. "Then we need to get out there again."

Stephens groaned.

"That's what we do." Alba sat back in her chair. His desire to avoid fieldwork was almost comical. But it was also getting in the way of their closing this. "We trudge around, knock on doors until our knuckles bleed, and if we still come up empty...we twiddle our thumbs until someone else gets murdered or we file it under 'unsolved mysteries' and pretend we never cared anyway."

"We have a second crime." Stephens' face shifted to a deeper layer of glum.

"Which apparently still gives us nothing," said Alba, trying to stop her lip from curling back in a snarl. "And...why attack her? What does she know or what does the killer think she know?" Alba rose to her feet. "Let's go."

Stephens' stooped shoulders stooped even further.

Alba ignored his physical plea not to go outside and grabbed her coat. "She should be out of emergency by now.

After that, I want to talk to every shop owner we listed as away or closed."

She led the way out. The wind had picked up again and Stephens followed with a heavy plod.

"We need underground parking," said Stephens in a high-pitched tone that Alba labelled whining.

"The car's right here," said Alba, enjoying the scent of water in the air.

"If I get ill from this, I'm putting in a safety incident form, just so you know."

Alba unlocked the car and looked over its roof at Stephens. She had only one rule with cold weather.

"Are you cold?" she asked.

Stephens glared at her as he pulled another scarf out of his pocket and wound it around his face. "Yes, Inspector, I'm cold."

"Do you know that clothing exists that can keep you warm at this temperature?" asked Alba.

Stephens ignored her and pulled out a beanie, which he put on his head and attempted to pull down until it was in contact with his scarf. Once it was down as far as it would go, he wrapped his arms around himself, looking at her with accusing eyes.

Alba looked around. The wind was whipping at the trees and the clouds had covered the sun. "I know that there is. Therefore, I would suggest, Senior Constable Stephens, that you invest in some appropriate clothing for the location you have chosen to live."

Alba glanced across the car to find Stephens had not waited for her speech but was already in the car with its doors closed.

The hospital was a large brick building on the main road coming into town, which also serviced the smaller communities that peppered the shores of Lake Divan. As Alba drove in, she ignored the larger parking complex and took a spot in the short-term section near the main entrance. Stephens shuffled off towards the doors, but Alba had to double back as she had forgotten to put her police car sign on the dashboard again. It was always safest to assume Jeffrey was watching.

With the car now safe from being ticketed, they entered the hospital to find Ms Roberts, examined, drugged, and her shoulder manipulated back into place, assigned a bed in the general ward. A lift and two long corridors later, Alba nodded at the constable on duty. At least the superintendent had taken her concerns seriously, though she couldn't help noting the constable didn't ask to see her identification.

Alba hadn't missed that Greer Roberts favoured old-style clothes and bright colours that seemed slightly out of place in the casual Lakes End community. She had also noted that Ms Roberts went in for highly controlled waves in her hair and well-applied makeup—a level of effort that struck Alba as excessive. But then, Alba thought ironing was excessive.

Today however it was all stripped away.

Ms Roberts lay there with her eyes closed, wearing a pale hospital gown that had possibly once had a colour, surrounded by white sheets and white walls. Her black hair seemed to highlight the paleness in her ordinarily rich skin tone. For a moment, Alba thought she was looking at a corpse.

A rush of sound from orderlies, nurses and doctors at work followed them into the room through the open door and Ms Robert's eyelids lifted.

Looking at her, Alba wanted to say, sorry, I couldn't solve this fast enough. Sorry you ended up here.

"Did they give you the good drugs?" asked Alba. She had been twelve when she had dislocated her knee during a soccer game, and the years had done little to dull the memory of the pain.

"Yes, the lovely Dr Yardley has been checking on me regularly and has given me some very nice drugs."

Alba bet he had. She had forgotten he worked at the local hospital a couple of days a week. Still, that wasn't her problem. Murder, and attempted murder, were.

"Are you up for some questions?" Alba realised she had forgotten her tablet, so took out her pen and an old-fashioned notepad.

"I want this person found as much as you do." Ms Roberts gestured rather regally Alba thought, towards the only seat in the room. Stephens left the chair to Alba and went over to a heating vent.

"We need to go over what happened again," said Alba. She looked at Ms Roberts and paused. "Are you sure you are up for this?"

Ms Roberts smiled at them. "No need to tread lightly. Fire away." Alba watched as Ms Roberts pressed buttons until her bed had her sitting up.

How heavy was this medication?

"What led to your being in the laneway this morning?" asked Alba.

"I'd just arrived at work when..." her fingers plucked at the sheet, and her gaze flicked towards the door, "Fran came by to talk."

"Fran," said Alba. She kept her voice neutral and left sharing what she thought about that for later.

"Yes." Ms Roberts rested her head back against the pillow and closed her eyes. "She wanted to talk, wanted help."

"Did you offer any?" Out of the corner of her eye, Alba could see Stephens taking notes on his tablet, so she just focused on the unreliable woman in front of her.

"No, just an ear." She gave a wry smile. "Too hypocritical of me to pretend to offer more."

"After that?"

"We left the trattoria. I watched Fran walk down to the esplanade, and I headed back to the bookstore." Her mouth twisted, but she opened her eyes and stared directly at Alba. "And at the entrance to Merchant's Lane someone attacked me."

"There was no one else around?"

"No, it was pretty quiet, not unusual."

A summer town closed down by winter.

"Might I suggest you keep out of the laneway?" Surely she could start entering her store from the front for a while? Some self-preservation would help.

"I should start sleeping in." Ms Roberts gave a soft chuckle. "Avoid the morning rush of attacks."

Alba surprised herself with a laugh. "You've my permission to sleep in every morning until we solve this."

Ms Roberts gave her something of a smile. "Thanks. Can I have a note to give to my accountant?"

Alba gravely wrote out the note, handing it over to her. The laughter put more colour in Ms Roberts' cheeks.

"I promise to be a good citizen." Ms Roberts sat up and awkwardly used one hand to shove the note in her phone case.

"Can you describe the attack again?"

"I leant forward to throw my coffee cup away, and something landed on my shoulder. I hit the ground."

"So, at around nine-thirty in Merchants Lane, someone snuck up and potentially went to whack you on the head, missed and hit your shoulder instead." Which she already knew. This wasn't helping.

"Pretty much. I saw someone running away, a dark figure." She frowned and slumped slightly. "I keep running it through my mind trying to think of something, anything."

"What type of shoes did they have on?" Alba figured if anyone would notice someone's shoes it would be Ms Roberts, even if she was on the ground in pain.

A blank expression stared back at her. "Not heels."

No heels. Perhaps she should have been more specific in her wish for new information. Yet someone believed Ms Roberts knew something. If only they knew how little that was

"How long are they keeping you here?" asked Alba.

"They just took another scan. If it looks okay, I'll be home tonight."

"The question is, were they targeting you? Or did you interrupt something?" Right now Alba was thinking more the latter. "If they think you know something...well there's a concern about your safety."

"Yes, I can tell that by the fact you put Frank on the door."

Alba stared at her. Who else was getting involved in this? "Frank? Who's Frank?"

"The constable."

Which she should have known. Alba clicked her pen and frowned. "Yes, of course." She clicked her pen again. "We can organise a button."

"A button?" Ms Roberts blinked at her with a confused expression on her face.

"A wearable alarm, Stephens, can you..." Stephens stepped forward and handed Ms Roberts a chain with a fob and a big red button on it. "Do you just carry them around with you?' asked Alba.

"Figured you might want it," said Stephens, shuffling back to the heater and reminding her that despite his obsession with the weather, a competent police officer was hidden under the thick coat.

Ms Roberts looked at it, looked at Alba, and her eyebrows rose to an impressive height on her forehead. "This is my protection? You know that there have been technological advances in the last few decades, right?" She sat up higher and winced.

"Better than nothing," said Alba.

"Is it?" Ms Roberts stared down at the button in her hand, her expression dubious at best.

Clement's arrival stopped Alba from having to think up an answer.

"Greer, how are you feeling?" He turned towards the two police officers and raised his eyebrows when he spotted her. "Hi Alba."

He smiled at her. Alba did not smile back.

"Dr Yardley." She gave him a small nod. "We're here investigating the assault on Ms Roberts."

"So formal." He grinned. "You're rather dashing when you go all police inspector."

Stephens coughed and mumbled to himself and, thankfully, gave Alba a reason to look away from Clement.

Smiling, Clement turned towards his patient. "Okay, Greer, from what I can see, everything is looking good. Do you have your outpatient schedule?"

She nodded. "Thanks, Dr Yardley. I appreciate you looking after me so quickly."

"See you in two weeks," said Clement with a smile, and then he left the room to go save someone else.

"Need a lift?" asked Alba.

Ms Roberts blinked before shaking her head. "Thanks for the offer. I've called Victoria. She and Kendall are picking me up."

Stephens scowled.

"Right. The constable will follow you and check the house for you before you go in. Lock up and don't be afraid to press the button."

Clearly there was nothing useful to be found here. Alba gestured to Stephens and left.

When Alba returned to the police station, it was to find out her preliminary toxicology results were in. The forensic pathologist who had undertaken the autopsy was also ready to speak to her at her earliest convenience.

They had a traffic camera photo of Michael Williams in his car running a yellow light at quarter past six that morning. Significantly closing the potential time of death. Alba forced herself to send a silent thank you to Jeffrey and his anti-yellow light campaign.

Before she could call the pathologist, the superintendent signalled he wanted another update. Alba asked Stephens to pull together any reports or information that had come in from the other techs before heading into the superintendent's office.

"Do you have anything to report, Inspector?"

Alba shut the door behind her and carefully took a seat.

"The attack on Ms Roberts is a concern," said Alba.

Russell drummed his fingers on his desk. "How much danger do you think she's in?"

"Not sure." Alba leaned back in her seat. "I just can't work out why someone attacked her. She has no special knowledge. Sure, she discovered the body, but that could have been anyone. Maybe she discovered it earlier than expected? We have narrowed the time of death to between six fifteen and Ms Roberts stepping on the body."

A crease deepened on his forehead. "I don't want any harm to come to her on our watch."

"I've asked for a few more patrols near her house and Stephens gave her a duress alarm."

Russell frowned. "Will that be enough?"

Not unless he wanted to pay overtime.

"Unless you want to assign full-time protection—"

"What about Michael's murder?" he shot her a glare. "Any more progress there?"

Alba tensed and focused on the superintendent's forehead. "There might have been some dodgy business dealings."

Russell stilled. "When you say dodgy..."

"Some significant differences between the purchase and sale price of second-hand or antique goods. I suspect misrepresentation, possibly fraud."

Russell's face still didn't move. "Anything else?"

"Some rumours about an affair. I haven't any evidence."

He sighed and sat back in his chair.

"I expect this to be handled with care and respect, Inspector. I understand you need to follow those paths, but let's avoid any assumptions until we have more information."

Alba kept her gaze on the superintendent's forehead and concentrated on keeping her own face immobile.

"Yes sir. The pathologist is ready to give a verbal update on their findings. We also have some of the early toxicology reports back, which I'd like to review."

"Keep me in the loop. I've a lot of stakeholders to manage."

"Of course, sir." Alba stood up.

She pivoted and exited the office with hopefully the right balance between running and dawdling on the job. By the time she got back to her desk she had nailed the long strides of someone in control.

"Do you need to use the bathroom before we leave?" asked Stephens. He sat at his desk, his hands wrapped around a mug with steam coming out of it.

"No, thank you, Stephens." She would have to work on her stride later. "I'm fine, and we aren't going to the lab."

"The pathologist wants to give an update."

"There's this wonderful thing called technology."

Stephens, torn between disapproval and relief, divested himself of his outdoor clothes.

Ignoring two more missed calls from the Mad Cutter, Alba called the pathologist. The news wasn't great. Something heavy had clocked Michael Williams on the head. Something metal, or at least metal-adjacent. The bit that made contact had been curved with an edge—the techs reckoned ten to thirty centimetres and weighing one to three kilograms. Two blows had done the job. The only thing toxicology identified was more alcohol than you'd expect at dawn.

Michael was having an early celebration—or a very late one.

Regardless, a big load of niente.

After dumping the paperwork on Stephens and leaving the others to track Michael's movements from the night before, Alba fled the station.

Even though she had been here for a few months now, she hadn't really explored, too tired to feel much curiosity about the town she had chosen. Or fate had led her to.

When she had seen the advert for an inspector role a few months ago, her sole criteria had been that Lakes End was far enough away to avoid everyone. She had applied and been accepted with a minimum of fuss. A quick sale of her apartment, an even faster purchase of a car, and she had hit the highway.

Alba's feet took her down to the water's edge and its well-maintained esplanade. Despite a sense of a divide between the older and newer parts of town, the esplanade kept everyone connected.

The park across from the police station was crawling with lunchers, so Alba aimed for the smaller Broadview Park instead. Half-circle shaped and mercifully empty. The clouds were clearing, and as the trees came into focus, she let her pace drop from escape velocity to merely brisk.

She looked past the park towards an old two-storey building near the lake's shore split into four sections with wide verandas on both levels. Once upon a time, it might have accommodated stores or apartments. Today it was bars. Each with its own style and together the total of the town's nightlife. It was close enough to lunchtime that they were open. Tempted to stop and have a beer, Alba forced herself to turn away and find a bench. Sitting there, she let her mind go blank and gazed over the lake, enjoying the combination of sun and icy wind on her face. The trees creaked in the wind waving what few leaves they had left.

"It's a beautiful day, isn't it?"

Alba sighed and turned to see an elderly well-dressed gentleman with a cheerful smile take a seat next to her.

"Yes, it is."

The lake sparkling under the sun was almost sickeningly picturesque. She had never lived so close to water before, and she constantly noticed the scent. Presumably, one day it would just smell like home.

"I always love this time of year." He gazed out over the lake.

Alba followed his lead and looked at the water sparkling in the sunlight. She had nothing useful to add, so she arranged her face into something vaguely supportive.

"It's strange to me that this is when most people leave town." He glanced at her. "Are you visiting?"

She didn't think she gave off an approachable vibe. A lot of her colleagues had joked about her resting bitch face over the years. And yet, strangers walked right up to her. People were weird.

Alba didn't feel like making small talk. She just wanted to sit and be quiet for a moment. She imagined telling him to fuck off, but she took in his friendly countenance and couldn't bring herself to do it.

"I just moved here."

"How wonderful," he smiled at her, apparently genuinely happy she was now a resident. "Welcome." He held out his hand. "I'm Kendall. Pleasure to meet you."

Kendall, Kendall, where had she heard that name before?

"Alba," she shook his hand and gave him a reluctant smile, accepting she would not get out of this soon.

He looked at her quizzically. "As in Alba, the new Inspector Alba Mauzer?"

She stifled an exhale. She wasn't sure which was worse, the tenacity of her work or pocket-sized towns.

"That's me. Have we met?" Surely her brain hadn't gotten so bad she was forgetting faces too.

"No, no, but I believe you know my friend Victoria." His face glowed as he said her name but then the glow faded. "She told you what happened to me?"

Right. Kendall. Alba remembered now - something she'd meant to follow up before Greer Roberts had been knocked down. So much for lunch breaks.

"She did." Alba thought about dragging him down to the station, but he was here and talking. She pulled out her notebook. So much for time alone. "What happened exactly?"

Alba heard the story again from Kendall's perspective. The fundamental difference was that Victoria was apparently the most exemplary person ever. Since Alba had met Victoria, she took this with a grain of salt.

As Kendall talked, the sun ducked behind clouds and threw the park into shadow. The bare trees at the edge turned skeletal, like bones reaching out of the darkness with hollow spaces that could have been eyes. Alba shivered.

9

Greer

The mere click of her lock wasn't enough. Greer visualised all the moving parts fitting back into place, securing her from the rest of the world as Frank left. Hand still on the lock, she fumbled, triple-checking it with her one good arm. Miles sat on top of the fridge, glaring.

"I'm sorry, I didn't mean to get hit on the shoulder."

The cat huffed and turned his back to her.

Greer put her bag and phone on the kitchen bench and reached up to give him a soft pat on the back. He scooched further away from her. Best to ignore him until he got over his hissy fit.

She fumbled with her watch strap, her fingers still clumsy from the pain medication, and attached it and her phone to the chargers into the wall. A small red light blinked to life, a comforting pulse in the dim hallway. Even though the police had checked the house—tramping through with their heavy shoes and touching everything—she clutched the red *do not panic* button, as she had decided to call it, in her palm. Its smooth plastic surface already warming from her grip. The weight of it, no more than a matchbox, felt both reassuring and humiliating.

She shouldn't need this.

The stairs stretched above her like a mountain but she navigated them, driven by the need of a shower and clothes that weren't infused with that distinctive hospital smell—that nauseating cocktail of industrial disinfectant and something deeper, more organic that she could taste at the back of her throat.

The shower was a careful dance of hot water and awkward manoeuvring but getting dressed proved its own ordeal. Her injured shoulder protested as she wrestled with a fresh shirt. She finally dragged a chair from another room to lean against and when she managed to get fully dressed without toppling over, triumph bloomed warm in her chest. Such a small thing, but it felt like a minor victory worth celebrating.

Exhausted and famished, Greer headed downstairs but paused on the bottom step.

She glanced at her empty hand and tensed. The button was upstairs in the bathroom. For the first time her home with its floor-to-ceiling windows looking out over the lake left her feeling exposed rather than joyful.

She turned to go back upstairs and jumped at what sounded like a tree scraping at the window. Two steps later realisation struck—there weren't any trees near the house.

The sound of glass breaking cut through the silence and sent her scrambling. If she hadn't started sobbing, she would have screamed.

Greer clutched at the wall, struggling to remember which way the bathroom was. Heavy footsteps on the stairs cut through her confusion. This time she did scream, running into the bathroom and locking the door behind her.

The room was small enough to wedge her chair under the doorknob with its legs pressed up against the vanity. She tossed clothes and towels around until she saw a glimpse of red. She grabbed it and pressed it as if it was the only thing keeping her heart going. What sounded like a siege weapon rammed the door.

She gave a hoarse cry and looked around for somewhere to hide or something to protect herself with. Her brother had taught her better than this, however she couldn't think, and it took every ounce of willpower she had just to breathe.

"I've called the police." She croaked out. Something heavy slammed into the door again making the wood squeal. She cleared her throat and tried again, pushing out her words with more volume. "I've called the police."

There was silence from the other side of the door, followed by an even louder bang and what sounded like a swear word. The handle of the door jiggled.

She had a flash of her phone downstairs. Maybe they didn't believe her.

"I've got a button, and I'm hitting it." Okay, that hadn't quite come out the right way. "I have a mobile alarm. The police are on their way."

She waited. There was a pause, another bang, footsteps heading down the stairs, and a cat's screech. *Miles.* She would have to trust him to look after himself for the moment.

Greer grabbed a can of keratin hairspray and positioned herself in the corner behind the door. If they changed their mind and came back, she wanted to at least get a few sprays in. Ten minutes passed before the police arrived. Clearly, the attacker had been as optimistic about police response times as she was.

The inspector and Stephens weren't far behind.

"What the fuck happened?"

"I believe that someone smashed through one of the glass doors and tried to attack me in my home. Or isn't that obvious by the destruction and the button-pushing?" Sometimes the police really needed things spelled out for them.

The inspector stood there examining the room covered in glass and her. Greer tried to control her shaking.

"Are you hurt?" asked the inspector.

"Only my adrenals and my pride," said Greer, already dreading having to confess her lack of action to her brother.

The inspector looked towards the broken glass door.

"Well, you can't stay here. Do you have friends you can stay with?"

"Only a seventy-year-old woman who I refuse to put in danger." Greer really hoped Miles had found somewhere safe to hide. "I'll contact one of the rental agencies. They might have some accommodation this time of year."

"Stephens, is there a safe house—"

"No, not something we have." Stephens frowned at Greer. "Be tricky to organise for tonight." He shook his head. "Especially with a cat." Stephens looked towards the kitchen.

Greer glanced to see Miles pressed low against the top of the refrigerator with just the tip of his nose and eyes showing. Air flooded her body and she realised it had been a while since she had taken a proper breath.

She swallowed a sob. They were right. She couldn't stay here. But was she really willing to risk Victoria's life? Not that Victoria would mind. In fact, Victoria would have brained the attacker and be dealing with charges of excessive force.

"I want you to stay with me," said the inspector, staring at the broken glass.

"With you?" Greer parroted.

"You can't stay here." She glanced from the glass to Greer's sling. "If you're going to be attacked again, I want to see it."

"So...you want me to stay with you, hoping they'll attack me?"

"Gives you time to get this fixed and us time to work out what's going on. Win-Win."

"Ideally not attacked," said Greer, "just to be clear."

"We can't change what happens." The inspector kicked one of the larger pieces of glass. "We can only change how we respond. I've a spare room and very nosy neighbours. If anything happens, we will get information out of it."

In the end, Greer gave in to Stephens and the inspector's arguments. It was only one night.

After Greer rang the estate agent, though the chances of anything moving quickly seemed about as likely as Victoria admitting she was incorrect, she looked at the three boxes and suitcase by the door and then at the inspector's car. There was no way her things, including Miles, would fit, not to mention it would leave Stephens stranded. Constable Ceesay was volunteered to assist with his standard issue sedan, and they divided her belongings between the cars, with her boxes and bag going with Ceesay and Stephens, while she and Miles went with the inspector.

Greer was glad that the soft red top was up as a stiff wind had picked up again. She squeezed into the car with Miles on her lap. The long way down to the passenger seat, another reminder she needed to work on her core.

Miles ended up facing the inspector and alternated between hissing and howling his displeasure at the whole arrangement.

"Can't you shut him up?"

"Not used to cats, I take it."

Greer stuck her fingers in the cage and attempted to pat Miles. He pushed his nose under the tip of her finger.

"Are you sure he won't bite it off?"

"He's not at his best right now."

"So...he *could* bite your finger off?"

"Have you never had a pet?" asked Greer. It would certainly explain some things. She had grown up with a variety of them and sometimes she forgot that there were people out there who had never had that experience.

"What's the point of them? Anyway, my father was allergic."

"Having a pet is the same as having friends. They don't do things *for* you, however having them around makes life better."

"Even your fur bag of evil there?"

"Even this fur bag of evil." Greer smiled.

The inspector slowed down at a yellow light.

"No, don't slow down," said Greer and then sighed as the car stopped.

"Why not?" asked the inspector.

"These lights take forever to change."

The inspector's weight shifted, so more of her body faced Greer.

"This certainly explains Jeffrey's obsession with yellow light rules and regulations. If last month's stats were accurate, I think I have seen more yellow light tickets issued in this town than I would normally see in a year."

"Jeffrey cares a great deal about his work," said Greer.

"Oh, I know."

They sat there, the inspector's tapping on the steering wheel filling up the space. Greer wondered if the inspector had thoughts of *what was I thinking* running through her mind right now. Though, knowing the inspector, it would be more explicit. She certainly enjoyed the versatility of certain words.

The inspector's fingers stilled. "So," she said, "any thoughts on who's trying to kill you? Just asking for a friend."

Greer laughed, surprising herself.

"I don't know," said Greer. She took a deep breath. "Do you really think they'll come after me again?"

"Invading your home suggests a level of desperation."

"What I'm curious about is why they didn't stay and finish me in the laneway this morning," said Greer. "They also left my house as soon as I let them know the police were on their way. It suggests that not being seen is significant to them. So much so that they couldn't even risk a couple of minutes."

"They must think we have something on them," said Alba.

"Or, they're so well known in the town, even a glimpse means a revelation."

"Fuck."

"It's just a theory."

"They must think you saw them. Maybe you did and just don't realise it yet. I'm talking about from the moment you left the house, not just near the laneway."

Like trying to remember where you'd parked your car, Greer couldn't sort which memories belonged to that morning from all the other mornings that had come before. She closed her eyes attempting to piece it together. The car lurched forward and she opened them to see the green light had finally appeared. Despite their living clear across town from each other, the drive passed in only a few minutes.

"This is me." They turned into a wide residential street that ran all the way down to the lake. "I'm halfway down."

The inspector inched up towards some rubbish bins, and using the front of her car, pushed them out of her way and into a driveway.

"Why don't you just park in the driveway?" asked Greer.

"I'm over there, and we don't have them." She gestured to the series of small worker cottages across the road practically touching each other. Greer admired the attempts at privacy with ornate trellises of vines between the houses.

It took a while for Greer to get out of the car. With one arm in a sling and an unhappy cat in a cage, she wouldn't have made it without the inspector's help. Once Greer was standing, she looked at the bins.

"Err..." said Greer. "Why not park on your side of the street?"

"Public street, I can park where I want," was all she got back. The others pulled into the street and did a U-turn to park in front of the inspector's house. Greer looked at them and then back at the inspector, who ignored her.

With everyone helping, it didn't take long for them to get it all inside.

The residence was a two-storey house, and downstairs comprised a kitchen and living room that opened onto a back patio garden. The real estate advertisement would say it was quaint, with the warm woods and greenery making it quite beautiful. Not what Greer had been expecting at all. She would have guessed something very utilitarian, a place to eat, shower and sleep, and that was it. This was a home.

They took her things upstairs, and once they had dropped everything off, she went up to get Miles settled.

The narrow stairwell opened into a hallway with two doors on the left. Greer looked in and saw a bathroom and an office. She followed the hallway as it turned right and could see two bedrooms. Assuming the larger bedroom was the inspector's, she walked into the room on the right and found her boxes against one wall, her suitcase on top of the chest of drawers and an unhappy Miles in his cage on the bed.

The room, just big enough for a double bed and a chest of drawers, had its own cupboard-sized ensuite. Closing the door, Greer opened one box, awkwardly set up the kitty litter in the bathroom, and let Miles out of his cage. He immediately disappeared under the bed. Knowing that he needed a bit of time to recover, Greer put out food and water, preparing to leave him alone. The bedspread was a dark blue tartan, and the sheets were a soft flannel. She tested it out by lying down for a second.

Dale,

Well, you won't be happy with me. I am in the thick of it now. I have been putting off contacting you. First, I want to say that I am okay and safe. I am surrounded by police officers. You are wondering why? Well, someone attacked me. Now don't freak out. It is just a dislocated shoulder. The real problem is that they tried again at the house and broke a glass door, not an easy feat.

So, Miles and I are staying at the inspector's house. Just for the night. I will get everything sorted tomorrow. Right now, I have my duress alarm and people around. Which is about as safe as I can be.

Tomorrow's focus is on finding the person who killed Michael and attacked me. Assuming they are the same person, of course.

Wish you were here

Greer

p.s. The attacker ripped your coat. It is cold, and it is my only coat! I will repair it, I promise. You won't be able to tell the difference...hopefully.

Miles' eating woke her up, and she looked at her watch. She had been out for two hours. Someone had thrown a rug over her, so they must have checked on her when she didn't come back. Greer gave Miles a pat and splashed some water on her face before heading downstairs.

The inspector, seated at her kitchen island, was checking messages while eating cheese and crackers.

"Are you hungry?" she asked, looking up as Greer came into the room.

Before Greer could answer, there was a knock on the front door. The inspector grinned like a boxer before a fight and jumped up to open it.

"Henri, how can I help you?" her shoulders slumped.

A short woman with an enormous smile and white hair peered over the inspector's shoulder.

"Oh, I see you have a guest. How lovely that you're making new friends. Do you need dinner? Eli's been cooking again."

The inspector stood in the doorway, blocking her from coming in. Curious. Henri seemed to assume that the inspector would join them for dinner. Strange to imagine the acerbic inspector socialising with her neighbours.

"I haven't eaten yet," said Greer.

The inspector glared in her direction.

Greer shrugged her shoulder. "You asked."

Henri used the distraction as an opportunity to squeeze past.

"Since Alba seems to have lost her manners. I'm Henri, and my husband Eli does a food blog online. I'll send you the link. How do you know Alba?"

Greer smiled at Henri. "I'm Greer. I run the Book Distillery. My home—"

The inspector cleared her throat.

"I needed somewhere to stay tonight," said Greer.

"Welcome," Henri blushed slightly. "I'm embarrassed that we haven't met before. I've heard great things about your store though." Henri shook her head. "Serves us right for getting kicked out of the book club. Well, we've met now." Henri smiled, walked up to Greer, and took her hand.

Unfortunately, it was the hand attached to the recently dislocated shoulder and a sharp pain shot up Greer's arm.

"Argh."

"Oh dear, I'm so sorry."

"You couldn't see the sling?" asked the inspector, shutting the door.

"Greer, wait, weren't you the one to discover Michael's dead body? Such a shock for you." Henri manoeuvred Greer to sit down at the kitchen island on one of the high-back stools. Henri had pulled out her phone and sent a text before sitting opposite Greer. She did not appear to be in a rush to go anywhere.

"Who'd you just text?" asked the inspector, who stood with her hands on her hips, glaring at Henri.

Henri gave a beatific smile. "Just letting Eli know where I am. He worries so."

From the snorting noise from across the room, Greer guessed Eli had never worried a day in his life about the competent woman in front of her.

"What brings you here tonight? Not another body, I hope?" The bright light in her eyes and her body leaning forward ruined Henri's attempt to look concerned.

The inspector sighed. "Not that it is any of your business but someone put her in that sling." She frowned at Henri. "Probably best if you stay away."

Greer rubbed her left wrist. The tug by Henri still stung a bit.

Henri sat up straighter. "I could be in danger?" her eyes brightened even more but quickly dimmed. "Nobody's going to attack while there are so many people around, are they?" She turned her attention to Greer. "You must have read hundreds of murder mysteries over the years." She leaned forward again. "Where would you hide a body?"

Eli and Dr Yardley—Clement—who apparently also received the text, arrived. Greer watched the ping-pong conversation between them all as they discussed how they would get away with murder over Eli's amazing—just ask him—food and wine.

Strange that someone like the inspector could attract such agreeable company. Greer watched the easy humour between them all and realised that while she had always thought of herself as warm and friendly, she wasn't open. She didn't like people popping in uninvited. If it had been her, she would have politely sent Henri away. Which meant she missed out on nights like this. If any of her neighbours had made overtures when she had arrived, they had stopped trying years ago.

A loud knock on the door interrupted a discussion about the liberal use of lime and some Cayman Islands bank accounts. The inspector winced.

Henri's eyes narrowed. "Alba, what did you do?"

Greer smirked. This must be the neighbour with the bins.

"Nothing." The inspector slowly stood up and made her way to the front door. Taking a deep breath, she opened it. "Julius, what a pleasant surprise."

A man with long black hair pulled up in a bun and a clean-shaven face stood there looking ready to explode. The inspector gestured him inside. He looked confused but stepped in and she locked the door behind him.

"What the actual fuck, Alba?" he said. "You pushed bins into my driveway rather than do a U-turn. What's so hard about parking in front of your own bloody house?"

"It's a public road. There is plenty of space for everyone," said Alba, her arms crossed.

"Oh, Alba," Eli said with a shake of his head.

"Julius?" asked Greer.

He turned towards her, and his face shifted into a look of horror. Julius was not bad looking. In the scheme of things, he had all the features necessary to be reasonably attractive, but right now this was reduced as his lips were drawn back thin across his teeth, and his eyes squinty. It was not a good look.

"Greer," said Julius, choking. "What are you doing here?"

"She's here because she was attacked twice today," said the inspector, her voice sharpened with a dry edge that Victoria would have been proud of.

"Right," said Julius. His face smoothed out, and he tried to smile at her. "I hope you're.... okay?"

"Would you be okay if you got attacked twice?" The inspector snorted.

Greer felt sorry for him. He looked lost, all the righteous steam knocked out of him.

"Julius, how lovely to see you," said Eli, smiling at him and getting up to give him a hug. "I feel like we haven't seen you in ages. In fact, I think the last time was, well, it was my risotto night, wasn't it? The first one?"

Julius reddened. "Yes, I believe it has been some time."

"No offence, no offence taken," said Eli. "Life's all learning isn't it? Don't worry...tonight, tonight's a masterpiece. A massaman curry. Trust me, you don't want to miss it."

Julius let Eli drag him over to the table.

10

Alba

Alba lay there wrapped in her warm flannel sheets, wondering what the fuck just happened. It had been a fun night by most criteria. A pity it was on Wednesday in the middle of a murder investigation. She knew she shouldn't look. It would only make it worse the next day. Unable to help herself, she picked up her phone and saw it was almost two thirty in the morning. *Shit*, they had to be up in less than four hours. She was too old for this.

She made sure her alarm was up high and locked her phone, flopping her head back on the pillow. Sleep did not appear. Not surprising, considering how much sugar she had consumed.

Eli had insisted on making each of them a self-saucing chocolate pudding and on Henri filming him. Which considering how much wine he and Henri had consumed had turned out to be a challenge. Henri had stabilised the camera, but Eli was all over the place. Still, he had not let that stop him and when he dropped a measuring cup he had turned to the camera with a grin. "Don't try this at home, folks."

Every time after that—and Eli dropped things often—the entire group shouted it out in unison. Alba couldn't remember laughing so hard in months.

Thankfully, most of the neighbours were at the party. Otherwise, she'd have ended up with a noise complaint, and that would have been awkward to explain at work.

And who knew that once the rod from up his ass was removed, Julius could be such a hoot? When Eli had become set on making dessert, Julius and Henri had foraged across the households to find all the ingredients and he had attempted to be Eli's assistant. While he might have been willing, he knew little about baking and ended up mostly picking up the things Eli dropped and winking at the camera while drinking.

Ms Roberts, or now Greer, as she had permission to call her, seemed to loosen up around shared food and wine. Alba hadn't really seen her as the dinner party type and expected her to bow out early. Instead, despite having one arm in a sling, she had done some impromptu rounds of karaoke with Clement. Henri had captured it all. Another reason to be grateful she remained sober.

As sleep finally pulled at her, her mind imagined a weight in her bladder. Sometimes if she lay there long enough, her body would eventually accept she wasn't getting up and go to sleep. Instead, the weight seemed to grow. After a few minutes, she gave up and dragged herself out of bed and headed to the bathroom.

Greer's door across the hallway was open, and she could see her passed out on the bed, fully clothed. Someone, probably Clement, had put a pillow strategically under the arm and her body to support her shoulder. When she had bought the house, the previous owners had given her the option of buying the furniture in it, and she, with her whole life in a couple of bags, had purchased the lot, including the guest bed. Hopefully, it wasn't too uncomfortable. Alba walked carefully down the hallway to the bathroom. Despite her care, her footsteps made the whole house creak. She loved her house, but it wasn't modern or quiet.

The toilet trip was quick, and she made it back to her bed without Greer waking up. Able to relax, sleep got its hold on her, though not before flickers of Henri slapping Eli's ass flashed across the back of her eyelids. Her mind fled from them, straight into dreams full of elderly people gyrating.

Alba snapped awake. It felt like she'd only been asleep for seconds, but someone was in her room. She forced her breathing to stay deep and even.

A sneeze sprayed a light covering of snot over her face. She sniffed and got a whiff of tuna. She turned in the sneezer's direction. A massive cat—*had he been that big in the cage*—stared at her from the bedside table. He looked hungry.

"Nice kitty."

He made a noise. Apparently, he didn't appreciate his prey talking back to him.

Alba kept still. He shifted, lowering himself, so his weight was distributed evenly across his back and front paws. Was he going to attack her? And if he did, was she allowed to defend herself? She was pretty sure if she killed the cat, it would ruin her sheets, and there would be lots of paperwork to fill out.

She kept facing Miles as she slipped backwards out of the other side of the bed and inched her way to her bedroom door. He sat back down on his hind legs and tilted his head, watching her. Once she was close to the door, he jumped onto her bed, curling up in the warm spot she had left behind.

Asshat.

Alba glanced out the window while keeping Miles in view. A faint lightening of the sky made her think it was almost time to get up, anyway.

Fuck, the phone.

She looked at the giant cat in the middle of her bed and the edge of her phone sticking out from under a pillow. Who needed their phone anyway?

Pretending that she was happy to get on with the day, she grabbed her clothes and retreated downstairs. A flick of the light switch and her breath caught.

At least a break-in would have been covered by insurance. Alba scanned the flour over the bench, the floor, the ceiling, and what looked like thousands of glasses, plates, and bowls scattered everywhere. The entire room had a musty, sweet-sour smell that deepened as she walked into the kitchen.

She groaned. But the mess was future Alba's problem. Right now, the priority was coffee and breakfast.

With a quick change into her work clothes, and clearing just enough space for breakfast, she had started the coffee and toast when the alarm on her phone went off. Alba was about to give in and brave it when she heard Greer's feet hit the floor. The alarm stopped, and a few minutes later, a rather haggard Greer made her way down, one step at a time, with Alba's phone in her hand.

"Thanks." Alba smiled at Greer and took her phone. Greer had managed to get dressed despite the arm in the sling but did not look like she had fully woken up yet. She offered a cup of black coffee. "There's milk, normal milk, in the fridge if you need it. I doubt I've any sugar left."

"No, no more sugar." Greer's face took a greenish tinge. "Why are we up so early?"

"The whole murder thing? Not to mention that someone wants you dead." Alba blew on her coffee. "And we need to find out who quickly, mainly so you, and your monster, can go back to your ice tower."

Greer accepted the cup and took a sip.

"What?" said Greer, before leaning back against the wall, closing her eyes and cradling the cup. Alba had finished her own coffee and a couple of pieces of toast before Greer opened her eyes again.

"Can I have some toast?"

"Butter?"

"Yes, I think so."

Alba handed her a piece of toast with a smear of butter spread on it. After only a few bites, the green in Greer's face deepened. Avoiding her sling, Alba quickly guided her over to the toilet in the laundry and let her get rid of the coffee, toast and everything else in her system. They were going to need a proper hangover cure.

She left Greer to it and set up three drinks in a row. She could hear the running of the tap in the laundry and Greer hugged the wall as she shuffled back into the kitchen.

"Here," Alba handed her the first glass.

"I can't," Greer pushed further into the wall.

"Drink it." She forced it into her free hand.

"What is it?"

"A shot of coffee tequila...it's sweet."

"Alcohol? No, I can't."

"Stop whining. Drink it. Or do you want to be ill the entire day?"

Greer looked down at the glass and up at Alba's face. With a shudder, she knocked it back.

Alba steered her over to one of her armchairs and helped her take a seat.

"Give it a few minutes, and then I will give you the next drink."

"Will this really work?"

"I have spent years perfecting this, trust me. In half an hour, you'll feel...not great, but functional at least."

After giving her some lemon soda with a shot of vodka in it, she let her have another bit of toast. This time Greer held it down.

Alba handed her another soda for the road.

"Sip, don't drink it all at once." Alba looked at the time. "We can move to water when we get to the station."

If Greer didn't take too long, they should be on time for the morning stand-up.

She didn't know who invented stand-up meetings but they should win a prize. The whole principle was to make the meeting physically uncomfortable so it would be over sooner, and she appreciated that. A pity it didn't work on everyone. *Bloody Beitean.* She sent her thoughts out into the ether, hoping he wouldn't spend the first fifteen minutes talking about what his kids did that morning.

Alba picked up her phone and once again regretted her compulsive need to check her emails. The little badge on the corner showed that there were four unread. Three of them were predictably from stores, offering her clothes that would magically make her slimmer at incredible rates. The fourth was another one from her father. Unable to stop herself, she opened it.

My dear Alba,

You can't keep ignoring us. I have spoken to your friends, and they said you haven't contacted them either.

I just need to know you are okay. I need to know that, eventually, we will be okay too.

I know you are angry with me for not telling you that your partner was dishonest. Life is messy, and I made a choice, a wrong one. Remember, we are family, which means more than anything, even something like this.

If you don't contact me soon, I will find out where you are. I won't let this be the end of us.

Your father.

Alba cracked her neck and rolled her shoulders. *Dishonest, seriously?* He couldn't even call it what it was. How about corruption and criminality? Putting away her phone, she added that to the list of future Alba problems. First she had to get the slightly less green Greer into the car, so she wasn't late for her own meeting.

She turned to shut the door behind them and saw eyes watching her from the stairs. A shiver rolled down her back. As she was already outside, she took two fingers, pointed at her eyes and then at him. Alba thought she heard him hiss as she slammed the door closed.

When they arrived, it was to find that Beitean had organised coffee for everyone, including Greer. About to start the meeting, Alba remembered that one of their potential suspects was in the room. She must be more fatigued than she thought.

"Ms Roberts."

"Greer."

"Greer, can you wait outside until I'm done?" Alba looked around at the officers gathered ready to discuss the case. "You can't be in here."

Everyone frowned at her.

Alba addressed the entire room. "Whether she's a witness, victim or a suspect, she can't be in here."

Greer struggled to her feet. "I'll be at my bookstore."

It might end up giving them some more evidence. But only if one of them was there to see it.

Alba shook her head. "Can't you just..."

Greer stared back at her, her face set. Alba wanted to drop her head into her hands and scream. She was just trying to solve this thing and keep everyone safe.

"Stephens, can we swing some...protection?" The superintendent wouldn't want to pay overtime so it would mean losing one of the officers working on the case, which would slow them down and potentially leave the murderer out there longer. Why did everyone have to make it so difficult?

Stephens smiled. In fact, he looked almost cheerful. It filled Alba with trepidation.

"Inspector, as you requested, I researched Greer's background." His smile broadened. "Technically, Greer Roberts' arrangement with the police is active."

Alba crossed her arms and stared at him. "Is it?"

"Yes, which means if you wanted to, say, engage a Ms Greer Roberts to accompany you and assist with your interviews, you could do so with a simple order form. I have copies, just in case." With that, Stephens walked back to his desk at a brisk pace.

"Why's he so excited by this?" asked Greer, who didn't look happy.

"Reduces the probability of him having to go outside, Ms Roberts," responded Beitean.

Greer just looked confused, and Alba couldn't blame her, but she didn't have time to explain the nuances of Stephens' behaviour.

Stephens was back with the forms faster than she expected, and they were pre-filled.

Still he wasn't as clever as he thought he was. "She's still a person of interest in the case. Too much of a conflict of interest."

Stephens handed her a pen, showing her where to sign.

"Already logged, Inspector. The prosecutors won't like it, true. But I believe that as we are such a small community and with Ms Roberts' specialist skill set..."

"And what's that exactly? Being an ex-psychologist who owns a bookstore?" Alba glanced at Greer, who looked a mixture of annoyed and amused. "No offence."

The amusement appeared to increase.

"Still active and with police experience," rebutted Stephens, who seemed to have spent some time thinking this through. Perhaps if she engaged Greer, she should send Stephens out with her just to mess with him.

"I'm not sure that would be enough—"

"She has a doctorate in forensic psychology and over a decade of practical experience. Not something found locally," said Stephens.

"Err, did it cross anyone's mind that perhaps I don't want to work with you?" asked Greer.

"Someone attacked you twice yesterday, remember?" Alba's coffee was getting cold and they were losing time. "It's in your best interest to stay close to the police during this time." Great, now she was defending something that she didn't even want.

"If you can spare a constable to escort me to the bookstore, I am sure that I will be fine."

"The bookstore behind which you discovered a dead body, and someone attacked you? That bookstore?"

Sometimes she found she really had to spell it out to civilians.

Fuck it. It galled her to do it but if Stephens said it was possible, and she trusted him to know procedure, then he probably had found a solution to several of their problems, even if he had only been trying to resolve his own.

"The faster this is over, the better." And she could go back to having a quiet home with no monsters in it. "And the bonus of extra protection while you worked with us."

Greer's lips had almost disappeared, but she nodded.

Shit. Alba had only herself to blame if this went pearshaped. Well, herself and Stephens.

With Stephens clutching the signed forms, the stand-up finally began.

They had confirmed that Michael purchased secondhand furniture and décor around Lakes End, but so far, the owners all had copies of valuation certificates and everything seemed in order. Jayden hadn't turned up to make his statement yet, so Alba tasked Beitean and Kotowska to track him down.

They had just finished their updates when the superintendent joined them.

As soon as he saw Greer in the room, the superintendent turned towards Alba. "Inspector, a word."

As Alba left the room, she saw Stephens slip back to his desk to file the paperwork.

The door to his office barely had time to close.

"Since when do we let persons of interest in police briefings, Inspector?"

"Since we engaged her as a consultant, sir."

"We did what?"

"Stephens..." if she was going down for this, she was taking him with her, "identified that her standing arrangement with the police was still active. He submitted, and I executed an order form for her services, sir."

"And the fact she's a witness? ... at the least of it."

Alba kept her face blank, and her eyes trained on the superintendent's eyebrows. It was a trick she had learnt when she was a junior police officer. It looked like you were paying attention, but they couldn't quite stare you down. According to her former superior officers, it was very annoying.

"Couldn't avoid it because of the small community size combined with the uniqueness of her skill set, sir." Alba straightened. "Unless you want me to request help from the regional office, sir?"

If Russell said yes, that would actually work out even better. Alba could release someone to watch Greer and have experienced police officers to help with the investigation. If this resulted in the superintendent approving regional support, she would buy Stephens a bottle of scotch.

"I hope you aren't trying to strong-arm me, Inspector." She wondered if the crease lines on Russell's face hurt, all scrunched up like that.

"No sir, just being honest. Extra help would be useful, sir. Ms Roberts will undoubtedly have a lighter touch than me. It might make it easier for the family. Alternatively, I'll need extra bodies to assist with providing protection and with the interviews, sir."

"Very well, continue with your engagement of Ms Roberts. However, if this all goes to hell in a handbasket...it's your name on the order form."

Not waiting for the superintendent to dismiss her, Alba left the office. Buying that house was looking more and more like a mistake.

Everyone was waiting in the conference room, and she only had two steps in which to take a breath and re-centre. Never let them see you bleed.

"Right, Greer's in and Stephens, you're getting your wish of a day in the office."

Stephens grinned, and the constables all patted him on the back like he was some sort of hero.

She and Greer were going to meet with the family again. Beitean and Kotowska would continue to track Michael's movements the night before and bring in Jayden Merritt, while Grimaud and Ceesay would talk to Michael's clients. Stephens got to stay in the office and track down anyone around Merchant's Lane who might have left town recently.

As far as Alba could see, the only people who weren't happy were her and Greer.

11

Greer

Between her hangover and the pain in her shoulder, all Greer wanted was to head home and pass out. Instead, she was here, heading out to conduct a police interview.

Sinking into Alba's car, Greer adjusted her sling and rested her head against the seat.

"You up for this?" asked Alba.

"Do I have a choice?"

"Always... but your other options aren't great." Alba's tone was dry with an edge of humour.

Greer's lips turned up at the edges. She didn't even have the energy to squeeze out a chuckle.

"How about some food first?" asked Alba.

If she could hold it down, it would go a long way towards helping her feel better. That and maybe some painkillers.

"Sounds good."

"No worries, it's early. Let's get you sorted and work out our approach for the interviews. We need to get this right—the superintendent wants Fran and the family protected." Alba turned down a street heading towards the lake.

Greer closed her eyes. "Do you think Fran did it?"

"Too early to tell."

"Isn't it always the spouse?"

"Statistically."

Alba parked next to the trattoria. Pulling herself out of the car, Greer headed towards it, but Alba shook her head.

"Let's try the Vice & Virtue café. Stephens says they make a mean breakfast burger."

Soon Greer was sitting in a sunny spot, looking over the lake with a sweet, icy, caffeine-heavy drink and the recommended breakfast burger. She picked at it silently, focusing on making sure it stayed down.

Her cheeks puffed out as she stifled a burp. Alba, who had disappeared once Greer's food arrived, sat down and pushed some painkillers across the table. Greer took one gratefully.

"So, what do we want to get out of them today?" asked Greer.

"Where Michael was the night before—surely Fran or Gregory knows. I also want to confirm Fran's movements. She lied about what she had done that morning."

"What about Gregory himself? Is he a person of interest?"

Alba shrugged. "He's a beneficiary, so yes, and if anyone knows what Michael was up to, he would." But Greer could tell she wasn't convinced.

"So Michael's movements, Fran's movements and Gregory's movements? What about the kids?" Greer was exhausted just thinking about the conversations ahead.

"Nah, I can't see them involved and they won't benefit from any of this. Still, if something flags, we follow it."

"Now that I'm part of this..." How exactly had that happened? Stephens had filled in some form and she'd apparently suffered a momentary lapse of judgment, concluding that spending time with the police was a good idea. "How do you want to play it?"

"I don't know." Alba appeared to concentrate for a moment on pouring water into the glasses on the table. "It depends on how good you are or whether you're going to fuck it up."

Greer just raised her good shoulder and said nothing. It was Alba's call. If she could avoid doing anything, all the better.

"A doctorate in forensic psychology, huh? What does that mean exactly?"

It felt like a different era and for a moment Greer's mind was blank.

"Hmmm...there are lots of different subfields. Some act as expert witnesses on people's capacity to stand trial, research why people commit crimes, or advise on how best to interact with criminals. Crime is big business."

Which felt like part of the problem sometimes.

Alba continued to examine her. "Which one are you?"

"I researched criminal behaviour and its interaction with victim recall and advised on dealing with highly traumatised witnesses."

"Were you any good?"

"I thought I was," said Greer, sipping at her water.

"Why'd you stop?"

Her stomach churned. "I'm not up for this discussion right now." She put her glass down.

Alba tilted her head. "My guess would be some arsehole thought he, or she, knew more than you, ignored your advice, and someone got fucked up?"

"He, the witness committed suicide, and pretty much."

"Police officers can be fuckwits," said Alba with a shrug.

"Are you one, Inspector?" asked Greer.

"Sometimes. Look." Alba leaned forward, and Greer pressed back into her chair. "I want to get the person who's doing this as much as you do."

"Do you? Even if the superintendent ends up...unhappy."

Alba's gaze dropped to the glass of water in her hand. "Yes." She flicked a glance at Greer. "I've been fucked over before, and I won't let that happen here."

"We'll see." Greer took another sip and shifted so she was facing the lake. 'So back to my original question...how do you want to run today?"

"You take the lead. Better to start softer." Alba did not look impressed with her own words. "And if you make a mess of it, I'll come in with better questions."

Greer chuckled despite everything. "Fair enough."

She pushed herself up, paid for her breakfast, and shuffled her way back to the car with Alba following.

As busy as it got at Lakes End, navigating back to the newer side of town, Alba had to dodge pedestrians who acted like cars were a foreign concept and drivers that had apparently never heard of sharing the road. Eventually, they pulled into Fran's driveway.

It struck Greer that they'd designed this to be a family home, from front porch to backyard. The only reason you knew the kids weren't here anymore was that everything was tidy and well-maintained.

As Alba put the car in park, they saw Alex and Sam coming out of the front door. Alba stepped out of the car.

"Inspector, I hope you aren't here to harass our mother?" asked Sam as she approached them.

Greer opened her door and levered herself up to standing, her stomach lurching. She stilled and gave it a moment to recover.

"Just following standard procedures, I assure you," said Alba. She might have meant to sound non-confrontational, but Greer could hear the unspoken swear words.

"And I can assure you, Inspector, if you are anything less than polite to our mother, you can expect a formal complaint," said Alex, standing next to his sister with his arms crossed.

Alba's face flushed. "This is a murder investiga—"

"Sam, Alex, you're right." Greer—realising things were about to spiral—pulled herself together and stepped forward. "This is a tough time for everyone." She adjusted her sling and tried to look ill. It required very little acting.

"Greer." Alex's face softened as he took in her sling. "I heard about the attack. I'm so sorry. How are you holding up?"

"Not great, to be honest," said Greer, letting her shoulder droop. "Someone tried to attack me again last night."

"What?" Sam appeared distressed for her. "That's terrible."

Greer suppressed a twinge of conscience and swayed slightly on her feet. Alex stepped forward, hands ready to catch her if needed. Sam took her good arm and helped Greer towards the house.

"And this inspector seems to have you running around all over the place when you should be resting," said Sam, shooting a look of disdain towards Alba.

"Come in and take a seat," said Alex. He was about to take Greer in when Gregory opened the front door.

Sam and Alex handed Greer over to him and then, citing unavoidable work commitments, said their goodbyes and headed to their cars. A reminder that the world didn't stop, even for murder. Though perhaps it was more telling about Michael as a father.

Greer sighed. She was too tired and hungover to handle a conversation with anyone, let alone Gregory.

"Greer...with the Inspector...what's happened?"

Well, at least that was short and to the point.

"I mean, not that it isn't great to see you, and of course we expected to see the police again, what with poor Michael's death, such a tragedy. I think it's all caught up with Fran. She's here. Did you want to see her? She's napping, the grief you know. Not a big fan of naps myself, not that I'm not grieving. Terrible what happened to Michael makes you wish they hanged people."

Please be quiet.

"Gregory I don't want to interrupt, however, I fear I need to sit down."

"Yes, yes, of course, come in," Gregory stepped out of her way, "and the Inspector too, I suppose?"

"Oh yes, my protection." Greer couldn't help a small smile. Strange to think she needed protection, and that she qualified for a full inspector to provide it.

"What?" Gregory seemed to take in her sling for the first time. "Oh right, yes. I hope you're okay. It looks vicious. Come and sit down." He escorted her into the living space, leading her to a high-backed armchair near a window. Greer ignored him and sat on the three-seater couch in the middle of the room.

"Tea, everything's better with tea, won't be a sec," said Gregory, and disappeared.

Alba leant against the window, her gaze travelling the room cataloguing it and Greer wondered what she made of it all. She regretted not having taken the seat near the window. The sun was out, and the glass looked warm.

Greer let the couch take her weight. It was easy to sit there quietly, looking weak. She had leaned back and closed her eyes, only opening them again as Gregory entered the room. She smiled at him as he put down a small tray and joined her on the couch.

"How have you been going, Gregory? You were so close to Michael. I can't imagine what you're going through."

"Oh yes, well, it's left a bit of a hole, to be honest, not sure what to do with myself sometimes. Haven't had a chance to get to the store yet. With Michael gone, well, neither Fran nor I has the heart for it. The kids are going to help on Saturday. I mean, it must be done, and it's nice to have something to do. Especially busy work like inventory. Hilary and Alfie will need it for the will, you see."

"How long had you worked together?" Greer picked up her tea. Gregory hadn't offered Alba any.

"A lifetime, a lot of it informal in the beginning. I've been officially on the books at the Hidden Gem for about ten years now. His partner for at least five. On top of my real estate business, of course. Helps fill in the gaps when the market's tight."

Greer softened her expression. "I can't imagine working with a family member so closely."

"Ha, we grew up practically like brothers, you know? Drove each other nuts sometimes."

"Oh, I hope you have some final fond memories with him?" asked Greer.

"Yes, we'd had dinner the night before."

"Lovely." Greer forced herself to give him a warm smile. "I'm glad the four of you—"

"Just me, a bit of a boys' night." Gregory's face sagged.

"Even better." Greer went to smile at Gregory again however he was looking at a family photo on the wall.

"Hard to imagine I'll never see him again." Gregory rubbed his chest.

Greer knew she should ask more questions, but her brain was currently using its energy to keep her upright. Fortunately, Gregory didn't need prompting.

"It was a good meal. Macabre to think it was Michael's last supper, but it was a good meal. You know Le Perchoir de Paradis?"

"Very fancy. Were you celebrating?" The restaurant catered to the wealthier tourists, and she wouldn't have thought it Michael, or Gregory's usual style.

"Well, yes." Gregory paused.

Greer smiled at him expectantly whilst sipping her tea.

"We'd made a good deal the other day and wanted to celebrate his success."

"Really? That's wonderful." Greer didn't press the point. Alba could do that later. Her focus was on working out their movements that night.

"Did you have the matching wines? They always make the best recommendations."

"Yes, of course, fools not to." Gregory's smile was a sad thing to behold.

Greer tried to keep in him the moment. "I did the dessert tasting the last time I went. I practically rolled out of there."

Gregory laughed. "Yes, I'm not sure I could have completed that after a three-course meal."

"Anyway it was a chilly night, you probably both wanted to be home and warm before it got too late." Greer could have slapped herself. That was hardly subtle. In her defence, it had been many years since she'd done this kind of thing. Maybe she should just hand it over to Alba.

"Yes, well... normally I would have, but Michael was in a bit of a party mood that night, so we went down to that whisky bar near the park afterwards."

"What's that called? I remember it having a rather interesting name?"

"Cobbler. An excellent range of whisky."

She watched as Gregory tugged at his clothes and shifted away from her.

"How has Fran been doing?"

Moving the questions off Gregory and onto Fran caused his body to relax, and he leaned back towards her. "I worry about how much she's sleeping." He looked at the ceiling above him.

"A typical response. It's only been a few days, and it's important to let her feel her grief. Remember, though, that there's support there for her if it continues. I'll make sure she has the contact details for if...when she needs them."

"Thank you. They were together for over thirty-five years. No matter what, it's still an enormous loss for her."

"Of course it is."

"Poor Michael, he struggled to talk about his feelings." Gregory took a sip of his tea. "I mean, it's not my place to say anything, of course."

Then why are you Gregory?

Greer stopped herself from looking meaningfully towards Alba.

"Fran had nothing to do with this horrible business, of course. But the reality is Michael was distant." Whilst he'd been talking, Gregory had leaned in close and she got a whiff of a breath of someone who had had too many teas and coffees.

"I didn't realise. It's a sad thing that isn't uncommon in couples. Had they moved on..." Greer took a sip of tea and turned her face away.

Gregory dropped his eyes. "Michael hadn't."

At that moment, the squeak of old stairs signalled someone was making their way down.

"Fran," said Greer as she got up and stepped towards her with her good arm outstretched.

"Greer, my goodness, I heard about the attack. I just didn't realise you'd been so badly injured."

Gregory moved off the couch, offering Fran his place and saying he would make some more tea. Once Fran settled, Greer brought her up to date with the events of the last twenty-four hours.

"How are you holding up?" Greer asked.

"I identified the body. Had to really to make it real. Can't plan his funeral for weeks yet, but I am glad it gives us time to gather proper pictures of him. Take time to remember him. No point in being angry once they're gone, is there?"

"It doesn't mean our feelings of anger just disappear. I hope you're being kind to yourself?"

Fran was silent. She reached out and patted Greer's hand, the one that was sticking out of the sling. Greer controlled her wince.

"I'm lucky with my friends," said Fran.

"I can't imagine how much you miss him," said Greer.

"I'm not sure, maybe? He was there and had been part of my life for a long time. But lately...well, I feel the last years prepared me for this moment."

Greer would have reached out to hold Fran's hand, but between the sling and the tea, there wasn't much more she could do other than look sympathetic.

"I only ever heard about how devoted he was to his family." Greer took a sip of tea, but it couldn't mask the unpleasant taste in her mouth.

"True, I'm sure you're right." Fran looked tired.

"Gregory was telling us how they went to celebrate at Le Perchoir de Paradis the night before."

"Yes, Gregory mentioned that to me yesterday. I didn't know about it. Not that I would have minded."

Gregory came back into the room with Fran's tea.

Greer was wondering what to do with him when Alba stepped in.

"Mr Williams," said Alba, stepping away from the window. Fran gave a slight jump, but Gregory turned towards the inspector without a twitch.

"Yes, Inspector?" He stood awkwardly just near the chair that he had clearly been about to sit in.

"I just need to ask you some questions about Michael's whereabouts the night before he died. Perhaps we could step into the other room?" Not waiting for Gregory's response, Alba headed towards the office. Gregory followed.

Greer returned to the dilemma of how to ask a suspect whether she slept separately from her husband and for a summary of her movements in the twelve hours before his death.

"You think I'm oversharing, or as the kids would say, TMI," said Fran.

Greer would have been grateful if she had shared a lot more.

Fran sighed. "It's just that I've been turning all of this over and over in my head."

Greer cleared her throat. "I'm sure that none of it makes sense right now." Great, now she was down to platitudes. Okay, she could do this. "At least you got to say goodnight." She had always found that giving a story with incorrect details was one of the most effective ways of eliciting information. People didn't seem to be able to help themselves from correcting others.

Fran's teacup rattled against its saucer. "I never saw him that night."

"Oh, he came home after you'd gone to sleep? I'm so sorry. I didn't mean to bring back a sad—"

"No, not even that." Fran's eyes started leaking, and Greer cast a glance around for some tissues. Fran, prepared as always, pulled one from her pocket. "He didn't come home that night. We don't—didn't share a bed anymore." Fran said it as if she were confessing some terrible sin.

Greer—having met Michael—thought it was a very sensible choice. However now was not the time to say that. Putting her tea down, Greer reached out and held Fran's hand. She didn't have it in her to press for more details, so they just sat there silently. She really was useless.

Eventually, Alba and Gregory came back into the room. Alba took one look at Greer and suggested they take their leave. At least they might have some information to assist Beitean and Kotowska.

The rest of the morning passed in a blur. Alba had the crime scene unit dust her home for prints. A security company came around and gave a price for reinforcing the security on the house that Greer wasn't sure the real estate would accept, though Alba assured her it was reasonable. They also said that they wouldn't be able to install it until Friday. To be fair the agent had moved fast and already had the broken glass door sealed up. Still, without the extra security, she knew she couldn't go back, not yet. Which meant another night at Alba's place.

Did that mean she would have to help clean up?

12

Alba

Alba flipped through her notes and made herself another cup of coffee. Food would be needed soon unless she fancied the jitters.

Between Gregory's insinuations about Fran having an affair and Jayden's hints, Alba had to consider seriously whether she had, in fact, killed her husband. She didn't see it herself but noted it to go up on the board as soon as they got Jayden's statement.

She was also interested in Michael and Gregory celebrating at an expensive restaurant over some deal.

Money and sex—what was it with the money and sex that seemed to make people lose their minds?

Well, it was two more leads than they'd had yesterday. The superintendent would have been happier with a random kill, but there was something about repeated blows to the head that said it was personal.

Beitean and Kotowska had confirmed Michael's movements up to the Cobbler. They had witnesses stating that they'd seen Gregory and Michael leaving together in a rideshare. Stephens was tracking it down. There couldn't be that many here at Lakes End surely?

According to Gregory, they'd headed back to his place, and Michael had crashed there. It would be interesting to see if Hilary would corroborate this. Especially as this was not information Gregory had offered in the first round of interviews.

Grimaud and Ceesay had nothing, just legitimate purchases. Alba had them switch their attention to the buyers. Perhaps it was the people purchasing the items, not the sellers, who were being conned.

Alba had two goals today: to find out why Michael was in that blasted laneway and to get a feel for his financial situation. Leaving Stephens to battle with the lawyers and the banks she chose the laneway. Of course, Greer insisted on stopping at her bookshop first.

They arrived to find the bookshop open and Victoria behind the counter sipping a cup of what smelt like peppermint tea. Greer stopped to check in whilst Alba wandered through the bookshop. She'd been in here before, but this was the first time she'd stopped and looked. Full of velvet chairs tucked in nooks between wooden bookshelves, each with a lamp allowing the reader to stop and read if they wanted to, it seemed more like a library than a store.

It was also quiet. Leaving them to their conversation, Alba headed towards the back, choosing a chair out of view from the rest of the shop. She sat down and reached for a book that was at eye level.

She'd read an entire chapter without interruption, a first for her since arriving at Lakes End, when Greer found her.

"What the fuck is Toad News?" asked Alba, showing Greer the book's cover. Greer laughed.

"That's one of my all-time favourites," said Greer with a broad smile. "You can keep it if you like."

"I'm not in the market for a book." Alba closed the paperback and peered at the shelf trying to remember exactly where she got it from.

"Consider it a gift, a thank you for giving me a safe place to stay," said Greer.

Alba wasn't exactly sure when she would get time to read it but she had to admit to being curious about what happened next. "Thanks." She pushed herself to her feet, shoved the book under her arm and slouched behind Greer, somehow feeling like a kid following a librarian to the checkout area. She reminded herself that it was only this morning that Greer had thrown up in her laundry and straightened her shoulders.

"Have you worked out how to get Kendall his money back yet?" Victoria swivelled and gave Alba the full effect of her stare.

Alba shook her head. 'What is that?' asked Alba, pointing towards Victoria's computer screen.

"Since you haven't discovered who killed Michael yet,"—Victoria gave her a pointed stare—"the local newspaper's entertaining itself by revisiting the last Lakes End murder twenty years ago. Everyone thought it was a tragic accident until the doctors worked out it couldn't have happened without help."

"Who died?" asked Alba, squinting at the screen but unable to make out a name.

"Mr Beecher, Amos Beecher's father," said Victoria. "Apparently, there'd been some friction there. Never considered a suspect, even though he inherited everything."

"If anyone was going to kill, it would definitely be Amos," said Greer, her voice unexpectedly sharp.

Alba stepped closer and peered over Victoria's shoulder trying to skim-read the article. Nothing flagged, but she texted Stephens to get her a copy anyway.

Right now, they needed to work out why Michael was in that lane.

Leaving her book with Victoria, Alba dragged Greer out the back door and into the laneway.

Alba looked around whilst Greer, who still seemed to be under the weather, leaned against the wall with her eyes closed. Alba tensed. She thought that Greer's forensic psychology shit could be valuable. It would just be helpful if Greer realised it too. Stephens' text had said he was finding a lot of cash. So, they might have some money to trace. Another lead.

The laneway itself was narrow and only long enough to fit four small artisan shops on one side and The Book Distillery and the Mad Cutter on the other. But they were of no use. Everyone who could be talked to had been. And none of them saw anything. She twisted her upper body, trying to see every angle and guess where Michael might have been going. Or maybe Fran was why he had been here.

"Greer, if you were Fran and had to find somewhere to hide out at six-thirty in the morning, where would you go?" asked Alba.

"Coffee," said Greer.

"You've already had coffee. What I'm asking is..."

"Elvira's," said Greer. "If I were Fran, I would sit in her kitchen at the café whilst she got ready to open. She usually opens around six thirty, and that is when it gets busy."

"Which direction?" asked Alba.

"Elvira's Cravings, surely you know it?" said Greer.

"Maybe. How close is this café owner to Fran?" asked Alba, her back and neck tightening. She stretched her neck trying to loosen it.

"One of her best friends," said Greer.

Alba ran her hand through her hair. "And does everyone know this?"

For fuck's sake.

Did no one think the fact that Fran's best friend worked a block away from where Michael was killed relevant? Surely, one of the fuckwits would have known.

"Yeah, it is pretty common knowledge, and Elvira usually starts early. It is the one thing she hates about her job, especially in winter," said Greer.

"Well, let's get coffee," said Alba. Just what she needed. More caffeine.

Greer pushed herself off the wall and headed away from the lake. Alba noticed her eyes were a bit more open now and her stride a little longer. Progress of sorts. Despite being taller than Alba, Greer rarely walked with any kind of speed. Today was no different. Alba matched her pace, which meant they would reach the café before nightfall. Probably.

But it was closer than Alba had expected—*how had no one mentioned this*—they soon arrived at the hole-in-the-wall café with a few chairs out the front sheltered from the road by pot plants. Two mismatched downlights illuminated the tiny counter. Vases, sugar packets, and glass-domed trays with tasty treats were highlighted by the overhead lights. Alba was pretty sure one plate had homemade doughnuts on it and her mouth watered.

After everything that had happened with her old department and her father, she'd developed a dangerous habit of *fuck it* food choices. Which for her meant large amounts of bread, cheese, and any deep-fried tastiness, as well as an entirely new wardrobe. It was amazing how quickly her body had let go of years of hard physical training, eager to replace it with extra bits that moved separately from her body when she ran. She didn't like it. Not enough to give up doughnuts, of course.

"Hi," said Alba with a smile. She could be nice when food was on the line. "Can I have a latte and one of those doughnuts? They look amazing."

The barista smiled at her warmly. "Thank you. We make them in-house." She gestured behind her, and Alba could make out a doorway leading to a small kitchen.

"Wonderful. Greer here was just telling me that this was the best coffee in town."

Elvira's face cooled as she turned her attention from Alba to Greer, who'd put two reusable cups on the counter. One had large purple dots on it and the other, multicoloured squares. Alba wasn't sure she wanted to use either.

"I'm Elvira," she seemed to remember herself and smiled again at Alba. "And as much as it pains me to say this, Greer's right. What brings you to Lakes End?"

"I'm Alba." She watched Elvira use the tongs to put one of the doughnuts in a paper bag and her mouth watered. "I moved here a few months ago now."

"A new resident? That's exciting. How'd you get stuck with—" she paused and restarted, "...know Greer? Are you a reader? If you are, Amos, he is the owner of the Mad Cutter, runs the biggest book club in town."

"I'm Inspector Mauzer with the police department. I'm sure you've heard the sad news about Michael Williams?"

Even if she hadn't been Fran's friend, in a small town like this, Alba was sure that everyone had talked about it at length by now. Stephens had found at least three local blog sites that had polls on who they thought had done it with the local townspeople voting as if it was a game. She hoped that Fran, the front-runner on two of them, hadn't seen them.

"Yes, poor Fran, it has been truly awful for her." She filled both cups with coffee.

"Have you seen Fran recently?" asked Greer.

Alba got nothing antagonistic about Greer's tone, but Elvira straightened and turned towards Greer, her face significantly less warm.

"What's it to you?" asked Elvira.

Alba shifted so that she was between them. Greer might be a shit-hot forensic psychologist, but she didn't appear to be much of a people person, or perhaps it was the hangover.

"Greer, why don't you take your coffee and head back to the bookshop? I'm sure you've work to do," said Alba.

Elvira looked pleased, Greer less so. Regardless, Greer took her coffee and left while Alba took a bite out of her doughnut.

"Oh my, these *are* amazing," said Alba, and she wasn't just buttering Elvira up. It was fluffy and had a slight lemon zest to it, which, when combined with sugar and cinnamon, put her in donut heaven. They were even warm.

"I have to be careful not to eat too many *testers* or I wouldn't be able to fit behind this counter," said Elvira and gave a small laugh.

They shared a smile.

"It's good to know that Fran has friends, especially at such a stressful time for her," said Alba, leaning against the counter, hopefully signalling she was up for a chat.

Not that friends always made it better.

"Absolutely, I have attempted to be there, especially lately," said Elvira.

Alba nodded knowingly and tried to keep the interest out of her face.

"Not that there was anything in it," said Elvira. "He was just busy at work."

"Of course," said Alba. She smiled as she took another bite, her eyes closing. "Doughnuts make everything better."

"Fran helps with the first batches. My own taste tester. Saves my hips," said Elvira.

"A nice way to start the day." Alba took another bite of her doughnut and a sip of her coffee. "I can imagine she has been here all week with everything going on." Alba could see some people coming along the street and suspected her quiet moment at the café was about to come to an end.

"Well, no, not since that morning." Elvira's eyes widened. "I mean, I can't remember which morning she was last in. She hasn't been here this week, though. Staying home, understandable of course, so sad to lose Michael so young. I think he was only in his early sixties."

Alba stayed focused on the doughnut and tried not to look eager. Jayden put Fran in the area that morning. It also made a lot more sense than an affair.

She decided it was best to leave it at that and not play her hand too early. She was finally onto something. There must have been others at the café on a Monday morning. She would send the constables to check it out.

"Thank you so much for this remarkable coffee and doughnut. I know how I'm going to be starting my day from now on," said Alba.

Elvira gave her a second doughnut to welcome Alba to the community, and Alba went away smiling.

When Alba entered the bookshop, Victoria was talking with a customer and Greer was hard at work, curled up in an armchair with her eyes closed, taking the occasional sip of coffee. Alba followed her lead and sat in another nook, enjoying a rare moment of peace whilst finishing her second donut and coffee. The sound of the customer leaving roused her.

"Come on Greer, we have to visit the Joneses," said Alba, getting up and heading to the shop's front door. She had a potential explanation for why Fran was here that morning, but she still didn't know what brought Michael here. If Stephens was finding more cash than expected, then she needed to understand what exactly he had been up to.

"The Joneses?" asked Victoria. "Would that be the delightful Hilary Jones and her even more delightful brother Alfie?"

Alba grinned at Victoria's false enthusiasm. To be honest she wasn't looking forward to this interview either. "Yes, why?"

"No reason, just they have my vote, in case you are interested," said Victoria.

"And on which poll would that be?" asked Greer as she joined them.

Victoria had the grace to blush. Alba dragged Greer from the bookshop. A quick drive and she found a park a few doors down from Next Level Law, Hilary and Alfie Jones' practice.

Stephens had served the warrants on the Jones' law offices for all of Michael's papers and was navigating professional privilege to see what they could get. But Alba wanted to talk to Hilary and Alfie, not as Michael's lawyers, but as his family.

It was messy, and she didn't like it.

A receptionist greeted them as they entered, and they followed his directions to a door marked with Hilary Jones' name. Alba noticed that there didn't seem to be any other administrative employees. Strange for a legal office.

Alba knocked but didn't wait for a response before opening the door.

Hilary, seated in a high-backed office chair behind an oversized desk with only a laptop and a wide monitor on it, sat back and examined them.

"Inspector." Her gaze flicked to Greer and her eyes narrowed. "And Greer...this is a surprise."

"Morning," said Alba, keeping her voice cool and professional. "I'm here to talk to you as a family member of the deceased."

Hilary's body stiffened, and a flush of colour flooded her cheeks. Not waiting for an invitation that was unlikely to come, Alba and Greer took seats in the visitor chairs facing the desk.

"I'm clarifying Michael's movements before he died," said Alba.

But before Alba could even ask her first question, Hilary's brother came storming into the room.

"What's going on here?" Alfie might have been attractive in his youth. No doubt a footballer or the big man at school.

But a sedentary lifestyle and too much alcohol had aged him, leaving heavy jowls and broken capillaries on his face.

"I'm merely trying to establish Michael's movements before he died, and I believe Ms Jones has some relevant information," said Alba.

"If you have questions"—Hilary glared at everyone, including Alfie—"you'll need to provide me with a date and time, and I'll attend with legal representation if I deem it necessary."

"That's what I was about to say," said Alfie, crossing his arms.

Hilary flicked him a glance. "I can take care of myself," said Hilary.

"Fine," said Alba. "Three this afternoon to give a statement on your knowledge of Michael's movements in the twenty-four hours before his death."

Pounding started in Alba's ears.

"Don't go down there without a lawyer," said Alfie, his voice filling the room.

Greer winced but Hilary didn't seem impacted by its volume.

She frowned at her brother. "I've been a lawyer longer than you."

Realising nothing was going to happen here, Alba gestured to Greer and stood.

Lawyers, they always made it fucking harder.

Seriously, how hard was it to say yes, he slept on our couch, or no, he didn't?

Hilary and Alfie continued arguing whilst Alba and Greer mooched their way out of the office. Regrettably, Alfie had the mind to shut the door behind them.

As they were leaving, three people were coming in.

"You, Jayden," said Alba. "We've been looking for you." She stared at the man in front of her. He looked better in activewear.

His trousers were unironed, and his long hair was tied up in a messy bun. A turtleneck jumper and an old plaid jacket with leather patches on the elbows finished his rugged look.

"Inspector, please accept my apology." The rueful smile he gave Alba lit up his face and transformed it into charming. "I'd every intention of attending the police station earlier. One of my elderly clients passed away and duty called. I'll head there straight away." He paused and stepped away from the couple next to him.

Alba did not return the smile and turned her attention to the other two who'd entered, Fran and Gregory Williams. It made sense for them to be here, yet it was rather unfortunate timing.

Greer stepped up. "Fran, Gregory, hello again, everything okay?"

Fran stared down at her hands. "It's overwhelming how much there's to do. Gregory and Hilary have been so helpful in getting it all sorted for me."

Alba looked at Gregory. He cleared his throat and scraped a hand through his hair.

Alfie, whose life's mission appeared to be getting rid of police, threw open Hilary's door and came storming out.

"You should leave," shouted Alfie. "If you wish to talk to anyone, schedule a time."

"Mr Jones, please calm down," said Alba. She wasn't sure, but she thought Greer sighed. "We're just trying to locate Michael's killer."

Alfie did not calm down.

"By harassing the grieving widow, you mean." His face was getting redder, something Alba hadn't thought was possible.

"Yes, we'll need to talk to the family," said Alba dryly. What did he expect was going to happen in a murder investigation?

"It's all about how fast you can get that paperwork off your desk. All so you can stay within budget," said Alfie with no noticeable attempt to decrease his volume.

"And lawyers are known for their altruistic approach to life." Unhelpful, but she couldn't stop herself.

He looked like he was going to explode and everyone was staring at her unsure what was going to happen next.

Alba knew she'd fucked up. The problem was she was treating the case like Fran wasn't a suspect. But she was. There was now the evidence from Jayden and Elvira, putting her near the scene of the crime.

Alfie was right. Fran was the easiest to suspect.

13

Greer

Greer blurted a goodbye and followed Alba out to the car. With the pain throbbing in her head and shoulder, Greer couldn't keep up, and Alba was about to pull away as she reached for the passenger door. The car jerked to a halt.

"Sorry," said Alba.

Greer jumped in before Alba changed her mind. "Who was that?"

"Who? Jayden? A witness."

"You know, with his hair in a bun and that thick jumper on he looked like a lumbersexual," said Greer with a small smile.

"What the fuck is a lumbersexual?" asked Alba. Horns blared as Alba crossed lanes.

Greer thought for a moment. "A lumbersexual is like an outdoorsy metrosexual. Super-hot."

"He's a lawyer who works next to Hilary and Alfie Jones." Alba thumped the steering wheel. "He also saw Fran close to where her husband died. I don't like coincidences."

Greer looked over at Alba's hands squeezing the wheel.

"You know what Stephen King said about coincidence don't you?" asked Greer.

"Is it relevant?" asked Alba, her fingers relaxing.

"Sometimes a cigar is just a smoke, and a coincidence is just a coincidence," said Greer.

"So no."

Greer watched Alba sit back further in her seat and throw a snarky look in her direction.

"I'm assuming you're not happy with how things turned out?' asked Greer.

She could hear Alba sigh as she slowed down to under the speed limit.

"I made a hash out of it."

"You've got lawyers who are both legal representatives, family members and potential suspects. It was never going to be clean."

"Maybe." Alba lifted one of her hands off the steering wheel to run her fingers through her hair, her shoulders slumped.

"Once you take Jayden's statement and get Elvira's corroboration on record, you can work out the next steps from there." Not that Greer wanted it to be Fran. And to be honest despite the way things were adding up it still felt wrong.

"I know how to run an investigation," said Alba, her voice rather tart.

Greer jumped a little as Alba slapped her hand back down on the steering wheel.

"I was just reminding you of the next steps." Greer muffled a sigh and let the weight of her head fall back on the car seat. Her brain wasn't firing on all cylinders, and she spent some time in her own wallow. She had been of little use in the interviews.

"Need some food?" asked Alba.

"I could eat." Greer rolled her head to face her without having to lift it. "Aren't we in a hurry to get back to the station, though?"

"Jayden won't rush there, and I don't mind if he has to wait."

"Food and water would be useful."

"There's a Tex-Mex place a block back from the station." Alba's face relaxed into a broad smile. "The beef verde burrito makes everything better."

Alba took the next right and parked in front of a small bistro. Greer followed her in and they took a table near the back.

"Any reason you don't sit near windows?" asked Greer as she sat down across from Alba.

"Don't go psychoanalysing me. I've just learnt that if you sit near a window, people come and say hello in this town."

"Is that such a bad thing?"

Alba ran her hand across her face.

"It is when they don't go away."

A server came over.

"Hey, Paulina."

"Hey Alba, the usual?"

"Yeah, two and a couple of your best beers—"

"Oh, not for—"

"You need it," said Alba. "Two beers, thanks Paulina."

"No worries, anything else?"

"Nah, that's all today. Busy morning?"

"Always, you know that." Paulina laughed and thumped Alba on her shoulder before heading off towards the kitchen.

What was it about Alba that people responded to? Greer was used to smiles and hellos, but Alba seemed to convert those into friendships.

"Paulina owns the place. Trust me, the food's excellent."

Greer just nodded, she had been here once or twice before. Not that Paulina seemed to remember. She sat back, too tired to make polite conversation.

Paulina dropped the beers off first. Greer tried to take a sip, but it was like razor blades down her throat. She put it aside. Maybe it would be more palatable with food.

The Tex-Mex bistro had avoided chain-restaurant tackiness. Greer admired the mosaic made up of tiny pieces of glass and tile, forming a bird in flight over a waterfall on the brick wall near their table. She wanted to touch it.

"What do you think of Fran?" asked Alba.

"I've shared with you what I know of her."

"No, not what you know. What do you think? If you had to give a psych eval right now, what would you say?"

"That's like asking you to give a cause of death before you have a pathology report."

Alba laughed. "We do that all the time."

At that moment, Paulina brought over two massive plates.

"They're hot." She smiled warmly at Alba and gave a friendly nod to Greer.

It was like Greer was in an alternate reality where grumpy, abrasive people were valued.

Alba gave thanks and started on the rice.

"I don't think she did it," said Greer, pulling apart the burrito to help it cool.

Alba paused mid-shovel and glanced at her. "Why not? If Jayden and Elvira are telling the truth, it looks like she lied about where she was that morning. Not a good sign."

"Unless she is a seasoned killer, I can't imagine her reacting the way she is. There is no paranoia—"

"She came to see you...wanting to be involved in the case."

Alba was right. Greer braved a bite of food. It was delicious and full of spices which made her mouth water. She took a couple more bites.

"True, however, she hasn't tried to insert herself in the case or give irrelevant information that implicates others."

"I'd have to check my notes," said Alba. She poked at her food.

"Furthermore, she's stayed home quietly and grieved. Fran's an admirable woman, however I'm not aware of anything that suggests she has nerves of steel."

Alba and Greer finished their food in silence. Greer looked down, surprised to see she had eaten most of it. She felt uncomfortably full, but her brain was happier.

"Better?" Alba glanced at Greer's plate.

"Compared to this morning...yes." Greer shifted so her sling wasn't pressing on her full stomach. "I don't remember drinking that much."

"Alcohol hits us harder at different times."

"Perhaps," said Greer.

Alba's plate was empty and she sat back. "Do you have any other thoughts about the killer?"

It was a good question. Greer tried to remember all the chess pieces she had contemplated the other night sitting alone in her room with her cat. It seemed so long ago, almost out of reach.

"I'm not actually sure whether it is a man or a woman. Usually, with the violence of these crimes, I would suggest a man. However, an implement was used every time. Something to bash the head, something to help break down my bathroom door. Why not just kick it in?"

Alba's eyes narrowed. "So...a man or a woman."

Greer glared at her. "No need to be sarcastic, I'm thinking. They'll value their fitness, not being skinny, but being strong. They won't have a tidy appearance. They are too messy for that."

"Seems a bit of a stretch."

"It's in the violence of the attacks. They're volatile and untidy."

"Your theory is that it's a man...or woman...who's fit but isn't a neat dresser."

"Exactly, I mean, I'm practically handing this to you on a silver platter." Greer waved her hand over the empty plates in front of them.

A broad grin spread across Alba's face, and she gave a loud laugh. For the first time, Greer understood why the locals had been so welcoming towards her. She was candid, and even if it was abrasive, the honesty of it was comforting.

"Thanks, I appreciate it," said Alba.

Greer glanced at the clock. "Do you think Jayden's been waiting long enough?"

"We'll see. You done?"

When they got back to the police station, Stephens was in the conference room preparing an update on the will. As suspected, Fran was the primary beneficiary. The surprise was that Gregory had ended up with the business.

"Strange." Greer turned towards Stephens. "How much do you think Fran will get?"

"The house, the superannuation and the life insurance. Nothing to be sneezed at."

"She's what? Early sixties? Maybe she didn't want the business?" asked Alba.

"Sixty-two," answered Russell as he entered the room. "Why wouldn't she want the business?"

"He left it to Gregory," answered Stephens.

"Gregory? Understandable in a way." Russell continued into the room and stood in front of their board.

"A sign of trouble in the marriage?" asked Greer.

"From what we can see, Michael updated it several years ago, changing it to Gregory. Before that, he had set the business to go to Fran," said Stephens.

Russell frowned.

There was silence as they all examined the board. Greer suspected they were all hoping for inspiration to strike. But the board offered no new insights.

"Do we know why Michael was in that laneway yet?" asked Russell.

"No sir," said Alba, her voice crisp and professional. "We've two witnesses placing Fran in the vicinity around the same time, though."

"And possibly a third," said Greer.

"What?" asked Alba, jerking towards her.

Greer stifled a wince. Perhaps revealing this without discussing it with Alba first was a mistake. It was too late now. For the last few days she had been trying to recreate that morning in her memory. It had been hard and she had worried that she was creating false memories. But her anchor had been the lack of coffee that morning, the interruption to her usual routine.

"There was a person, a man I think, walking their dog right on the edge of the park, so they would have had a view of the entrance to Merchant's Lane."

Beitean came to let them know Jayden was wondering how long he would have to wait.

"Jayden?" asked Russell. "Jayden Merritt the estate lawyer?"

Alba nodded. "The jogger who saw Fran, sir."

"We think Fran's a possibility?" Russell's face was grim.

Everyone in the room kept their eyes on the board.

Russell exhaled audibly. "If we are going down that path, make sure you cross your t's and dot your i's. I want it iron-clad."

"Of course, sir." Alba turned to Stephens. "We need a statement from Elvira about Fran's movements that morning. I want to know when Fran arrived, what state she was in, and what time she left. Greer and I'll interview Jayden and maybe get some insight into the Jones siblings as well. Something's going on there, and it is not just the idiocy of acting for family."

Greer wasn't sure how much help she would be but accepted that she was along for the ride.

Kotowska had put Jayden Merritt in the main interview room and given him some water.

"Jayden, thank you for finally coming in," said Alba.

"Again, my apologies. I should've let you know about the delay. After all, it's not often you're a potential witness in a murder inquiry." Jayden settled back in his chair, his body relaxed. "But when faced with two deaths, well, I chose the family who was paying me. Unless they give consultant fees for witness statements now?" He flashed a smile at Alba.

Greer thought his attempt to charm Alba interesting. Why waste his time on a move that he had to know wouldn't work? Or was he just arrogant? His robust cologne suggested the latter—and made Greer's nose itch.

When Alba didn't respond, Jayden transferred his smile to Greer, and she smiled back at him. If they were going to play games, she was definitely playing good cop.

"Could you please go through your movements and what you saw on Monday morning?" said Alba.

"Yes, I jog most mornings. I leave around six and return around seven. I circuit through the town first, then along the lake edge. That morning, I noticed Fran walking across Lakes Way. I've seen her before hanging about with the café owner who makes the doughnuts. Have you tried them?" He smiled at Alba again. "Give them a go if you haven't."

Greer updated her analysis of him to fool. Alba ignored his play and asked him to continue.

"That was it really." Jayden shrugged.

"And you didn't think to come in?" asked Alba.

"It wasn't until later that day that I heard what happened to Michael." Jayden shrugged again. "And no, it wasn't my first thought."

However relaxed he was trying to appear, his gaze never left Alba's face.

Alba sat there and clicked her pen, staring at him. Greer could feel each click reverberate through her head.

"Do you work with the Jones siblings often?" asked Alba.

"The Jones? No, I mainly do estate law, and they're more commercial."

The only evidence of Jayden's discomfort was the occasional adjustment of his cuffs.

"And Michael and Gregory?" asked Alba.

"Sometimes they've purchased items from my estate clients, but that's all."

"Ever seen anything unethical, perhaps under-pricing an antique?" asked Alba.

Greer tried not to blink.

"Always a risk, especially with estates." Jayden cleared his throat. "But I make sure everything gets valued appropriately." His fingers flexed.

"And who does that?"

"Theodore Lopez, a valuer who works for several auction houses." Jayden was no longer playing with his cuffs and instead sat with his shoulders back and relaxed, highly controlled.

Alba continued to question Jayden, trying to work out his relationship to the Jones and Williams with little success.

There were a few flags. She would like to see how he changed when he wasn't in control. Or maybe she wouldn't.

By the time Alba had finished with Jayden, Stephens, who apparently would go out into the cold when there was coffee, had returned with Elvira's statement.

It was loose. Elvira had tried to avoid committing to anything however admitted Fran often met her there to help her open the café. Greer hoped Alba wasn't expecting any more doughnuts.

Grimaud had also found another jogger who verified seeing Fran, and this one could place her in the area at six-thirty. While it wasn't in the laneway itself, Alba seemed to think it was enough to support a search warrant for Fran's home.

They arrived in style, with four police cars and a crime scene van. Greer would have been happy to wait at the police station, but Alba insisted she come along.

"Fran has given us permission to search without her present, so your only job is to keep Fran in a quiet part of the house. The last thing we need is her running around hysterically."

Greer shot Alba a glance. "Since when has Fran ever been hysterical?"

"You never know. People can go a little crazy when suspected of murder," said Alba. "Here goes fucking nothing."

"That's the spirit," said Greer and in they went.

While the police searched the house and emptied cupboards that had so much stuff in them, it was a miracle it fit in the first place, Greer was having one of the most awkward conversations of her life.

"So, now you are working for them, and they think I did it?" asked Fran.

Greer couldn't say anything about witnesses putting Fran at the scene of the crime. Still, she wasn't about to lie.

"I think the term they use is a person of interest."

Greer and Fran sat in the kitchen. Greer shivered. The late afternoon sun wasn't strong enough to provide any warmth and asked Fran if they could turn the heating on. Fran just looked at her and then dropped her head into her hands.

"What am I going to do?"

Greer's mind raced, and her chest tightened. Who was she in all of this? Fran's friend or police consultant? Could she be both?

"Listen to what they say about your rights and use them."

Fran didn't raise her head.

Sometimes, there is wisdom in just keeping quiet and the teacup full. Greer also found the heating controls and some biscuits.

14

Alba

The search dog raced along an invisible thread, its large wet nose pressed to the ground. It laid down on a patch of flowers in the garden, crushing them completely. Alba bounced on her toes, her heart racing. She called the forensic team over, and they started digging.

Of all the things she had expected to find, a sizeable metal pigeon statue buried in the widow's garden had not been on the list. But the fact that the techs said it had blood—and of Michael's blood type—on it was enough for her for now.

Alba walked up to the house, taking a breath to calm herself down. Her palm pressed flat against her stomach, lest her lungs bottom out. Greer wouldn't be happy. Not that it mattered.

She found Greer and Fran sitting around the kitchen island, sharing tea and biscuits.

"Fran Williams," said Alba.

Fran lost a bit of colour at the formality of the tone. She put her cup down and met Alba's eyes. "Yes?"

"I'm formally detaining you for questioning. You do have the right to remain silent, and any statements you make might be used as evidence against you. You also have the right to obtain legal advice or contact a support person. I will ask that you come with me, and we can organise for you to contact whoever you need to at the station."

Greer frowned but thankfully didn't raise any useless objections.

Fran stood, swaying a little before taking a deep breath and following Alba.

Alba left the techs to finish searching and followed the police car with Fran back to the station, taking Greer with her.

Fran had sought legal advice and, in a show of good sense, had not called in one of the Jones siblings and engaged a criminal lawyer from Mountview.

The woman played it smart. When she said that she wouldn't talk until the lawyer arrived, she meant it. Not that it would help her. They had discovered a text on her phone to Elvira, asking her not to say where she was that Monday morning, just after the superintendent's visit advising her of Michael's death. Which would explain why Elvira's statement was so ambiguous.

Finally the lawyer arrived, and they began the interview. But despite her best efforts they couldn't establish all of Fran's movements that morning. Primarily because of Fran's unfortunately competent lawyer, who wanted to avoid any accidental admissions.

Did they have enough? She called a meeting with Russell and Stephens to step through their evidence.

The superintendent was in the conference room when Alba arrived.

"So, you've formally brought Fran in. Are you looking to charge her?"

"The evidence is circumstantial, but we have three witnesses—her friend and two people jogging in the area—who place her near the murder. We found the pigeon statue with blood on her property, and the techs confirmed it matches the victim's blood type. We know she's the primary beneficiary. We also know that the marriage was in trouble and that she lied to us when we asked her about her movements that morning."

"There are gaps," said Russell. "How did she know Michael would be in the laneway that morning? And she isn't the strongest woman. Do you really think she could have brought that statue down on the skull of a man with sufficient force?"

"The pathologist said there was a hit across the back of the head, potentially the first blow which would have dropped him down for the killing one. Maybe she got lucky, or maybe she knew what she was doing."

Russell sighed and looked away from the board towards Alba.

"Draw up the charges." Russell's movements lacked their usual energy, and his voice was soft.

"Yes, sir."

Stephens rocked up with a cup of tea in his hand.

"Stephens, some more paperwork for you. We're going to charge," said Alba.

"Woop, Woop."

He was a weird one.

Alba advised Fran and her lawyer that they would progress to formal charges.

She found Greer in the visitor's seat at her desk.

"Thanks for your help with this," said Alba.

"What for?" Greer folded forward as if the weight of her head was too much. "Contributing to the wrong person being arrested?"

"It doesn't say much for marriage, but the spouse is the prime suspect for a reason," said Alba, her stomach hot and jittery. She hoped she was right on this one. Despite the gaps there was also too much information to ignore.

"I just don't see it." Greer rubbed the back of her neck. "There's nothing for Fran to gain. She would've gotten enough if she'd just divorced him."

Alba ran a hand over her face. "Maybe...maybe, it wasn't about the money. Maybe it's about the fact that he cheated on her, and she couldn't take it."

Greer straightened, her free hand falling into her lap and her fingers curling. "Have we confirmed there was an affair?"

Alba's mouth was dry. "No, but we don't need it to charge Fran."

"You have it wrong."

"Can you say—absolutely—that she's not the killer?"

"No, I can't." Greer rose to her feet. "However I can say it is unlikely and is not in alignment with the behaviour we have witnessed."

"Which changes nothing." For fuck's sake, a bloody weapon trumped an opinion any day of the week.

Greer put her free hand on her hip. "If you really think Fran is the killer...then I assume it is safe for me to go home?"

Fuck.

Alba could see Fran killing her husband but struggled to see her running around, swinging at Greer's head, and attempting to break through doors.

"I'd feel more comfortable if you waited until tomorrow."

"You agree it's unlikely Fran attacked me?"

Alba glared at her. "Don't assume it's the same person. Maybe someone was protecting Fran."

"Surely the risk is less now you have arrested her?"

Alba grabbed a glass of water and took a sip.

"We're both shattered. It won't kill either of us if you crash at my place one more night. Did the rental agency confirm they have secured the house?"

"The reinforced locks should be in tomorrow." Greer stared back at Alba her face expressionless. "I need to stop at the bookstore."

Alba took that as acceptance of her offer of one more night.

"Give me a few minutes. I need to see if Stephens needs a hand." Alba's lips tightened. Maybe she should just let her go back to her place. If she did though, Alba had a sinking feeling that the next dead body would be Greer's.

The front door had a closed sign hanging on it. Greer fumbled with her bag and keys with one arm, refusing Alba's offers of help.

Apparently, work did not include serving customers as Greer locked the door once they were inside. Alba found her book and returned to her chair. The lamp next to it was gone, so she had to move a few around to have enough lighting. She managed to read another chapter before a knock on the front door pulled her out of the book. She could hear Greer foolishly opening it. What was the point of having police protection if you didn't use it? Alba closed the book and started to stand when a familiar nasally voice cut through the air. Alba paused in her half-standing position and then sat back down.

"Your shop has been closed again today. Closed at two in the afternoon."

"I'm sorry, Amos, about the murder and the two attacks on me. You have heard about them, haven't you? Perhaps you didn't see the sling on my arm?"

"It's not my problem if you have...issues. Under your agreement with me, you keep the same business hours as the Mad Cutter."

"I have kept to those terms for five years."

'Well, I'm cancelling your lease.'

"You can't cancel it. Have I ever missed a payment?"

"Not the point, you've breached it, and I am cancelling it."

"It doesn't work like that, Amos, and you know it."

"Fine, well then take this as notice that I won't be renewing it."

"What?" said Greer, her voice rising and ripping through the store and Alba's eardrums. "Amos, you can't be serious. I'm the only bookstore in town, and you run the local book club. How does that make sense?"

"Got an offer from another bookstore. As a bonus, they won't be as interfering as you are."

"You really are a piece of work. You know that? And who is this magical offer from?"

"Your lease is up in two months."

The sound of the door slamming reverberated through the store. Alba wasn't sure if Amos was leaving or Greer had slammed it behind him.

Alba pushed herself out of the chair.

"Swearing may help," said Alba.

Greer's laughter had a slightly hysterical tinge.

"He's the worst," said Greer. "I used to love this bookstore. With everything that has happened...." She paced in front of the doors, wringing her hands.

Alba put her book down and leaned against the counter. "Where will you move the store to?"

Greer stopped at the end of a bookshelf and started picking up and putting back books. "I'm wondering whether I even want to stay in Lakes End."

"They say not to make any big decisions quickly."

"What made you move?" Greer looked over at her with a raised eyebrow.

Alba could see where this was going. "I needed to leave my old department in a hurry."

"What did you do?" asked Greer.

"What did I do? For fuck's sake, what makes you think it was me?"

Greer raised her right hand and took a step backwards.

Alba grimaced an apology. "My partner turned out to be a corrupt asshole. Worse, everyone seemed to know, including my father, who is an ex-cop. That is everyone—except me."

"Hmm, layers of betrayal. It must have been hard."

Alba pointed her finger at Greer. "Don't psych me with your empathic bullshit."

Greer appeared amused. "I was merely stating a fact."

"Yes, but you don't care if it was hard, so don't pretend to."

"I can still feel empathy because the foundations of your relationships and profession took a beating, even if I don't particularly care about you." Greer smiled. "I won't waste too much time on it, though. After all, you have a job, a house and the ability to make friends. When did all this happen?"

"What did I say about not psyching me?" Alba's eyes shifted around the store, noticing that everything that made the bookstore work was Greer's and had little to do with the space. There was no reason she couldn't take it all with her. Anyway, maybe Amos would calm down.

Greer cleared her throat, but the smile stayed on her face. "I take it you didn't wait before making any major decisions? You what? Changed jobs and rented a house in Lakes End within a few weeks? You know what hypocritical means, right?"

"Bought." Alba picked up her book and pretended to study the cover and hid the crease she had put on a page.

"Bought." repeated Greer. "Don't preach to me about hasty decisions." She threw up her good arm and returned to the counter, packing up and shutting down the computer.

Alba shrugged. "It seemed like a good idea."

Greer gathered her keys in her hand and stood there looking at them. She raised her gaze to Alba. "Do you regret it?"

"I don't know yet." Alba loved Lakes End. It was the police department that she had an issue with.

Seeing the darkness under Greer's eyes, Alba called it a day and once they had double-checked that the bookstore was secure, they headed back to her place.

Alba did a U-turn and parked in front of her house.

"I know that hurt you somewhere deep within," said Greer, her voice full of amusement.

At least she had succeeded in being entertaining. Maybe if the police thing didn't work out Alba could join the paramedics on the comedy circuit.

"Hell yeah," said Alba as she climbed out of the car and headed inside.

The mess in her kitchen had been waiting for her all day. She stood looking at it. She didn't know what she had been expecting. Maybe deep down, she hoped Henri and Eli would break into her house, and she could pretend to be mad at them. In fact, she had the entire speech planned.

"Close the door," said Greer, pushing in behind her. "Miles will get out and he might get hurt."

Alba snorted. "Yeah right. He's bigger than the dogs in this street."

Greer laughed. "Don't let his size fool you. He is a soft fur ball, really. Miles." Greer's voice lifted in a singsong chant. "Miles, I'm home."

A thump-thump vibrated through the ceiling from the direction of Alba's room, and what sounded like a herd of elephants followed by an air-raid siren descended the stairs.

Greer squatted down to fuss over the furry killing machine, who flipped on his back and let her rub his tummy. Alba didn't move as Miles swivelled his head towards her and flicked his tail.

"I'll clean up the kitchen," said Alba, wanting to get it over with.

"Ah, do you want me to help?" Greer's voice had a hopeful tone in it.

A knock sounded before Alba could answer.

"Wait," said Greer, pushing Miles into the laundry. "Okay, you can open the door now."

"Thanks," said Alba, her tone flat. She opened it to reveal Henri and Eli, who had grins on their faces and dishwashing gloves on their hands. Alba's body relaxed, and she gave them an enormous smile.

"You didn't think we would just hit it and leave, did you?" said Eli.

"Please never say that again," said Alba. "Thanks." She stepped back and waved them in.

"Greer, no offence, you look like death warmed up," said Henri after one glance in her direction. "With one arm in a sling, well, you won't be much help, will you?"

"No, possibly not." Greer gave a wobbly smile. "I'm happy to try, though."

"Nonsense, go upstairs and rest, and take that fine furry gentleman with you. Poor thing has been on his own all day. We can take care of it."

As soon as Greer opened the laundry door, Miles bolted out and ran upstairs.

"He needs some food and fresh water," said Greer. She thanked Henri and Eli again.

Alba watched her follow Miles upstairs and turned back to Henri.

"Please tell me you caught Eli on film last night," said Alba.

Henri assured her she had and that it was superb.

With that the three of them, it didn't take long before the kitchen was clean. Henri and Eli didn't stay afterward though.

Greer hadn't returned and even though it was too early Alba showered and crawled into bed. Even with her brain shouting all the unanswered questions about the case, she couldn't put sleep off any longer. Alba could feel her consciousness slipping away when a large, warm, furry body flopped down next to her back but she was too far gone to feel alarmed. And she wouldn't admit it to anyone but the vibrating warmth was soothing.

15

Greer

The chilly air against Greer's face contrasted nicely with the warm cocoon she was in. She stretched out her legs and toes, trying to do soft stretches without aggravating her throbbing shoulder and her eyes drifted open. There was just enough light for her to make out her suitcase, overflowing with clothes, sitting on top of the dresser and the slightly ajar bedroom door.

In too much pain to go back to sleep, she went to the bathroom to find her painkillers and face the day. It took her a while, but once dressed, she headed downstairs.

She found coffee, hash browns in the freezer, and some eggs that didn't float. By the time she had the coffee on and hash browns in the oven, Miles had come out of hiding. He weaved around her ankles, talking to her, and put his paws on the countertop, giving a big stretch, reminding her he was here and hungry. Finding a plate, she put some food out for him in the laundry.

Greer was whisking the eggs when loud thuds started moving down the stairs. Looking up, she saw Alba, still in her PJs and a robe wrapped around her for warmth.

"What the actual fuck?"

Greer recoiled.

"I'm sorry?" asked Greer.

"Do you know what time it is?"

"Not specifically." Greer looked out the window. There was less light than she expected.

The coffee started making bubbling noises. Greer grabbed some old-fashioned brown cups decorated with bright orange flowers and poured.

Alba glared at her cup before accepting it and collapsing into a chair.

Miles walked over to Alba, sniffed her legs, and jumped onto the chair next to her. He sat there staring at Alba until she turned and stared back. Happy that he had her attention, he purr-meowed and lay down but monitored her and Greer.

"I've got hash browns and scrambled eggs if you want some?"

Alba waved her free hand, which Greer interpreted as acceptance.

"What's the plan for today?" Greer pulled out the pan, hoping the conversation might distract from the clanging sounds.

"We'll process Fran's arrest."

"That's it? What about all the other unanswered questions?"

"We'll continue to track Michael's movements. Close any holes for the prosecution. I'd like to know how his car got home."

"His car?"

"We have him driving through a yellow light just after six in the morning. I still don't know how his car got back home, though. Of course, Fran would have the keys."

"So, she kills him, visits her friend, taste tests some doughnuts and then somehow gets her own and Michael's car back to their house?" asked Greer, stabbing at the eggs in the pan with the spatula.

"People can surprise you," said Alba, her shoulders stiff.

It was a relief when Alba's phone went off. Apparently, others were early risers too.

"Mauzer...yes and... are you sure...yes...okay...send it...good..." Alba hung up.

"There's a phrase. You get more flies with honey than vinegar," said Greer.

"Yes, and I never understood it. Why would you waste good honey getting flies?" Alba finished her coffee and joined her in the kitchen. Greer put down two plates of hash browns and scrambled eggs and poured them both a second coffee.

Greer drank black coffee the same way she drank whisky, with a mixture of pleasure, pain and a liberal use of water. She shuddered slightly as she knocked back a shot.

"I'm going to head home today," said Greer.

Alba sculled the rest of her coffee. "I can't force you to accept protection."

Apparently, that was all Alba had to say on the matter. In the end, Greer organised her own transport. By the time most people were arriving at work, she and Miles were once more in their house looking down on the town with the lake sparkling in the morning light.

Miles was ecstatic, running from room to room and calling for Greer to follow like a little kid. After he settled, Greer got changed into her smartest work clothes. It took a while with the sling, but she felt more normal than she had in days. With that, she headed into the bookstore.

With Amos already set to kick her out, Greer decided not to rush and took the long way in. The wind had died down, and the sun was out, giving the town a crisp, clean feel. As she walked along, she could see people smiling as they went about their business, a spring in everyone's step. If this was a movie, everyone would probably launch into a dance number about how great it was to live here about now.

She smiled and nodded to people she knew, or even people she didn't. It was that kind of day. Inside, her muscles quivered, and her throat was tight. How could they charge Fran on such little evidence? Admittedly, the bronze pigeon in Fran's backyard wasn't helpful. It just seemed insane that they would arrest her when they still didn't know so much.

At the shore, continuing out onto a small jetty, Greer leant against the railing. The warmth of the sun on her face bringing a moment of peace. Only the throbbing in her shoulder disturbed the tranquillity. She reached up to touch the injury and winced. None of this had been her choice.

Looking out over the lake, Greer took a moment to absorb the beauty. The view helped her step back from it all and calm herself down. After all, calm is clever. Unfortunately, the world couldn't be forgotten forever. One more large breath, and then it was time to head back to work.

Victoria had opened the store and was in her usual reading spot. Greer wasn't sure what to tell her about Amos' threat. Was it even real? Maybe he would calm down. Or if he didn't, perhaps she could find somewhere else. She couldn't imagine going back to a life where she didn't have a bookstore. It would feel like a betrayal to Dale.

She watched Victoria, who had to know she was there by now, ignore her and continue to read. It was a good advertisement for the books. Maybe she should employ readers? Get some people to come in to sit and read, give the place, or the next location, a vibe.

"Thanks for opening up."

"No worries, I got the newsletter off to ISite Design. Windary said he would have Tanya drop them over as soon as they did the print run and once I have the electronic version, I'll email it out."

Greer laughed and took a seat on the stool. "What would I do without you?"

"I honestly don't know." Victoria glanced up. "Which reminds me...I need a raise."

She picked up a book and gave it to Victoria. "Here's a bonus." Victoria sniffed and went back to reading her book.

Greer shifted a few books around. With Fran charged, technically she was free from the whole sordid mess.

"Do you know where Kendall is?"

Victoria kept her gaze fixed on her book. "Kendall? No, why?"

"It was on one of the blogs." Victoria put the book down. "The odds are definitely on her, though I think there is still one pool going that has the Jones siblings as the frontrunners."

"Your pool?" asked Greer, her lips twitching.

"No comment. The spouse with the murder weapon in her backyard...she's definitely the fan favourite."

"The evidence seems to be pointing to her." Greer examined the bookstore. Maybe she should just stay here? Warm, safe and away from all the murder business. However, it wasn't really safe anymore, was it? This too was about to be taken away.

"I want to talk to Kendall. The police have largely dismissed that angle however I think something was going on."

"I said that at the beginning," said Victoria with a sniff.

"Yes, oh great all-knowing Victoria, you did. However, it wasn't my responsibility then. It was police business."

"And now it's yours?" asked Victoria, leaning back in her chair like a queen on her throne.

"They attacked me, remember? I need to know what's going on."

"And free Fran."

"Sure, that too. So, Kendall?" asked Greer. She had to do something.

Victoria made a phone call and after a brief argument about whether someone should stay, the Book Distillery's closed sign went on the door. The clincher being that Victoria had her car.

Kendall's place had once been the home of a large and hopeful family. Now that it was just Kendall, he had moved unnecessary furniture into the garage. The result was that Greer's hello almost echoed back to her.

"Greer, Victoria, welcome. I just heard about Fran, such terrible news," said Kendall. Despite his obvious distress he smiled warmly at them.

"Thank you. I hope you don't mind my asking about Michael? Even though the police have arrested Fran, I'm still assisting them with the investigation," said Greer, which was technically accurate. "I want to make sure we have all the facts."

"Of course, of course, I know you've been helping them," said Kendall.

The entire town probably did.

"Would you like some tea?" he asked.

Greer smiled. "That would be delightful."

Victoria made herself useful by offering to do the making and disappeared off into the kitchen. Kendall led Greer into a room with an old wooden table and four white wooden chairs in a bay window area looking out over a beautifully maintained garden.

"What a wonderful spot," said Greer, taking a seat in the winter's sun and enjoying the feel of its faint warmth on her skin.

"Yes, I often start the day here. It's so pleasant you almost forget that the rest of the world exists."

Greer settled herself in the chair, but it was hard to keep her arm from being squashed on the wooden arm. "When Victoria told me he bought all your furniture. It surprised me."

Kendall's chin dipped downwards. "I thought he was going out of his way to help me out. Naïve, I know."

"Do you know what he did with it all?" asked Greer.

"After he got it valued, he took it away. I don't know what happened to it. It certainly wouldn't fit in his store..."

"So you did have it valued?" asked Greer.

"Yes, though Michael organised it all." Kendal smiled at her, his expression sad. "I really thought he was doing the right thing, you know."

"Of course." Greer adjusted her arm again. "Do you remember who did the valuations?"

"I don't remember his name. But I took photos of the valuation certificates for my records." Kendall picked up his phone.

"You don't have the originals?" asked Greer.

"No, Michael kept those for when he sold the items."

Of course he did.

Greer watched Kendall flick through his photos. He finally paused and held out his phone for Greer to see.

There were twenty formal valuations. Six pieces of furniture, ten lamps, and four statues. Most were only worth a few hundred dollars and for one statue, fifty. The valuations themselves probably cost more than some of the items.

"That's a lot of lamps," said Greer.

Kendall laughed. "Yes, Winnie hated having the overhead lights on and liked rooms to be lit by lamps. Dust collectors the lot of them."

Greer suspected she would have liked Winnie. She zoomed in to see if she could identify who the valuer was. Kendall was not the best photographer, but she made out a name, Theo Lopez.

"Do you mind if I take a picture of any lamps you kept? I think my next step is to talk to this Theo valuer person."

Kendall looked excited. "Ah, the investigation's afoot." He took back his phone and found the relevant valuation certificate. "But I can do better than a picture. I have one you can take with you."

"Even better," said Greer. "I'll see what I can find out."

"I have to say this is all rather exciting." He grinned at Greer as Victoria returned with the tea. "I feel like I am in a game of Cluedo, and it was the Professor in the library with the lamp."

Victoria rolled her eyes. "Of course you do."

A phone call secured them an appointment that morning with the valuer and after finishing tea, Greer and Victoria set off to meet Theo Lopez.

"I'm surprised that you didn't stay with Kendall," said Greer. "I would've thought you'd want to be there curling up with him on the sun lounge I saw in the other room."

As soon as she had spoken, Greer realised she didn't want to know the details of their relationship and was grateful Victoria ignored her.

The mountain area where Theo lived was popular with weekend inhabitants, offering views across the lake and a ten-minute drive into the town centre. As they followed the road up, the houses became sparse. Theo's house turned out to be a well-constructed, mid-century modern home perched on poles welded into the mountainside with panoramic views.

They pulled into a park next to a door with a sign that said *Theodore Lopez, valuer of antiquities and art.*

A clean-cut man opened the door—early thirties, Greer guessed. He didn't smile on seeing them, however his brown eyes were friendly.

Greer beamed at him while Victoria's face moved to the more extreme end of her dour spectrum.

"Mr Lopez? I'm Greer Roberts. We spoke on the phone?" She held up the lamp in her hand in case he missed it.

"Ms Roberts—"

"Greer, please." She flashed an even bigger smile at him.

"Please come in." He stepped back and gestured towards another door.

The large room beyond had a worktable running slightly off-centre down the middle, stocked with tools and implements for examining finer details. The entire room had a steampunk vibe that Greer loved. At Theo's request, she placed the lamp on a wooden stand.

He picked it up and examined it. "I think I valued this one, or a comparable one, recently."

"Yes, from a similar set I believe, that's how I got your name." Greer widened her eyes in an attempt to look harmless. A faint snort from Victoria was quickly muffled with a cough.

"Ah. Just the one to be evaluated today?"

"Yes, for now." Greer stepped closer, though careful not to enter his personal space.

Theo got to work examining the lamp, taking pictures of it at all angles.

"So, Mr Lopez."

He paused and glanced at her. "Please call me Theo."

"Theo." Greer tried not to sound too enthusiastic. "I got your details from a client of Michael Williams. I believe you have done valuations for him in the past?"

"Yes, I've been working with Michael for years now."

"And you'll still issue a certificate for this lamp? Even though I'm assuming it's not in the higher-end bracket?"

He smiled at her. "It looks in the same condition as the others so you can expect a similar amount."

Greer tried to ignore Victoria, who was poking her in the back.

"I have to admit I'm not sure what to expect," said Greer. She shifted away from Victoria before she started stabbing her in her sore shoulder.

Theo laughed. "A bit of an antique roadshow moment for you then. The lamp has an estimated value of around a thousand dollars."

"Oh my," said Greer. That seemed like a lot of money for a lamp, especially as the other had been valued closer to a hundred dollars. Was it that simple? Did Michael just shave off a zero? It was hardly Machiavellian.

Looking at the lamp, Greer wondered how she would get it back to Kendall safely. Putting it on the back seat of the car seemed foolhardy now.

"Thank you, Theo," said Greer.

"My pleasure. It usually takes me a day or so to organise the formal certificate. I'll let you know when it is ready."

"Oh," Greer laughed self-consciously. "I thought you'd issue it now. I mean, I am happy to come back, of course, it was just I thought…"

"It's possible to produce it straight away, for emergencies like Michael's earlier this week. But there are extra charges for quick turnarounds and odd hours, and if you aren't in a rush, I wouldn't recommend it. I can pack the lamp safely for you."

"Odd hours?" asked Greer, feeling adrenaline rush through her at the words *Michael* and *earlier this week*.

"Some people might be morning people." Theo turned his attention to Greer and flashed her a smile. "But I'm not."

"Me neither." Greer smiled back perhaps a bit too enthusiastically. "It's all too traumatising."

"I was up at six in the morning to do an evaluation the other day."

"Six? in winter? That's horrific." Greer shuddered. "Why would you agree to do that? For any amount of money."

"I was flying out, and Michael had a buyer for that day. It happens, though thankfully not often."

Theo carefully wrapped up the lamp. "I swear the whole town was up that morning."

"The whole town?" asked Greer.

"I had to stop at the service station. You know the one just outside of town? Anyway, Fran, Michael's wife, was there getting milk. It makes sense, I suppose, once one is up, the entire household is."

Greer frowned as she tried to remember the timeline Alba had put together. Victoria seemed to have wandered off. Where was she? This was good stuff.

"I know you said he had a buyer, however if it was a lamp like this one, I might need to contact Michael and see if it is still available."

"Sorry, it was a metal statue. A pigeon in the art déco style. Most likely one of a pair." Theo's weight shifted onto his heels, and he stared off into the distance. "If he had both, I would have bought them myself...a beautiful piece."

Victoria came back into the room, her heavy footsteps muffled by the thick rugs.

"Sorry, needed to use your restroom. Age, you know."

Theo didn't seem worried and handed over the now-packed lamp to Greer. She thanked him for his time.

Once they were back in the car, Greer turned to Victoria. "Where'd you go?"

"I did actually need to use the toilet. You know, some of us need to use the restroom every now and again."

"Really?" asked Greer, her eyebrow raised.

"Okay, fine, I couldn't stand the two of you making googly eyes at each other. It was nauseating. And I wanted to have a snoop."

"Find anything interesting?"

Victoria sighed. "No, his place is practically a museum."

"Well while you were snooping, Theo told me he saw Fran at the service station near Mountview after six in the morning. How could she be there and be in the centre of town to kill Michael before six thirty?"

The last time she had felt like this was on a roller coaster ride her brother had convinced her to go on. It was that moment, after taking so long to get to the highest point, when the carriage paused.

"Service stations have CCTV, don't they?" asked Victoria.

"Yep," said Greer, a grin breaking out across her face. "We might get Fran out of this mess after all."

"But if Fran didn't do it, who did?"

"One step at a time Victoria, one step at a time."

"You're the one who's going to step in it if you aren't careful," drawled Victoria.

Dale,

I only have a second. I am out fighting crime again today and rescuing damsels in distress. I might have to order a cape.

Admittedly, Fran is not exactly a young maiden, and they haven't released her yet. Still, I don't think the police will ignore this evidence. This must count towards my good deeds, right? Averting a miscarriage of justice! Sorry, I am giddy.

We might not know who killed Michael, but I am getting a clearer picture of what he was up to that morning. He definitely ripped Kendall off, and who knows how many others. Tomorrow is another day, and I am excited to see what I can find!

I can hear what you are thinking, so I will be careful. I promise my goal is to resolve this as soon as possible and return to being a lowly book pusher.

It will devastate you to know that you are missing out on the latest shipment, including a new Harry book. Maybe I should change my name to Harry? You know, because I kick ass at the last minute!

Wish you were here.

Greer, aka Harry, the last-minute kicker of asses.

16

Alba

Alba ran her hand through her hair for what felt like the thousandth time and tried to stay focused on the investigation. The pigeon used to kill Michael was in Fran's backyard, for fuck's sake. What was she meant to do?

Alba worked her way through the paperwork, filling in the forms and getting the necessary approvals. Her background check on Fran included criminal history checks, domestic violence orders and traffic offences. While there wasn't anything in the criminal history or domestic violence space, apparently Fran had a bit of a lead foot.

There had been over six speeding tickets, usually on the road between Lakes End and Mountview. The Mountview Police Department had just finished processing her latest offence. Alba glanced up from it as Greer and Victoria entered with a lot of energy and a box. She looked at their faces and at the speeding ticket in front of her.

Fuck.

"Alba," said Greer as she came up to her desk with more animation in her face than Alba had seen so far.

"Are you here to tell me that Fran was at a service station near Mountview at around six-fifteen? Which would mean there was no way she could get back to the laneway and then to Elvira's by six-thirty?" said Alba.

Greer and Victoria stared at her.

"You had to ruin it, didn't you?" said Greer.

"Mean, that's what you are, mean," said Victoria.

Alba couldn't stop herself from smiling even though she was screwed.

"Sorry. Please share your news," said Alba, sweeping her hand in front of her in invitation.

Greer huffed. "Not much point now is there? You already seem to know. How do you, by the way?"

"Fran got a speeding ticket. What about you?"

"Michael was using a valuer, Theo Lopez. He saw him that morning. Theo left for the airport at six, running into Fran, buying milk at the service station just after," said Greer, her brows furrowed.

"Lopez, isn't that the valuer Jayden Merritt mentioned?"

Greer's eyes widened. "Yes, yes, it was."

"So, two eyewitnesses, one a police officer, and possibly some CCTV for before six-thirty."

"Is it enough to free Fran?" asked Greer.

"Technically, Elvira's the only witness to her movements between six-thirty and seven-thirty." Both Greer and Victoria looked like they were about to object, and Alba raised her hand to stop them. Alba felt her throat tighten, and she rubbed her face with both her hands. "But you're right, it makes it implausible."

"Which means the case is open again," said Greer, her voice full of unexpected enthusiasm.

"Yep." said Alba. Somehow she didn't think the superintendent would be as thrilled.

Greer tapped the box she was holding. "And we now know he had a buyer lined up."

"And that he was changing the valuation certificates," said Victoria.

Alba examined them. They were practically humming with excitement. "What valuation certificates?"

Greer put the box down on the visitor's chair and leant against her desk. "Apparently, they were knocking off some zeros on the evaluations given by Theo. We took this lamp." Greer patted the box. "His valuation, which he said was the same as before, was around a thousand, but the valuation certificate that Kendall took a photo of is only in the hundreds."

Greer pulled out her phone and showed the picture to Alba.

"What's this got to do with being in the laneway at six-thirty in the morning?" asked Alba. It wasn't that she didn't think it was interesting but it was hard to imagine antique deals going down in an alley that early on a Monday morning.

"Well, he was in a rush, wasn't he? He had a buyer waiting, so he would have had a limited amount of time to doctor it."

Alba ran her hand through her hair, turning it into a scratch at her scalp.

"It's a theory," said Alba.

"The question is, what or who could help Michael change the valuation certificate in that laneway?" said Greer, stabbing her finger at the window. Alba wondered if she saw herself on a crime TV show at that moment.

The actual work was less glamorous.

"Stephens." Alba projected her voice across the room.

There was no immediate response. The sound of a cup being put down and the slow shuffle of feet approaching closer preceded his coming into view. He inched his way over until he saw Victoria, at which point he stood up straighter and lengthened his stride.

"You hollered overlord." Stephens smiled at Victoria.

"Michael might've been visiting someone to help him change a valuation certificate. Find out who could do that and I'll let you sit at your desk all day."

"On it, boss," said Stephens, still smiling at Victoria. "Happy to contribute to the course of justice in whatever form it might take."

"Right..." Alba wasn't sure what to do with this enthusiastic version of Stephens. "Also, we need to look at releasing Fran from custody. We have evidence placing her outside of town just before six thirty." A frown gathered on her forehead. Was this the right thing to do? But if she held her unnecessarily that could cause all sorts of problems. "She's still a person of interest though."

"Knew she didn't do it," said Stephens to Victoria. Victoria just raised her eyebrows, and Stephens flushed. "Have to follow the evidence you know."

Alba took a breath. "Never mind that. Get started on the release paperwork."

Stephens gave a salute and a click of his heels before sitting down at his desk, looking like the enthusiastic police officer he wasn't.

"If the wheels are in motion, I'll head," said Victoria. "The last thing I want to do is hang around and watch people do paperwork." Stephens' shoulders slumped.

"You're heading back to the store?" asked Greer.

"No, taking the lamp back to Kendall's," said Victoria, and with that, she and the box were gone, and Stephens was back to showing his usual level of eagerness, or perhaps even a little less.

Alba called over Beitean and Kotowska and sent them to get a witness statement from Theo Lopez.

Alba wasn't looking forward to fronting up to the superintendent. At least they might finally have a reason for Michael being in that laneway.

Take a breath Alba. Just because you fucked up with Fran doesn't mean you are a shit investigator. You've made mistakes before, and you'll make them again. That's life.

Taking Greer with her, not for protection or anything, she knocked on the superintendent's door.

"Inspector, Ms Roberts."

"Sir, just wanted to give you an update. We've a speeding ticket on the road and an eyewitness putting Fran at the Mountview service station between six and six-thirty on Monday morning."

"A tight window to get back to the town, park your car, find your husband, kill him and rock up to your friend's café at six-thirty," said the superintendent.

"Yes, sir."

"What's the time on the speeding ticket?"

"Six seventeen."

"The statement you are getting...you think it'll verify her at the service station just before that?"

"Yes, sir, apparently she was buying milk," said Alba.

"Ask Mountview to send someone out to the service station to see if we can get a statement from who worked that morning and a copy of any CCTV footage. You'll need a warrant."

"I'll get Stephens on it."

The superintendent's face was once more carved in stone. He tapped his fingers on the table. "Back to the beginning, are we?"

Alba cleared her throat. "Not exactly, sir. The witness will also verify that Michael had a valuation of the pigeon statue done that morning. We suspect Michael was doctoring valuation certificates to reduce their value. It's possible he was getting a certificate changed before an early morning meeting with a buyer."

The superintendent examined her. His gaze flicked to Greer who had been standing next to her watching their conversation like a tennis match.

"Ms Roberts, would you give the inspector and me a moment?"

Fuck.

"Of course." The door closed with a snap behind her.

Alba looked at the wooden walls, empty of any photos or paintings. The only things up there were the professional certificates and awards given to the department. She didn't think this was going to be an award-giving type of day.

"Inspector."

Alba forced her gaze to finish its assessment of the room and to attach itself once more to the superintendent's eyebrows.

"I don't want to release Fran until we are a hundred percent sure of her innocence."

Alba's stomach was suddenly full of lead.

"I believe Stephens has already begun the paperwork, sir."

"On whose order?"

"Mine." It wasn't like it would have been anyone else's. But the superintendent knew that. He just wanted to hang her out to dry, but surely Russell would want her out of custody as soon as possible.

"While I am, of course, pleased that Fran is most likely innocent, I'm not happy with your cowboy approach to handling this case."

"Yes, sir." Alba kept her eyes on the deep crease in the middle of the superintendent's forehead.

"I expect major decisions like this to be run past me first, Inspector."

"Yes, sir."

The superintendent gave a curt nod but didn't dismiss her.

"On another note. I understand you questioned my husband recently."

"He's a local business owner—"

Russell raised his hand. "I appreciate your enthusiasm, Inspector. I really do. My husband..." He sighed and sat back in his chair. "If you need anything from him, you'll let me know, and we'll organise a formal interview with appropriate support people." He smiled at Alba, inviting her understanding.

What the fuck?

"He's not a person of interest, sir, so I don't think we—"

"I hope I'm not leaving any room for uncertainty?" Russell didn't raise his voice, but it was clear the invitation had been replaced by an order.

"No, sir."

"If it's something you are capable of, I'd like this wrapped up sooner rather than later. It's almost been a week, and I know the community is eager for this to be resolved."

If it was something she was capable of? *What the actual fuck?*

"Yes, sir." There wasn't really any other response that she could think of giving. Not one that wouldn't get her fired anyway.

Russell stared silently at Alba, and Alba continued her staring contest with Russell's eyebrow.

"Please let me know if you need anything, Inspector."

Alba left the room. Her stride was long, and she pushed her weight forward over her toes to give her extra momentum. She gestured to Greer to follow her and headed out to the car park.

Alba wanted the day to be over. Instead, she stood at the laneway entrance and watched Greer pace.

"Why are we back here?" Greer paused and put her hands on her hips.

"Because we need to find out why Michael was here." Alba pushed herself off the wall and started walking picking a direction at random.

"Okay, why am I here?" Greer shuffled along behind her.

"Because you're good with people." Alba slowed.

"Are you serious?" Greer threw up a hand. "People are the worst. No one's good with people, not really. There are just different levels of delusion."

Alba stopped and turned back to Greer, a slight tuck appearing in the corner of her mouth.

"Fuck yes, all people are the worst. But if you don't want to connect with them, at least watch them and let me know if any of them flag killer."

They stood there looking at each other.

"Am I included in that *all*?" Greer's eyebrows rose, creating wrinkles on her forehead.

"Sometimes." Alba grinned, but it didn't last. "Look we need to find out why Michael was here."

"We know why, a certificate to change and a buyer," said Greer.

"Yes, but was it a regular thing? Elvira said that Fran often visited early in the morning when she woke up and Michael wasn't home."

"You've already spoken to everyone here," said Greer, pointing out something that Alba was very aware of. She felt she was stuck in a Groundhog Day situation considering the number of times she had been in this laneway over the last week.

"We didn't ask the right fucking questions or people lied. They think it's protecting themselves or others. Whatever the reason, they lie. Fran wanted to conceal a potential motive, and Elvira worked hard to say as little as possible. We need to find out why he was here and who he was meeting."

Taking a breath, she started walking again. It was just after lunch on a Friday, and Alba had expected the stores to be open for once. The closed sign on the first one dashed these hopes. Probably off at a long pub lunch. How these store owners made money, she didn't know.

They checked all the storefronts before Alba walked across Lakes Way and found a set of corrugated iron gates that opened onto a small courtyard. It was a picturesque setting, with a small tree in the middle and a bench wrapped around it. Shingles hung above the four identically carved wooden doors that opened into the courtyard, guiding customers as to which business was which.

"Ah," said Greer.

"What do you mean, ah?" Alba glanced from the courtyard to Greer to find her examining one of the shingles with an intense expression.

"I forgot about ISite Design. Or at least didn't really think about it in context."

Alba looked up at one of the shingles. "ISite Design?" she asked. "What's that, a glasses shop?"

"Nothing that clever." Greer huffed a half laugh. "It's a graphic design business, does things like websites and posters. We use them for our newsletter, just to give it a more polished layout. I'm not a visual artist, and neither is Victoria, I can tell you."

Alba watched Greer ramble, not saying anything until she was sure she was finished.

"So, what you're saying is you use a local graphic designer for your newsletters...within walking distance of your store?"

"Yes, that's right."

"And we've a victim who was using someone to help him alter valuation certificates."

Greer just looked at her.

"And just so I have all the facts straight." Alba ran her fingers through her hair again. "We've just spent twenty minutes going from closed store to closed store before ending up here, in front of the said graphic design business."

Greer gazed at the door in front of them. "Yes?"

"Right, then to clarify my earlier statement, it definitely included you in the all." Alba pulled the door open and walked into a spartan room decorated with creams and pale blues.

Someone had livened it up with some posters that showed a sense of humour. Alba's favourite one was "Dare To Be Different! Be Bold Or Italic, But Never Regular!".

There was an abandoned reception desk with a tablet standing on it. The screen was awake and said, "You're one touch away from a great website" with a button icon.

Alba reached out and touched the screen. It didn't take long before a door opened and a man came out. He had a streak of white in his hair, an imposing nose and ageless skin.

"Hi! Welcome to ISite Design Inc. I'm Windary...Oh Greer, I didn't see you there. Everything okay with the newsletter I hope?"

He looked the embodiment of a respectable business owner, and appropriately dressed for winter, with a burgundy knit top, dark blue jeans and soft-looking grey boots.

"Everything's fine Windary, this is Inspector Mauzer. She's just trying to find out about the attack on Monday."

"Terrible business."

Alba showed her ID. "Did you know Michael Williams?"

"A bit of a shock that, not something you expect to happen here." Windary shook his head, his face sad.

"When did you last see him?" Alba watched as Greer walked around the room, picking up and touching everything. She made a mental note to never take her to a crime scene.

Windary blinked at her. "I've seen him around, sure. I don't think he was one of our customers, though."

"Where'd you see him? In this courtyard?" Alba shifted her weight slightly and tried to look nonthreatening. Just your friendly police officer asking questions, nothing to see here.

Windary looked out the door through to the courtyard as if imagining Michael sitting there. "Yes I suppose so. It's not uncommon for people to sit outside under the tree, taking a moment."

"Anyone else here who might have seen him?" asked Alba.

"Tanya, my part-time graphic designer." Windary jerked his thumb towards the back-office area. "I can get her if you like?"

"If you don't mind." Alba watched Windary turn towards the inner door.

"Tanya." Windary knew how to project.

As soon as Tanya stepped into the front room, Alba knew. She couldn't explain it, but this was Michael's accomplice. Besides, it was too much of a stretch not to think that one of them was somehow involved.

Tanya was a tall woman in her mid-thirties with long red hair and artificially tanned skin. She wore a tight purple top and jeggings. The only geeky thing about her was the Converses on her feet.

"Tanya, is it?' Alba pulled out her notepad.

"Yes." Tanya might have taken a position behind the receptionist's desk, but Alba could see she was shifting from foot to foot.

"What's your full name Tanya?" Alba clicked her pen. Greer, potentially picking up on the morph into police mode, had finally stopped touching things.

"Tanya Zuvic."

"How long have you worked here?" Alba kept her tone smooth and professional.

Tanya looked at Windary.

"About three years, mostly part-time." He smiled at Tanya. "A big help when the work gets a bit too much for me to handle on my own."

"Thank you, Windary." Alba made a note. "Would you mind if we spoke privately to Tanya?"

'Of course not. Just call out if you need me.' Windary wandered into the back room, closing the door behind him.

Alba turned her attention back to Tanya. 'Do you know a gentleman named Michael Williams?'

"The man killed, right? I mean, I know of him. He owns a store next to the shoe shop with that stupid name, Moonstruck Soles or something."

"Solestruck Shoe Shop," said Greer, giving a sympathetic smile.

"Yes, that's the one." She turned her attention to Greer. "I dropped those newsletters off but Victoria wasn't in, so I just put them in the delivery box."

"Thanks," said Greer, her voice friendly. "Appreciate the rush job."

Alba clicked her pen a few times, hoping Greer would get the hint. This was not the time for a friendly chat.

"How's your painting going?" asked Greer.

For fuck's sake.

"Great, my latest is epic, not that any of the old biddies here appreciate my kind of work. They just want pictures of the lake that tourists will buy."

Greer made sympathetic noises. "Maybe you could do a couple of landscapes, just to get your foot in the door?"

Tanya shook her head. "*I* do life in all its glory and mayhem. Not that anyone here has the level of sophistication to appreciate it."

Greer laughed. "Sadly most people have no vision. Don't get me started on the book club."

Apparently Greer was settling in for a full chitchat. Alba stifled her impatience. If she interrupted now she would probably spook Tanya before she got anywhere anyway.

Tanya sighed deeply. "Amos has a painting of a bird in his shop, *a bird*. I could do something so much more atmospheric for a place called the Mad Cutter."

"I know what you mean." Greer shook her head sadly. "I was at Fran William's place the other day. She had this turquoise and sand-coloured painting, pretty enough, I suppose, but hotel art."

Alba kept her face disinterested.

Tanya snorted and rolled her eyes at the same time. "Oh, I know the one you mean. Just dreadful. It always surprised me that Michael, who was so discerning, would have a wife with such little taste."

Alba's fingers tightened on her pen. Now, why would a part-time graphic artist know what kind of art was hanging in Michael Williams' house? It certainly suggested she more than knew of him.

"He made his business out of his good taste, didn't he?" Greer continued to look at Tanya with sympathy.

"Oh yes, Michael had a brilliant eye. He bought a few of my pieces and sold them for a pretty penny. Not in Lakes End, of course."

"No, of course not. I'm glad someone appreciates the work you do."

"Well, Michael appreciated all my skills." Tanya's lips turned up at the edges while her eyelids dropped, giving the impression of a pleased cat.

"What did you create for Michael? Other than your oils, of course," asked Greer with the subtlety of a sledgehammer. Pity she had done quite well until that point.

Tanya paused, looking towards Alba, and her eyes hardened. "I know what you're doing."

Not surprising considering Greer had practically sign-posted it.

"One might wonder why you felt the need to meet at a time when most civilised people are still safely tucked up in bed," said Greer, her eyebrows drawing together creating a sharp line in her forehead.

And now she was moving from sympathetic to antagonistic. That was usually Alba's role.

"It wasn't normally that early, and it was just normal...stuff."

Well they had one admission. She could work with that.

"Stuff? Seriously, if you didn't kill him, I really don't care what it's about." Greer shrugged her expression one of almost boredom.

"You might not, but she will." Tanya shot a glare at Alba.

Alba said nothing but clicked her pen, retracting its ballpoint and putting it and the notepad away.

Tanya crossed her arms in front of her, tucking her hands under them.

"It was Michael's thing," said Tanya, her voice becoming soft and high-pitched. "I wasn't doing anything illegal. He just wanted to use the equipment and for me it was just some extra cash off the books."

"Of course, perfectly understandable. It was Michael's thing," said Greer, smiling at her. Alba thought Greer had pushed her luck far enough.

"Ms Zuvic, now that we have established that you were working for Michael Williams, perhaps you could clarify an issue. Was he meeting you here the morning he died?"

Tanya shifted her weight and took a breath. "Yeah."

"What time did he meet you?"

"Just after six, he had texted me earlier saying that he had an urgent job. I just told him to come back to...well, not worry about it. It was cold, but he was super focused. He could get like that. He liked his work."

"And what time did you get here?" asked Alba bringing her notepad back out again.

"I don't know, six? Or close enough anyway." She uncrossed her arms and frowned at them."

"And Michael was here?" asked Alba.

"Look, he was here. He was in a rush and didn't have time to hang out or anything. I let him in, he did the job, and I left, and he left."

"What time did he leave?" asked Alba.

Tanya stood there, her lips tight and eyes narrow. "I don't know, a bit after six maybe. I know I was home and back in bed with a hundred cash in my pocket by six-thirty."

"Do you know where he went next?"

"I don't really know, do I? All I did was let him in to use our equipment." Tanya breathed in and exhaled heavily.

"Did you see the item he was selling?" asked Alba.

"Yeah, it was a statue of a bird. Michael had it with him."

"Something like this?" Alba showed a picture of the statue that they had dug up in Fran's Garden.

"Yeah, that was it. Look, I've told you everything I know." Tanya shifted her weight and crossed her arms. Her face was hard.

Alba could tell that the well had dried up for now, so she took a step back.

"Thank you, Tanya. That was very useful. We'll need you to make a formal statement."

"I've already told you everything." She huffed and glared at them.

"I'll get a constable to come in and get the statement from you," said Alba, keeping her tone low and calm.

Alba didn't trust her, so they waited with her until the constable arrived. They had some computer files to go through anyway.

Alba organised the warrants and had the computers and Tanya's files copied for evidence. She had also explained to Windary that it was unlikely Tanya would be back that day. She suspected he had heard everything, because while he didn't look happy he didn't object either. She almost felt sorry for Tanya. Almost.

Alba double-clicked a folder dated a month ago and wished she could unsee it. An invitation for a dress-up party where the host had put on a mankini which was, fortunately for everyone, over a bodysuit. Still, it wasn't a good look.

"What's that?" asked Greer, using her feet to push her chair over for a better look. "I certainly wouldn't be RSVPing, yes."

Alba closed the file.

"Have you found anything yet?" asked Alba.

Greer rolled her eyes and dragged herself back by the heels to her own monitor.

Windary had allowed them to use a couple of his computers. While the techs had a copy of the computer and files for evidence and were doing their own scans, Alba hoped to find something today that would tell her who he had planned to sell the pigeon to.

They had finally worked out why he was in this part of town. Great. But it still didn't tell her why he had headed down Merchant's Lane. She was also pretty sure Tanya was lying about her level of involvement.

Greer's laugh pulled her from her musings.

"I've just found a folder full of memes. Check out this one." Greer swivelled her monitor so Alba could see it. It looked like every other meme she had ever seen.

"Yes, hilarious." Alba didn't bother putting energy into her tone.

"So not a meme fan then?" Greer looked at her as if she were some kind of alien.

"Any fake certificates in that folder?" asked Alba as Greer continued to open files.

"I thought you wanted me to be thorough. How will I be a hundred percent sure that there aren't any certificate files if I don't open them?" Greer's eyes widened, and her face had an overly sincere expression painted on it.

"Just scan the thumbnails. We've a lot of folders to get through, and I'd rather not spend the entire day here while you look at funnies."

"Spoilsport." Greer sighed and closed the meme of a cat spread out in the sunshine over some clothes, which apparently represented life.

Alba opened another folder. This was for an online shop that sold hand-knitted toe warmers, not socks, individual knitted covers, for each toe. Well, to each their own, she supposed.

Greer laughed again. "Alba, you'll like this one." An image of a large black and white cat spread out over an enormous bed making it impossible for the human standing next to it to get in dominated her screen.

"Didn't Miles do this to you the other day?" Greer laughed like it was the funniest thing she had ever seen. It seemed absurd for such an uptight person to find cat memes a source of amusement.

"Yes, can you focus? We're here on a murder investigation, remember?"

"Sure, sure." Greer dragged the cursor to the corner of the folder and clicked close. "There, happy?"

"I'll be happy when we find the folder with the certificates."

Having killed the conversation, the only sound in the room was them clicking on folders and files.

Alba opened what felt like her hundredth file when a *wohoo* made her glance at Greer.

Greer grinned at her. "I'm a genius."

Alba turned her chair around but didn't let herself get too excited. "I require evidence, and a lot of it, before I agree with that statement. That said, if you've found them, I will buy the wine tonight."

"I'd like a grenache, a nice one. Check it out." Greer swivelled the monitor towards Alba and a folder with hundreds of files with large thumbnail images of valuation certificates displayed in a grid.

"Holy shit, how many are there?" asked Alba.

"About six hundred," said Greer.

"Can you find the pigeon one?"

Greer sorted by modified date and opened a file that had been changed, unsurprisingly on Monday.

"Looks like Michael would have made a ten-thousand-dollar profit on that bird," said Greer. She glanced at Alba her eyes bright. "Do you think I could see it, the statue?"

"The police evidence locker does not exist for your entertainment." Alba rose and walked over to Greer's computer.

Finding the certificate verified Tanya's story and surely there couldn't be that many buyers in the area who would be interested in a statue at that price?

"I thought you'd say that. You aren't much fun today. Just in case you weren't aware."

Alba shot Greer a glare. "Dial back on those pain meds."

Greer grinned up at her. "Okay, okay. We have the certificates...what next?"

17

Greer

Greer fell into step with Alba as they left ISite Design. Her good cheer faded as they headed back to the laneway entrance.

"So, here we are again." Greer gestured at the overly familiar lane.

"If he ended up in this lane, where was he going?" asked Alba. "And...where was the car?"

Alba and Greer looked back at the street they had crossed and the parking available.

"He could've easily walked over from the Hidden Gem. It really isn't that far, maybe fifteen minutes at most," said Greer. She was invested and wanted to know what happened just as much as the police did. But she had to admit this constant going over old ground was getting a bit tedious.

Alba shook her head. "He was carrying a heavy assed statue which was apparently worth thousands and he'd just left the valuer. He had his car...which was at his home when the superintendent arrived to give Fran the news."

"Then the killer must have driven it home." Greer paced, glaring down the laneway. They already knew this.

"What's in that direction?" asked Alba. She stood there her hands on her hips and appeared to be observing the laneway with dislike.

"No one with shops along here would buy an expensive art déco statue. They're small fry and mainly sell their own work anyway, and as annoying as Amos is, I can't see him being interested." Greer paused, and her eyes lifted, looking beyond the laneway to the other side. "The antique store, or is that too obvious?"

"Antique store? What antique store? I don't remember seeing one on the list." Alba turned towards Greer in a way that made her feel sorry for Stephens or the constables doing the canvassing.

"It's closed," said Greer. Which is probably why no one had mentioned it, though she wasn't sure Alba would see it that way. "Last time I saw Lona and Kolbein Gulbranson they were obviously getting ready to leave as they were putting away the smaller, more expensive items. They take them to be stored at the bank when they're away."

Alba was already on the phone with Stephens. She took some time in articulating that they should have mentioned the antique store when a man was murdered with a rare statue. She was emphatic in her language, though she showed little variety in her swear words.

At least Stephens had done a check to see if someone had stolen the statue from there. Once he had confirmed with their security company that there had been no break-ins, he hadn't pursued it further.

Alba turned her attention back to Greer. "When was this?"

"That I saw them? ... maybe last Saturday?"

"So... they might have still been here Monday morning. Maybe that was the rush? Maybe Michael wanted to sell the statue to them before they left?"

Greer lifted a shoulder. "Possible. But unlikely..."

Still Alba was right. Theo had admired it and maybe for a unique statue they might have made the time.

"I've Stephens tracking them down. Hopefully, we can talk to them today."

"Okay," said Greer, feeling her spirits lift again. She started imagining being home, petting Miles with a glass of wine in one hand and watching the night descend over the lake.

Alba took off down the lane. Greer exhaled heavily and followed.

"He has the certificate, the real and the fake," said Alba over her shoulder. "He's under the clock, presumably because everyone is leaving town. Theo was heading out too, remember? He wants to get this statue off his hands as quickly as possible before too many people know about it or start asking questions."

"Where did he get the statue from?"

"Stephens thinks it was an estate sale," said Alba.

Greer lengthened her stride, attempting to keep up. "This was a big score for him. It would have made him nervous...and excited. He would have been riding that adrenaline," said Greer.

"So, what goes wrong? Maybe he gets greedy? Has an argument with the antique dealers?" Alba reached the end of the laneway and looked at the antique store. Heavy red velvet curtains drawn on all the windows, and the store's name 'Precious Past' painted across the glass in dark swirly lettering. She turned back to Greer, obviously expecting an answer.

Really? How was she to know? She was an ex-psychologist, not a psychic.

Greer shook her head. "They aren't the arguing type. So why use it as the murder weapon and bury it in Fran's backyard? Why not keep it and sell it?"

Alba stood there, frowning.

Greer crossed the road to stand in front of Precious Past, Alba following her this time.

"Maybe someone became suspicious." Alba's eyes lit up. "Someone he'd previously ripped off. That could work. They don't want the statue, don't even know what it's worth. They confront him, he denies it all, they lose it, grab the statue and kill him."

"I don't know. It seems thin," said Greer. She felt she was going around in circles, and she was hungry.

When was the last time she ate? Breakfast?

"My gut's telling me Michael never made it here," said Alba.

"And there's still the car," said Greer, yawning.

"You know this is your safety on the line as well." Alba shot her a very judgy look.

Greer tried to force her jaw closed. "I know." Knowing your life might be in danger didn't make you less tired though. Sometimes the opposite. She was definitely suffering from adrenal fatigue.

"Do you? With Fran released and no other suspects, we have to assume that the person who attacked you is still out there," said Alba, peering up at Greer.

"I'm cognisant of the risks in the situation. Let's continue playing detective, shall we?" Greer didn't wait for an answer. "Lakes Way, the street between the offices and the laneway is broader, with street parking on both sides. He parks there. Why else would he be on foot?" Greer hoped her logical comments would distract Alba from ranting at her.

Alba grunted but gave a nod. "Easier just to leave the car there and carry the statue a few meters than move the car."

Alba sent another text to Stephens. The shops were opening up after their extended lunch breaks, hoping to catch the afternoon traffic. Which is what she should be doing. She needed to sell some books while she could.

"We need to talk to them again and find anyone who might have seen the Gulbransons that morning," said Alba.

Greer spent most of the afternoon wishing the day would end. Alba didn't look like she was having fun, either. On the upside, they had confirmed that Lona and Kolbein Gulbranson were seen driving off Monday morning. Alba texted

Stephens the update and advised that finding them was now a priority.

Greer needed food and water. She leant against the wall and looked towards the backdoor of her shop. That way lay water, however it didn't solve the food problem.

"Have you eaten?" asked Greer.

Alba's eyes were on her phone, and her fingers were flying. "We had breakfast."

"I'm pretty sure that was almost ten hours ago. I need food."

"Fine, we can grab something on the way back to the station."

"I'm not going back to the station."

Alba looked up from her phone. "What?"

"I'm going to the bookstore. Don't worry, I'll ask for a ride home. With Amos on the warpath, I need to look after my business."

"I thought you wanted to eat?"

"Yes, I need food, but on the way to the bookstore, not the station."

Alba frowned at Greer as if she were speaking some sort of alien language.

"I don't have time to stop for food," said Alba.

"That's fine. There's sushi only a block from here."

"Where? I—"

"What's happening?"

Greer and Alba turned to find Amos heading in their direction.

"I hope you've caught the killer, and we can rest safely in our beds tonight."

"Mr Beecher, I can't comment on an investigation," said Alba with a slight drawl.

"So, nothing." He peered at them with disapproval.

Alba's usually expressive face smoothed into neutral.

Amos turned his attention to Greer. "How's the packing up going?"

"I believe you have to give me notice in writing under our lease agreement," was all Greer could think of to say. So much for a witty response.

"Expect it today." Amos smiled cheerfully. Greer admitted to herself, for the first time, that this was really happening. "Perhaps I should wait until they arrest you for killing Michael, and the problem will solve itself."

"Ms Roberts's not currently a person of interest," said Alba.

While Greer was grateful for Alba's defence, she would have preferred that the word currently had not been included.

"Ha, though if she'd killed Michael, I might've looked on her lease with more favour. Good riddance to that blackmailing bastard."

"Blackmail?" asked Alba.

Amos huffed and muttered a few words about hearing things.

"Remember to order some boxes when you receive that notice today," said Amos, before turning and heading back to his store.

Alba and Greer looked at each other.

"Blackmail?" asked Greer.

"First I've heard of it."

"If it's true..."

Alba shook her head. "Not unless I've read the disinterest in his death wrong. I kind of thought it was just because he was boring."

"There has been a distinct lack of interest hasn't there?" Greer thought about everyone's reactions. So little emotion. Maybe some of them were working hard at it. "Really, you'd have expected a lot more questions and gossip, and he can't have been that boring if he was running a fraud and potentially a blackmail scheme."

Alba snorted. "You don't think criminals can be boring?"

"Well, yes, of course they can be. After all, they're people too and have the right to be just as boring as non-criminal people."

Alba laughed. "I'll start a campaign."

"I need to get back. I haven't told Victoria about Amos's decision yet." Greer's stomach twisted. Surely there must be a way through this? A thought of the space that might be available if the Hidden Gem shut down was quickly followed by a flash of guilt. The last thing she wanted to do was to profit off someone else's murder.

"Fine, but I'll escort you, and I want you to stay there."

"I promise, no more wandering through laneways on my own. I don't know what I would do if my other shoulder got hit."

"It's more likely to be your head next time."

Greer laughed. "Thanks for that comforting thought."

After grabbing some sushi, Greer headed back to the bookstore but felt Alba's hand reach out and grab her right elbow.

"Just stay with me, okay?" said Alba.

Greer examined her in surprise. "Do you really think that someone's going to—"

"Attack you in broad daylight on your way to the bookstore?" asked Alba, looking directly at her sling.

Greer touched her shoulder and sighed.

"Fine, so how does this work? Do you go first, or do I?"

"Just stay within reach," said Alba, moving towards the bookstore.

They proceeded down the laneway and into the store's back entrance, a decision that Greer came to regret.

Alba opened the door and did a quick glance before gesturing her through. Greer couldn't help rolling her eyes, which was the only reason she didn't see it at first.

Freezing, she stood there, too stunned to move. Thankfully, there weren't any customers. However that did little to console her at the sight of Kendall making out with Victoria, practically grinding her into the counter, now burnt into her retinas for all time. It was Alba's laugh that broke them up.

Greer knew her mouth was hanging open, but she still couldn't move.

"Alright, kids, let's break it up, shall we?" said Alba in a gruff, official police voice.

Victoria giggled, and Kendall blushed as they straightened their clothes.

"Greer, I didn't think you would be in," said Victoria.

"Obviously," she said, choking out the word.

"Greer." Kendall nodded towards her, still blushing.

"Kendall," she said, not sure what else to say. *How are you?* was not a question she wanted to know the answer to.

Tearing her eyes away, Greer scanned her bookstore. She had spent a lot of time and money creating the perfect atmosphere. Did she have the energy to start again?

"Okay, people, I have to head back to work. Greer call a constable or me when you want to go home."

Not one to waste time with goodbyes, Alba left. Greer, still traumatised by what they had walked in on, straightened her shoulders, ready to have 'the talk' with Victoria and Kendall.

However only Victoria, with a pleased look on her face, still stood there. Kendall had taken Alba's exit as an opportunity to escape out the front.

"Seriously, Victoria? What if a customer had come in?"

"We would've heard the front door. It was only because you came in the back that you surprised us."

Greer patted her hair. "I doubt you would've heard a stampede of elephants the way the two of you were going at it."

"It was..." Victoria's face went dreamy, and Greer's stomach tightened. "That man can kiss, let me tell you."

"Just...you both have your own homes...just not in the store, okay?"

Victoria blushed for the first time. "Fine, but when I walk in on you making out with someone, admittedly not likely to happen soon, I promise not to be judgy judgy."

Greer walked through the bookshelves, randomly picking up books and putting them back again. As she came near the counter, she stopped and stood there tapping the top of a book spine with her index finger. Should she wait for it to be in writing from Amos? He seemed pretty sure.

"So...Amos came to see me." Greer's finger stopped tapping., however her hand remained connected to the book.

"What did the prick have to say this time?"

"He isn't renewing the lease." The books captured Greer's attention again, and she rearranged them, making sure they were aligned perfectly.

"What?"

"He isn't renewing the lease." Greer moved along to the next shelf. "He's got another offer, from another bookseller."

"I don't understand." Victoria came around from behind the counter. She walked towards Greer, stopping next to her with her arms crossed.

"What's there to understand? The lease is up for renewal, and Amos won't be renewing it. He even tried to cancel it early because we have been closed a lot this week."

"He can't do that."

"No, he can't. Which is why he has given me verbal notice about the renewal. I am expecting it in writing today."

"So, where will we go?"

The sound of the front door opening caught their attention. Elvira was standing there, holding one of her pastry boxes. Greer's mouth started watering on cue.

"Elvira." Greer smiled at her, not willing to antagonise her until she was sure the box of pastry wasn't in play. "How can we help?"

"I was closing up, and I thought you might like the last of the doughnuts and muffins."

While Greer had hoped the box was for her, she could feel her eyebrows trying to climb her forehead again.

"Err.... thank you...doughnuts are always welcome."

"I heard what you did for Fran." Elvira walked over and rested the box on the counter.

"The police would've gotten there as well."

"Maybe, but you helped them get there faster, which got Fran home quicker. Especially after I put my foot in my mouth."

"Fran being at your café was a good thing. If she had just told the police, she was out and about..."

"She didn't know what time Michael had been killed, she thought..." Elvira looked down at the box under her hand.

"What do you think about all of this Elvira?" asked Victoria, her tone angry. Greer's eyes widened, and she turned to shush her.

Elvira took a bit of a step back at the force behind Victoria's question. "About the murder?"

Victoria was not someone to be muted.

"No, about Amos not renewing Greer's lease. Apparently he has another offer. I bet it's from one of those soulless chains."

"Any platform that makes books accessible is to be lauded," said Greer.

Victoria's hand dismissed this with a wave.

"I hadn't heard that." Elvira's brow furrowed. "Do you know which chain?"

Elvira's fear that Greer would attach a café to her bookstore might be realised just not the way she thought.

"No, Amos didn't say," said Greer.

"I'll find out," said Elvira.

"I'll put out my feelers as well," said Victoria.

Between the two of them, it would be all over town within the hour.

Elvira took her leave, now focused on this new threat.

They agreed to close the shop, freeing Victoria to find out all the gossip. Greer's excuse was pain and exhaustion. Now she just had to work out how to get home safely.

18

Alba

Alba made herself a coffee and joined Stephens, Ceesay and Grimaud in the conference room.

"I have to say I'm impressed by Michael's enterprise," said Stephens.

Alba grunted. Not that she disagreed. "Do you know how much he would've made?"

"On these certificates alone...I would estimate over half a million dollars in the last year."

Alba shifted her attention more fully towards Stephens.

"Half a million, and no one noticed?"

"He was clever, choosing pieces that nobody really cared about. Old people clearing garages, estate sales where they just wanted it all moved as quickly as possible."

"Still...how long do you think it's been going on?"

Stephens shrugged. "We're looking for older files."

"So, we know what Michael was up to." Alba turned to face the board. "We also know why Michael was in the laneway. But…" Alba caught herself rubbing her face again. "No one even knew it was going on."

"Except for Kendall," said Stephens. Alba could imagine he was envisaging arresting Kendall and removing him from the competition for Victoria's affection. She didn't have the heart to tell him he had lost that race, at least on the evidence of what she had seen earlier.

"Kendall was aware something had happened, but even he didn't really know, and he didn't seem that upset about it."

"Still…" Stephens stared wistfully at their board, no doubt imagining Kendall's face up on it.

"What else have we got?" asked Alba.

Ceesay cleared his throat. "The local police took a statement from the Gulbransons. They say Michael was to meet them at the store at six-thirty that morning, before they left Lakes End. He never showed. After doing some final packing up, they left after seven."

Alba glanced at him and Grimaud. "Can we verify that?"

Grimaud nodded. "The security company has video feeds confirming their statement. Shows them leaving down the road, and the camera at the lights captures them running a yellow. And no, none of the cameras show the laneway entrance or into the laneway itself."

Alba's face twisted in thought. If they were in the shop until seven and caught on camera leaving afterwards, it was unlikely they would have had time to kill Michael. Which meant they were back to square one.

"What about the financials?" asked Alba. "Have we found where he was keeping the money yet?"

"We've found a series of bank accounts held in both Michael and Gregory's names." Stephens couldn't quite contain his excitement.

"Gregory? Really? Grimaud, I think it's time to invite Gregory in for a chat," said Alba. "And why was Gregory a business partner to begin with? Isn't he a real estate agent?"

Grimaud nodded and hurried off, hopefully to track him down.

"We think they were using the houses he had for sale as a front for selling the antiques," said Ceesay, apparently convinced of his own brilliance. She wondered who had actually come up with the theory.

"Possible," said Alba.

"If they shared bank accounts, he already had access to the money. Why would he need to kill for it?" said Stephens.

Alba considered Gregory. Unless he was the world's best actor he came across as relatively harmless and a bit useless.

"How much are we talking?" Alba ran her fingers through her hair.

"Over a million and a half," said Stephens.

"How did they accumulate that much with no one knowing? What were they going to do with it?" asked Alba. What would she do with a million and a half dollars? She wouldn't continue working in a dead-end store in a small town that's for sure.

Stephens looked down at his notepad. "It appears their goal was two million dollars."

"Why two million?" Alba could feel her face scrunch.

"Because there are four accounts, and they have saving goals of five hundred thousand each."

"Saving accounts? What about interest? Surely..." She took a breath. She was getting off track. "We need to find Gregory as soon as possible." The adrenaline pumped through her body. "Stephens, please tell me we have a freeze on those accounts."

"Yes, of course."

"Then I want—"

"Inspector." Grimaud stepped back into the conference room, but her expression was not the eager face she had hoped to see.

"Yes, Constable." Alba's body braced itself.

"Patrol can't find him. He isn't at his home or office, and he has no appointments. We even had one patrol drop in on Fran Williams, and she said she hadn't seen him today."

Alba wanted to growl in frustration. How had she missed this?

"Get a list of all the properties he has on the market. I want them thoroughly inspected. See if you can convince the real estate agent's office to give you the keys. Stephens, get the relevant warrants just in case they hit any roadblocks."

"Will do," said Stephens.

She pulled out her car keys.

"Where are you going?" asked Stephens.

"To visit the Jones siblings. Maybe the delightful Hilary and Alfie know where Gregory has gone." Alba picked up her coat and prepared to leave.

"Do you want me to come with you?" asked Stephens while holding a large file, presumably to look like he was too busy to go outside chasing people around the town.

"No, stay here. If the constables bring Gregory back, start the interview and get the preliminaries out of the way."

Alba headed out into the wintry afternoon.

Her adrenaline was running hot and caused her to misjudge and slam the car door. She struggled to do some deep breathing and calm down. The last thing she needed was to be walking into the Jones' office all revved up. Calm, cool and collected, that is what she was. Just dropping in to see how things were going and check on Gregory and Hilary. Been a rough time for the family.

She hoped the constables had been discreet, but she was possibly delusional in thinking that it wasn't all over Lakes End and the odds in the betting pools were being updated. She had heard from Stephens that Fran being released had upped the stakes.

Maybe Gregory was the killer. Were they close enough to the goal that had kept them going all these years that they were about to call it? Maybe Michael hadn't wanted to share.

Had the plan been to keep the money hidden and divorce Fran? Maybe Gregory would divorce Hilary too. That marriage wasn't exactly full of rose petals and poems. The two cousins are heartbroken. They tell everyone it is too hard to stay here. They're leaving, selling up their business. Off they go together into the sunset. What great cousins they are.

It was a good plan, if that was what it had been. Greed, desire for more and a lack of honour among thieves, their undoing. She laughed at her own melodrama.

The laughter calmed her down and helped her compose her face as she walked into the offices of Next Level Law. She passed the empty reception and opened the doors to both Hilary and Alfie's rooms without knocking. Empty.

She was about to leave when she heard a noise from Jayden Merritt's office.

"Mr Merritt, Jayden?" She added a few knocks on his door for good measure. She was reaching for the door handle when Jayden half-opened the door and leaned against it.

"Inspector, how can I help you?"

She assumed he had a client with him, although from his ruffled appearance, perhaps it was a more informal meeting. He was an attractive man, so it wasn't hard to imagine, not that you had to be attractive to get your freak on. Still, it increased the chances.

"Sorry if I'm disturbing you. I'm looking for Hilary, Alfie or Gregory. We have some information and are having trouble finding them."

Jayden looked down at her with a lazy smile that should have been sexy. Alba's instincts kicked in, and she casually shifted her weight for a better view into the room while pulling out her phone as if to check for something.

Apparently, she would not win any acting awards. She only caught a glimpse, but it wasn't a pretty sight. There was a lot of blood, a body on the floor, and two others tied up. Realising she had seen into the room, Jayden acted faster than she expected. He knocked the phone out of her hand, pulled her into the room, and rammed her face up against the wall, locking the door behind him.

"Now, Jayden." With her breath knocked out, her voice was shakier than she liked. "Everyone knows I'm here."

The only evidence that her words had any impact was a slight increase in pressure of his arm against the back of her neck. She tried to get her legs under her, however with her upper body pressed against the wall and her arms trapped behind her, it was an awkward angle. Jayden kicking at her legs to keep her off balance didn't help either.

He pulled her back only to smash her face into the wall again.

"Don't fucking try anything. There's only one way out of this, and that's me with the money. Or you're all joining Alfie."

Well, that answered the question of who was on the floor. Which meant that it was Gregory and Hilary tied up. Where was the receptionist? She hoped Jayden had sent him away, and he wasn't dead in a bathroom somewhere.

He slammed her head against the wall again, making it difficult to concentrate. She needed him to stop that.

"Are you talking about the million dollars?"

He might be a runner, but he obviously didn't spend enough time on his arm days. All she needed was one opportunity.

"No, I'm talking about the millions, as in plural." Jayden leaned in close to her ear. "Did you know he only paid me a measly three thousand for letting him know about prime estates? Three thousand, and I find out that they were making millions off it when I was the one who made it all possible."

Nothing quite like a self-righteous rant to distract someone. As Jayden waxed lyrical, he didn't notice he had put his head a little too close to hers. With a headbutt that would have made her instructors proud, she dazed him enough to break free. She grabbed one of his shoulders and pushed it down while kicking his legs out from under him. Using her body weight to hold him face down on the ground. She was looking for something to tie him up with when the sound of a door breaking made her glance up and Constables Grimaud and Ceesay appeared.

"Need a hand Inspector?"

It turned out that Jayden drove a red roadster, which was well known in the neighbourhood. Once they found out that Gregory had been seen in Jayden's car that morning, they'd remembered Jayden was near the scene of the murder and had tried to contact Alba. After a call and an SOS ping asking her to check-in, they became concerned and dropped by the law offices.

Alba was bruised both physically and in the ego. Of course, Jayden had been there that morning. She couldn't believe that she hadn't put two and two together.

He clammed up and got a lawyer, of course. He wouldn't get away, though, not with a badly hurt Alfie, the restraining of Gregory and Hilary and an assault on a police officer. Hopefully, his lawyer would discuss the benefits of a guilty plea rather than drag everyone through a trial. They didn't have enough to pin Michael's murder on him though.

If her theory was correct, Michael or Gregory must have let it slip they were leaving or Jayden discovered by accident how big a difference there was between their purchases and sales and started following them. She would never know how the exchange went down. Jayden must have confronted Michael in the laneway, and in the end, Jayden had left with the bloody statue. He would have to run pretty fast to get back to the esplanade after he took Michael's car home. But it was technically possible. If Jayden had stashed the statue somewhere, they might get lucky and find some traces of Michael's blood at his home or in his car.

With Michael dead and Jayden not talking, it was their only shot. If Alfie, Hilary and Gregory knew anything, they certainly weren't sharing it with the police. But there was so much evidence on the other charges that the prosecutors were sure to be pleased.

Despite the bruises, she was smiling as she pulled into the station car park.

Alba's desk phone rang. She almost answered it before checking the number—The Mad Cutter. She didn't have time for him today. The bruises forming on her face would worsen tomorrow, and right now she had paperwork to get done. She sent the call to voicemail.

"Inspector, there's a man here to see you."

A man? Outstanding. Good to see that the front desk was vetting visitors. Alba turned her chair, and for the second time that day, had the wind knocked out of her.

Martese Mauzer, the man who had bandaged her skinned knees as a child, who she had hero-worshipped and followed into the police force. The man she had spent most of her life working to make proud, only to find that it was him she couldn't be proud of.

"Alba," said Martese. She couldn't blame the officer for bringing him to her desk. Martese could always convince people to do things, whether it was giving him the best seat in the restaurant, a free dessert or access to a police station. Alba had tried to be charming like him in her early twenties. It hadn't worked out well.

The bags under his eyes were fuller, smoothing out some of his laugh lines, while the creases in his forehead had deepened. His eyes, dark without their usual sparkle, sought hers.

Alba didn't know whether to call him Dad or Martese, so she said nothing. The others in the room picked up that something awkward was going on and stopped to watch.

Not wanting to be the day's entertainment, Alba stood up.

"Let's go for a walk." She glanced across the desk. "Stephens, if you could—"

"I've got it, Inspector."

Alba smiled at him, gratitude flowing through her. Everyone has value, and sometimes it is just about putting the right person on the right task.

Turning back to the wrong person at the wrong time, her smile leached away.

She said nothing to Martese, just walked out of the building and across the road to the park. Unlike the smaller semi-circle Broadview Park, this one was longer and had several walking paths through it. She waited at the start of the main one for Martese to catch up. He fell into step with her.

"How did you find me?"

"What happened to your face?"

"The job. How did you find me?"

"I asked a favour."

"Of course you did." Alba's lip curled up in a snarl.

"Would you stop?"

Alba halted and looked up at him. It wasn't just his face that looked tired. His shoulders were more stooped, and his usually robust body somehow managed to look frail. She suppressed a twinge of guilt. She wasn't the one who needed to feel remorseful.

"Fine." Alba stopped walking and spread her hands out from her body. "Say what you have to say."

Martese sighed and looked away. Alba watched him take in the park before turning back to her.

"I'm sorry. I should've done something, stopped Jonas if I could. Most of all, I should've told you."

They stood there staring at each other when the ring of a tinny bell interrupted them. A family on bikes was coming through, and they stepped off each side of the path—away from each other.

"Yes, you should've, but you didn't."

"I can't change that."

Once the bikes passed, they didn't move, leaving a distance between them.

"Some things can't be fixed. You just have to accept the consequences," said Alba.

"I refuse to believe that we can't heal this."

"Do you want to know what I think?"

"Probably not." Martese gave a quick, if tired, smile.

Alba ignored the attempt to engage her sympathy. "I think you're an arsehole."

Martese gave a rough laugh.

"And you know what else I think? I think..." She had spent hours, days even, going over exactly what she would say. Time wasted. Now she was like a tongue-tied teenager.

"Why don't you tell me?" asked Martese.

She could tell he was uncomfortable, but that little smirk made the blood pound in her ears and heat flood through her. Her blood probably couldn't actually boil, but it seemed to be giving it a red-hot go.

"You're as corrupt as those who took the bribes and cuts. Maybe you didn't take any cash...not that can be proved anyway...but just because something isn't a criminal offence doesn't mean it's lawful or right."

"How can you say that?" Martese stepped back, his shoulders dropping further forward.

It might hurt but it didn't stop it from being true.

"You're here, aren't you?"

"What, it's illegal to want to talk to your own daughter now?"

"I'm guessing you've used police resources to hunt down another adult who doesn't want you to know where she is. They've fired people for less. You have literally put someone's career at risk to satisfy your own desire. Am I right?"

Her father's face paled during her rant, highlighting the broken capillaries from too many rounds at the pub.

"You're *my* daughter. What about the years I sacrifi—"

"Don't fucking start with that. You had an obligation to raise me—congratulations on meeting your legal requirements. You're also the one who taught me not to lie. How many times did I get grounded for a small fib?"

"I'm just saying that life isn't black and white, and sometimes there's grey."

"When Jonas was taking a cut from the local drug dealer, was that grey? It looks pretty fucking black to me. And you knew, not in a I heard a rumour way. Amy, your old pal had told you outright."

If it had just been a rumour, maybe she could have understood why her dad didn't share it with her. But when Amy told Martese what was happening, he still didn't warn her.

Martese's hand curved into a fist, and he thumped his thigh.

"You're right. I knew, and I knew if I told you, you wouldn't be able to let it go."

"That." Alba pointed at her father's face. "That right there's our problem. You should've railed at it, fought against it."

"You can't turn on your own squad like that. It's not how it works."

"Jonas betrayed the squad the first time he took a cut. Don't you see that? He was the one who betrayed the team, not me."

"And you think this station will magically be better? That it won't have its own shades of grey?"

"Corruption is not grey." The words echoed through the park. Exhaustion settled on her like a heavy blanket. "Just go. Let me rebuild my life."

Martese's eyes filled with tears, and he sucked his lips inwards. Taking a wobbly breath, he nodded. Without another word he shuffled back up the path.

Alba turned away from the police station and went deeper into the park.

Beitean and Kotowska had gone home by the time Alba returned. A few of the other officers looked up as she walked in, but seeing her alone, they returned to the tasks in front of them.

Alba sat at her desk and stared at her screen numbly.

"You alright?" asked Stephens.

"If Jayden's not admitting to the murder...did Tanya give us anything other than the antique fraud?" asked Alba.

"No, only that she let him use ISite Design. What are you thinking?" asked Stephens.

"Blackmail mainly," said Alba. "Maybe he, or he and Tanya. She's involved in this I know it, had something on Jayden, something that—"

"What's this about blackmail?" asked the superintendent. Alba forced herself not to jump. She had assumed Russell had already gone home.

"We heard a rumour today that Michael might've had a hand in blackmail, as well as fraud. I was just asking—"

"Can I speak to you, Inspector?"

The superintendent turned towards his office and Alba followed, shutting the door behind her.

She took a seat, suddenly too tired to stand.

"Inspector, tell me about this blackmail."

Alba looked at Russell and realised she had a problem. If she said she heard it from Amos, she would have to admit that she ignored a direct order. Also, if Amos was being blackmailed, did that mean that the superintendent was a victim too?

Fuck

"Mr Beecher mentioned it wasn't a bad thing Michael was dead as he was a blackmailing bastard, or something to that effect, sir."

"I wasn't aware that Mr Beecher had been in for questioning."

"He approached Ms Roberts in the laneway. I don't know if you are aware, but he's ending Ms Roberts' lease and wanted to confirm that fact with her."

"Is he? No, I wasn't aware of that." His forehead's crease deepened ever so slightly. "Amos and I don't discuss work, as I am sure you can understand."

"Yes, sir." Alba kept her gaze up and her face bland.

"I'm still not clear how this led to a conversation about the case."

"He said he might have extended the lease if Ms Roberts had killed the *blackmailing bastard*." This time, Alba could see the annoyance clearly on Russell's face.

Russell sighed and rubbed his eyes.

"Have you ever been married, Inspector?"

"No, sir."

"I can tell you that having a spouse can be both a blessing and a curse."

Alba shifted in her chair. The last thing she wanted to do was discuss the pros and cons of marriage.

"Do you know why he called Michael a blackmailing bastard, sir? I understand you have known him and Fran for many years." No one had ever said she was smart.

"Are you interrogating me, Inspector?"

Alba took a breath, but Russell held up his hand and smiled.

"No need to argue your point. It's a valid question. There's some bad blood. Michael wasn't perfect by any means. I believe he got a sense of satisfaction from holding Amos's IOUs from some bets when they were younger over him. Hence the blackmailing bastard comment." Russell gave a soft laugh and sat back in his chair, inviting Alba to laugh at the folly of others.

Alba pulled back her lips and gave a few huffs of breath.

That was a laugh, right?

Russell examined her and was apparently satisfied that she accepted his explanation as he relaxed more in his chair.

"I understand Jayden's been formally charged?" asked Russell.

"We've arrested Jayden for the assault on Alfie Jones, myself, and for the assault and unlawful detainment of Gregory Williams and Hilary Jones. While he was near the scene, I've little evidence concerning Michael's murder, though we are searching his car. If there was blackmail, that might give us a motive."

"If you're pursuing this just off what Amos said, I don't think you have much to justify putting resources into it. See how the search on the car goes first." Russell drummed his fingers on the table and took an audible breath. "Unfortunately, I also have something serious that I need to talk to you about," said Russell. 'I've had some complaints.'

The adrenaline made her muscles contract but went as quickly as it came, leaving her both tense and tired.

"Complaints?"

What the fuck? She was a fucking delight, or at least she had been trying to be. She hadn't even called them ignorant fucksticks yet. Not that she remembered anyway.

"Yes, apparently, you've used some inappropriate language when talking to the other officers. I'll give you some slack because I know your old department, but you need to know that we speak with respect here. As the second highest ranking officer, I expect you to model that."

Okay maybe one had slipped through.

"Yes, sir, it won't happen again."

"In the meantime, I have allocated the constables back to Senior Constable Savas."

Savas ran the roster for all patrols, community engagement and handled all the minor crimes. Which basically
meant the entire station. Alba had sometimes wondered
what Stephens had been doing before she arrived.

"Sir, you don't have to—"

"It's for the best Inspector."

How exactly? There were two words for this and one of
them was cluster.

"Yes, sir." It was the only response she could think
of—again—that would not get her fired.

"On a better note, I'm pleased to see Stephens' level of
engagement. It's been a long time since I have seen him put
this much effort into his work."

So what? Russell had been okay with his doing nothing?
But he had a problem with her expressing frustration about
work not being done? Good to know.

"Thank you, sir," said Alba and used her arms to push
herself up from the chair.

"Inspector?"

Alba paused awkwardly in her half-standing position,
unsure which way to go. Russell just looked at her, so after a
moment, she sat back down.

"I want you to succeed here, and I like to think I create a
happy work environment."

"Yes, sir."

"But make no mistake Inspector, when I give an order, I
expect it to be followed." Russell's voice was calm and soft,
and he smiled warmly at Alba. "I just want to make sure
there is no room for ambiguity."

"Follow orders, yes, sir." A wave of anger rolled through Alba.

"Excellent. I look forward to the next update on the case." Russell smiled again, but this time, it did not fool Alba.

She left the office with her stomach a few steps behind her. As she opened the door, she could see Greer pushing her way into the station, her hair frazzled and without a coat.

"Alba..." Greer scanned the room only stopping when she saw her. "Someone tried to kill me...again."

19

Greer

Greer locked up behind Beitean and Kotowska, who had reluctantly escorted her home via the grocery store, and turned the new security system on. How had her life become so dramatic that she now required bodyguards to buy milk?

She started unpacking her groceries without Miles getting in the way, which was a relief. He had a dangerous habit of lying precisely where she was about to walk, then looking up at her expectantly, waiting for pats and food. He seemed to trust that she wouldn't step on him—confidence that was largely misplaced, especially when her hands were full.

The fridge door was slightly ajar, and the oat milk had spilt on the floor. Who knew how long it had been like that? Grateful there was not much left, she threw it all out and rinsed out the coffeemaker. After putting away the groceries, which took a lot longer with one hand, she poured herself a generous glass of wine and put her phone in her pocket.

Once she found Miles, they would settle down in the armchair and watch funny video clips together and try to forget the past few days.

She heard the rhythmic banging of blinds as she moved through the house and hurried down the hallway into her lounge room. One of her favourite lamps was lying on the floor, and the blind moved as icy gusts found their way inside. What was the point of a security system if someone could enter by a window?

Miles. He must have gone outside. She put her wineglass on the coffee table and pulled the cord on the blind, sticking her head out the window. Her breath caught on seeing his still body and the puddle of vomit next to him. Swinging her legs out the window while holding her sore arm, she dropped to the pavers, the jar of the landing making her tear up. She stumbled forward and touched his body. Warm. A good sign, right?

She kept patting Miles, refusing to believe that he was dead. She looked up at the window. What had she been thinking? There was no way she could climb back in with one arm.

Her phone.

She inhaled—in what felt like the first time in a while—and pulled the phone out of her pocket.

The vet took one look at her with Miles in her arms, Isaac on one side and Lucinda on the other, and rushed her through, allowing them to follow while they questioned her, then dismissed them to the waiting room.

"It's going to be okay," said Lucinda, sitting next to her and navigating her sling to give her a pat on the back. "How's the shoulder going, anyway?"

Aggravated and throbbing.

"Oh, you know, painful, annoying, the usual."

"Have you taken any painkillers lately?" asked Lucinda. Greer shook her head, and Lucinda clucked her tongue and dug some out of her jacket.

Greer waved them away. "I need to think."

"These aren't prescriptions. They'll just help it settle down a bit. If the pain gets worse, you'll need to see your doctor...consider that an order."

Greer tried to twist her lips into something resembling a smile.

"Thanks." Greer knocked them back with a small cup of water from the fountain in the waiting room. "Will you get in trouble for using the ambulance for a cat?" She did feel a bit guilty about calling them and hoped their kindness didn't create any difficulties for them.

Isaac settled next to her non-injured side and put his arm around her shoulder.

"Don't worry, once Lucinda disinfects the—"

"Hey bro, I'm not doing that on my own."

He laughed. "As I was saying, it'll be fine with a little elbow grease from sis here." Isaac grinned at Greer and was about to say something else when he and Lucinda got an alert.

"Our public awaits, it seems." Lucinda smiled at Greer. "I hope Miles is okay."

"If he is, it will be because of you." Greer thanked them again and watched them leave as they argued about who would drive and who would clean out the back. As they stepped out the vet's front door, Isaac turned, giving her a wave and a thumbs-up, making her smile for real.

When she had come to Lakes End, Greer and Miles had found a home in each other. She wasn't sure what it said about her life. With the risk of losing him in front of her, she realised he was the only being in her life that she loved. He was hers to look after, and she had failed, failed to keep him safe.

Her face was fiery and wet. She battled with it, trying to regain control. Every time she thought she had it, a thought of Miles dying or Miles in pain would enter her mind, and the process would start all over again. No matter how real the emotion was, it wasn't what she needed right now. She needed to find out who had done this to him.

Instead of doing anything however she sat there in the waiting room that time seemed to have forgotten. When the vet finally came out to talk to her it was to advise that they suspected Miles had consumed antifreeze. They were optimistic that they might have caught it in time, but it would be touch and go through the night.

There was nothing more she could do. Miles was unconscious, and in the best care she could provide. Her emotions swung from guilt and grief to anger. How had they poisoned him? Why would they? She saw in her mind the spilt oat milk. He always did need to put his face in everything.

She just hoped she hadn't been too thorough in her clean up and there was enough left to test. If they were trying to kill her, why move from physical force to poison? And she wanted to ask them what made it so vital that she died.

Greer didn't want to go back to her house, so she rang Kotowska and gave her the alarm codes. She mentioned her suspicion about the oat milk, and Kotowska said she would organise testing, though she didn't sound too optimistic considering Greer's clean-up. Alba wasn't answering her phone, so Greer called a ride and headed to the station. As she rushed in, she saw Alba standing in the superintendent's doorway.

"Someone tried to kill me...again," said Greer, throwing her voice across the office. "Miles got poisoned instead, and now..." She ran out of breath.

Russell joined Alba in the doorway.

"Is he okay?" asked Russell.

"It'll depend on his kidneys." Greer stood there. She wanted the police to ride out as Valkyries, slaughtering anyone in their way as they found out who did this. Russell and Alba did not look like they were going anywhere. Greer walked over to them.

"Poison?" Alba stepped forward. "I'll send out—"

"Beitean and Kotowska are already on their way to my house and are organising testing," said Greer.

'Testing?' asked Russell.

Greer wondered if his first thought had been about his budget but dismissed it just as quickly. He was just as much of an animal lover as she was.

"The oat milk. I think that is where the poison was, probably intended for me, but Miles, he likes to lick it, anything really. There was a spill, and the fridge wasn't fully shut when I got home."

"They left the fridge door open?" asked Alba.

"Yes, I think so. I mean, it could've been me, but I don't think it was."

"Interrupted again." Alba frowned, her eyes unfocused.

"What?" asked Greer.

"I think they were interrupted again. Hence the open fridge door."

"And the open window." Greer tried to remember whether she had heard anything when she had gotten home. "Beitean and Kotowska escorted me home. But I swear no one was there when I went inside."

"Close," said Alba, rubbing the back of her neck.

"But—"

"Best go into the conference room." Alba glanced around. "Stephens, you too."

Stephens stood up from his desk and headed over to join them.

Greer looked around the open-plan office. While there weren't many still here this late on a Friday evening, she was definitely the centre of attention.

She followed them in and slumped in the conference room chair. Any energy she had deserted her.

"Tell me what happened," said Alba.

Stephens set up his laptop, and since Russell had followed them in, the four of them sat there and tried to work out what Greer knew that was worth killing her for.

Alba and Stephens also brought Greer up to speed on Jayden's arrest.

"It couldn't have been Jayden, not this time anyway," said Greer.

She was disappointed that he was involved at all. A waste of a nice face.

"Maybe not this time," said Alba. "But the other attacks? It makes sense. People would recognise him if they saw him."

"How's that relevant?" asked Russell.

"Greer has a theory that our killer is well known," said Alba. "Which's why they ran as soon as the police were on their way."

"Indeed," Russell's body sat up straight, and he clasped his hands in front of him, using them to rest his chin on.

"But I didn't see him." Greer slumped deeper into her chair.

"He obviously thinks so," said Alba.

"So, what about this attempted poisoning?" asked Greer. Could she really have more than one person trying to kill her? In Lakes End? She ran a bookstore, and she was hardly Kinsley Millhone.

"Fuc—I...don't know, potential accomplice maybe?" Alba cleared her throat.

Russell flicked her a glance but turned towards Greer. "Ms Roberts, I'm so sorry to hear about Miles. I believe there's a special circle of hell reserved for those who hurt animals. I hope he's okay."

Greer's eyes teared up, but she swallowed it down and nodded.

"Superintendent." Alba leaned forward. "With this latest attack, perhaps I could keep Beitean and Kotowska for a few more days? At least until we've checked the neighbourhood out."

"You and Stephens can handle it and Savas will keep the patrols up near Ms Roberts' house." He examined Alba. "I want you to check her security system yourself."

"Yes, sir."

Russell looked around at Greer, Alba and Stephens.

"It might seem counterintuitive, but I suggest you all go home and get some rest. Jayden's in custody, and you all look like you need it." With that, they watched him leave, taking his own advice.

"Why did he say it like that? You and Stephens?" asked Greer.

"The constables are back reporting to Senior Constable Savas."

"What? Why?" asked Greer. What plausible reason could Russell have to reduce the resources on this case, which was obviously still very much active?

"I...let's just say that Stephens and I will continue investigating this case unless we need the extra help, of course."

There were still so many unanswered questions. Heat and electricity seemed to run through her body, and she stood.

"What does that mean...really?" she asked. She paced towards the window, looking over the car park in time to see the superintendent's car drive away.

Greer heard an exhalation and the creak of a chair.

"It means we stop canvassing the neighbourhood looking for witnesses." Alba came and stood next to her, looking at the fascinating car park.

"What because Lakes End is a hotbed of crime, and you have a lot of other things to investigate?"

"You'd be surprised." Alba's mouth curved but didn't quite make it to a smile before settling back into a flat, hard line.

Greer clenched her teeth. Miles was almost killed, and they reduced the number of officers on the case? It was absurd.

"Look." Alba reached out and rested her hand on Greer's good shoulder. "With Jayden in custody, I can't continue to throw the resources at it, but it doesn't mean we stop."

"What about the attacks on Miles and me?"

"Stephens and I've got this." She glanced over at Stephens who had remained seated. "Don't we Stephens?"

He nodded but didn't get up and join them, instead focusing on the screen in front of him.

Greer didn't trust herself to say anything.

"Which brings us to the question of your safety."

"I don't think she should go home." Stephens looked up from his laptop. "We don't know why they targeted Greer, and she's right. We can't assume it's only Jayden involved."

"I can see him carrying out an attack on impulse..." Greer tried to visualise him again. A tall and physical man, smart too. "But poison?" It left too much to chance. He would want control over the situation.

"I think you'll have to stay with me for a few more days. Stephens and I need time to work out what is going on," said Alba, returning to the board.

"Okay," said Greer with a large exhalation. It was easy to say. She didn't want to go back to her home. It didn't feel safe anymore. Regardless of the outcome of this case and what was happening with the bookstore, she was going to move. Preferably to a house with solid walls and bars on the windows.

"Let's follow the superintendent's advice. Stephens, you go home too. I suspect tomorrow is going to be a big day." Alba turned towards Greer. "Do you need anything from your place?"

Dale,

Why do I make the same mistakes repeatedly? Why do I trust that this time the police will do the right thing? I am a fool and Miles is badly hurt.

They were after me and this time it was poison. We don't have any lab results back, but the vet thinks it is antifreeze. Why else would it be there?

One of the players in this comedy of errors is in custody and I get the impression that the police think it will all stop. Maybe they are right. Maybe I am being too critical. It is not like I have been that useful. I am rusty, out of practice.

The question is, am I safer to cut my ties or stay close to the investigation? For now, I am back staying with the inspector, Alba. I don't feel safe at my place anymore. At least with Alba, I am surrounded by people.

On another note, because when it doesn't rain, it pours, Amos is ending my lease for the Book Distillery. Would you forgive me if I walked away? Gave up our dream of a bookstore?

I am going to shower and change. Hopefully, that will clear my head.

I need a hug right now.

Wish you were here.

Greer

20

Alba

Well, what a fucked-up day that had been.

Alba took her laptop and some files home. If she could work from home tomorrow morning, she would. The last thing she wanted was to spend any more time at the station than she had to.

Alba didn't want to ask for help, so they had to pile Greer's things around them in her car. She was glad they didn't run into Jeffrey. To top it all off, Greer had insisted that they U-turn and park in front of Alba's house.

With Greer unable to assist, it took her a few trips to bring everything back inside. They had both been on the go for over twelve hours, so a shower and change were necessary. Unfortunately, because of the age of the house, using both showers resulted in alternating blasts of hot and cold before settling down into a lukewarm trickle. She didn't linger.

Alba made her way back to the kitchen and poured them both a glass of whisky. She kept looking out of the corner of her eye for Miles and had to remind herself he was still at the vet.

She sat down and waited for Greer. If she went outside, there was a chance that Henri and Eli would pop round. She kind of hoped they would. Alba didn't want to cook or be with her own thoughts tonight. But she wanted to make sure Greer was up for it.

Greer took her time and came downstairs dressed like she was about to lounge around drinking cocktails. Did she even know what casual clothing was? Alba looked down at her own. She was wearing the same clothes as she had every night this week, old warm tartan leggings, an oversized shirt and her warm robe with its hole in the shoulder. Alba tried to keep the laundry to a minimum. She quickly took a sniff of the shirt to make sure it was still okay.

It was fine.

"How are you feeling?" asked Alba.

"In pain, weary and hungry." Greer took the whisky Alba offered her and collapsed into the vacant armchair. "To make it worse, I just realised that I left Elvira's doughnuts at home."

Alba laughed. "Don't worry. I grabbed them."

Greer mimed wiping her forehead in relief.

"Before he went home, Stephens asked Beitean to follow up with the vet for an approximate timeframe for the poisoning. Kotowska is checking out the red-light cameras as well. Considering everyone here seems to think yellow is a suggestion, we might get lucky."

Stephens asked because she couldn't fucking talk to her own team anymore. All Russell had to do was say, don't swear. Better to fire her than leave her there, unable to interact with anyone but Stephens and Savas.

"Unlikely," said Greer, her head resting on the back of the armchair.

Alba finished her glass of whisky. Why use poison? And even if Greer died, what would it change?

"Do you want to sit outside? I can turn the heater on, and if we're lucky, Eli and Henri might come over and feed us."

A tired smile appeared on Greer's face. "Do they usually feed you?"

"Hmm, there is about a sixty percent chance. Eli cooks every day for his show, so they usually have plenty of food."

"What do they do with it if you don't eat it?"

"A food bank. Henri used to work for the local council so has all the contacts. Don't worry. They give them more than they can handle."

Greer took a sip of her whisky.

"So, what you're saying is that we are going to sit outside in the cold hoping your neighbours will feed us."

Alba's cheeks heated, but she couldn't stop the grin.

"With wine."

"Oh, I'm definitely in," said Greer, returning the smile.

Gathering glasses, cutlery and extra bottles of wine, they headed outside.

Alba turned on the heater and the light.

"Bat-Signal engaged."

"Of course, you like Batman," said Greer, laughing.

"Who doesn't like Batman?"

As Alba had hoped, it wasn't long before Henri and Eli let themselves through the garden gate. They weren't carrying food but taking in the two women, wine and cutlery, they laughed.

Henri tsked. "Eli, I'm concerned we're encouraging dependency in the children."

Eli just grinned.

"Why wouldn't they become dependent? My food's amazing. Give me a second." And he disappeared back into the hedge.

Henri sat down, and Alba offered her a glass of wine, which was graciously accepted.

"You've been busy, haven't you?" said Henri. "Greer, how are you holding up?"

Greer took a sip of her wine and huffed out a breath. "To be honest, I thought I was okay, but with what happened to Miles...and I swear my shoulder is throbbing more now than it did two days ago. I'm exhausted."

Henri blinked at her. "Miles? What happened to Miles?"

"Someone tried to poison Greer and ended up poisoning Miles instead," said Alba.

"Will he be okay?" Henri rested her hand on Greer's left wrist.

"Argh."

"Sorry dear." Henri removed her hand and patted Greer's knee.

"The vet's optimistic. Fortunately, I came home early. If I hadn't..."

A clang of the garden gate saw Eli come through with a tray with three serving dishes and some bowls. Alba jumped up to help him.

"Did you see my latest clip?" asked Eli, maintaining a singular focus as always.

"No one cares about your clip. Someone poisoned Miles," said Henri.

"You said it was my best one yet." Eli bit down on his lower lip. "Will he be okay?"

"The vet thinks so," said Greer.

"Glad to hear it. Thank you," said Eli to Greer, who had handed him a glass of wine. "When he's feeling better, I'll make him the fish dish of his dreams. In the meantime, tonight, we will enjoy a beef bourguignon with mashed potato and broccoli sides."

Clement, who Alba suspected waited to hear the menu, stepped through the gate. A bottle of wine in hand.

"Ah, my fellow neighbours, so good to see you." He smiled warmly at all of them.

Alba smiled back. "Clement, join us." She gestured at one of the remaining chairs.

Before sitting down, Clement crouched next to Greer.

"How's the shoulder going?" He held his hand just above the shoulder before touching it.

"It hurts today," said Greer, her face scrunching up.

"To be expected." He adjusted her sling slightly. "I want you to come in and have it checked out. Just to make sure it is healing right." He took a seat at the table. "I have to say that it's all over the hospital today that Fran's out, and Jayden's in."

Clement smiled at Alba, and she felt a warmth that she usually associated with the first sip of wine.

"Yes, it's been a tough time for the family," said Alba. She still felt bad about Fran's arrest. But really what was she meant to have done?

"I'm glad that the police released her." Clement shook his head gravely before taking a sip of his wine. "Several people in the community, namely the Lakes End book club, were outraged at the original arrest."

"Okay." Alba wasn't sure why she should care about a book club and turned towards Eli to ask about his latest clip, a guaranteed conversation changer.

"The book club, oh dear, that's not good, Alba," said Henri, her eyes wide.

"It's just a book club, Henri," said Alba, taking another sip of her own wine and feeling the exhaustion of the day slowly fade. She looked over at Greer, who had taken the time to dry her hair and wished she had done the same. It was cold. She pushed her fingers into one pocket of her robe, hoping that she had, yes, left a beanie in there. She pulled it on, and while it didn't feel terrific against the wet hair, it was definitely warmer.

"No, no, no." Henri shook her head with force. "The book club in Lakes End is mighty."

She had handed everyone else their bowls heaped with tastiness but still had Alba's in her hand. Alba watched it, wishing that Henri had made her point *after* handing it over.

"Who's in it?" asked Alba.

Greer's laugh was loud in the quiet night air. "Feels like all of Lakes End sometimes."

"Well, Eli and I aren't. We got kicked out after the food poisoning incident," said Henri.

"How was I to know they would leave the salmon mousse out until the club meeting was over? Which took hours, by the way." Eli stared down at his food. "Amos can rattle on."

Alba watched him take a big bite of his stew with envy. She looked back at Henri, who still held Alba's bowl in her hand.

"I believe the standing member list is currently at almost fifty people. Not everyone turns up, of course," said Clement, who also had his bowl and was happily eating away. The bourguignon looked good.

"There used to be several smaller ones," said Henri, gesturing with the bowl towards the town. "You know, friends hanging out with friends. But when the last bookstore closed, Amos organised an official book club for bigger discounts and cheaper shipping. It's why he'll only rent out his space to a bookstore. He was so thrilled when the Book Distillery opened." Henri flicked a sad glance towards Greer who just shrugged and kept eating.

"I can't imagine," said Alba, picking up her spoon, hoping it might prompt Henri.

"Then..." Henri leant forward, holding the bowl almost absentmindedly. "Suddenly, Greer was recommending books for people to read. Amos did not like that at all."

Henri looked down at the bowl in her hand and handed it over to Alba.

Finally

"Don't worry, Henri." Eli patted her knee. "I'm due for a trim soon. I'll go to the Mad Cutter...see if I can smooth-talk him."

Henri smiled at Eli and ruffled his shaggy hair. "If anyone can smooth-talk him, it's you."

Eli smiled back at her and handed her a bowl, seeing she had forgotten to serve herself.

"How did that recording go today?" asked Alba.

This was enough for Eli, who explained his cooking technique and the successful filming of his latest video clip while they finished their meals.

A sound came from the front of the house. There was only one person who would knock this late at night. Groaning, she pushed herself up and shuffled over to the front door. Opening it, she could see she was right.

"I parked on my side. What more do you want?"

Julius smiled at her.

Wait, what?

"Greer sent me a text that she was back staying with you. Is she here?"

Alba looked up at his face, which was much less pinched than usual. She checked his pupils to make sure he wasn't on drugs.

"Sure." Alba stepped back and gestured him in. She had the whole gracious-host thing down pat.

Seeing everyone else out the back, Julius headed on out to say hello.

Alba still wasn't sure how her place had become the community house. The previous owners hadn't been overly social. According to Henri and Eli, they had barely said hello in the entire six years they had lived here. Alba tried to remember what she had done in her first few weeks that had made them feel so comfortable.

As Julius sat down, Eli brought out a self-saucing lemon pudding. Alba pushed her spoon through the rather dry cake to find a lake of thin lemon curd below. Possibly not what Eli was going for, but it was still tasty though.

After dessert, the conversation returned to murder.

"I heard Tanya got taken in for questioning about some false certificates," said Julius.

"Poor Tanya," said Eli. "She's done well to get herself set up again. Though her paintings are still a bit on the dark side."

"I can't imagine what she went through," said Henri.

Alba just nibbled at the lemon pudding and waited.

"Her husband." Eli addressed Alba. "Took all their money, left a load of debt and ran off with some tourist who was here for the summer...she didn't take it well."

"It would be enough to knock anyone off their feet," said Clement.

"Still, she got them back under her," said Henri, with an edge of admiration in her tone but then sighed. "To lose it all again because she helped another asshole fudge a few numbers on a certificate..." Henri scooped up the rest of her lemon pudding on her spoon and ate it in one go.

"How *is* the investigation going?" asked Julius.

Perhaps it was the wine, maybe it was her anger about the complaints or frustration at the attacks on Greer. Whatever the reason, Alba broke her own, and several departmental, rules.

"We've charged Jayden Merritt today with several offences. While technically the charges don't include Michael's murder, we suspect he was helping Michael find antiques."

Michael's certificate fraud scheme was now known to the community. Stephens had shared that once Tanya had given her statement, she had apparently needed a drink and ended up telling the whole story. Small towns really weren't all they were cracked up to be.

"Who got his money?" asked Julius, just in case anyone forgot he was an accountant.

"I think it's strange," said Greer, "that Gregory shared accounts with Michael."

Henri and Eli both leaned forward. This was obviously new information. Alba stifled a groan.

"Do you think Gregory was involved?" asked Henri.

Alba had enough self-control not to offer any further information.

"Gregory's someone we're talking to. I think we should leave it there for the night." Alba tried to bring the conversation back to the dinner and thanked Henri and Eli for the lovely meal. While it wouldn't help her get back into her good activewear, she had enjoyed it thoroughly.

"Personally, Alba." Whenever Henri had had a bit of wine, she started using the word personally a lot. "Personally, I'd try to stick it to the Joneses. Never liked them, and if we could get rid of Alfie especially, the town would be a lot better off."

"I can't just charge those who we don't like," said Alba. "I'd also like to point out that Alfie is the victim here."

"With him out of the way, we could definitely get back into the book club," said Eli.

Alba blinked at her. "What?" It was hard to imagine any book club being worth this much attention.

"Alfie had terrible food poisoning," said Clement. "I remember putting him on a drip."

"Alfie and Hilary are in the book club as well?" asked Alba.

"Yes, everyone who is anyone is," said Henri with an overly loud sigh.

"*I* heard they have a flamenco guitarist coming to the next mixer," said Julius.

Eli and Henri both groaned. Clement solved their sadness by pouring more wine and reassuring them they weren't missing out. He also seemed to pick up on Alba's exhaustion and organised it so that it wasn't long before everyone was saying their goodbyes.

The food had made Alba mellow enough that she could say a somewhat friendly farewell to Julius. He must have felt the same as he reciprocated.

It wasn't a late night, but it had been good to talk, laugh, and share food. As she loaded the dishwasher and secured the house for the night, she was grateful for being here and making these friends. Even Greer, while annoying, wasn't the worst company in the world. But right now she needed some sleep and suspected she had a big day tomorrow.

"You know where we haven't checked yet," said Greer, handing her a glass to put in the dishwasher.

"Where?"

"The Hidden Gem."

"Michael's store? We got all the paperwork pretty much on the first day, and the constables have checked it out. Nothing flagged."

"Maybe they missed something. I mean, they didn't know to look for antique fraud and hidden bank accounts, did they?"

Alba sighed. Another thing she should have thought of—and didn't.

"Stephens and I'll go back and have another look tomorrow."

"What if tomorrow is too late? Remember Amos' blackmail comment."

"The superintendent didn't think it was anything." Considering Russell knew the players and having met Amos herself, Russell's explanation seemed reasonable. Or at least that was what she had been telling herself.

"Of course he wouldn't. If Amos is being blackmailed, he's being blackmailed as well,' Greer banged down the plate she was holding a little too forcibly. Alba turned as the sound echoed and picked it up to check for cracks. Reassured it had survived, she gave Greer a reproachful look and added it to the others in the dishwasher.

"We can't go tonight," said Alba.

"We have to. The family's going to do the inventory tomorrow, remember?"

Alba closed the dishwasher door and exhaled audibly. She was right. But surely there would be time in the morning before the family descended.

"It wouldn't be illegal," said Greer. "You already have the search warrant, and you believe that there's a risk of destruction of evidence."

"Do I? Good to know. I'd still have a hard time explaining why I entered the property at nine o'clock on a Friday night after dinner and some wine."

"You barely touched your wine. We need to check it out tonight." Greer started pacing. Because of the size of the room, this required a lot of back and forth.

"Why do you care so much?" Alba realised why as soon as she spoke.

"Why?" Greer spun around and stared. Alba worried her eyes might bulge out of her head.

"Sorry, I—"

"Miles! He almost died, or have you forgotten that already?" Greer, who was usually a reserved person, the kind that you noticed when they smiled as they so rarely did, was windmilling her arm, and her voice was rising in pitch and volume.

"Look—"

"We need to find out who is doing this."

"We have Jayden, he—"

"Jayden? Do you really believe that Jayden tried to kill me three times? Why? He admitted he was near the crime scene, so if I saw him, so what? And he was busy attacking Alfie during the poisoning. No, it isn't Jayden or not only Jayden."

Alba stood there. She knew it wasn't wise to go tonight, especially considering the conversation she had today with the superintendent.

Fuck it and fuck them.

"Fine, but I have to change."

21

Greer

Both of them had changed into black jeans and black tops. Greer laughed when she saw them reflected in the mirror of the wall stand.

"This will not look good," said Alba with a shake of her head.

A bubble of excitement shivered through Greer. They looked like they were about to do a heist, not a search on a premise of a murder victim. Greer had even covered her sling with a black scarf.

Despite Alba's mumbling she led the way out of the house. It was a quick drive to the Hidden Gem and Alba found a park on the road behind the store. Greer walked up to its door before stopping. She patted her hair down and stood there, reluctant to ask the obvious question. She heard a jingle and turned to see Alba standing with a grin on her face and the keys in her hand.

"How—"

"I may have had a shitty day at work today, and I brought home a few of my files."

"And keys?"

"Okay, I brought everything home."

The bitterness in her tone made Greer shiver.

"What happened at work today?" And what exactly did it mean for her? If Alba was already in trouble at work perhaps this was not such a clever idea.

"Let's focus on searching the store, shall we?"

Greer stepped aside. Maybe this is just what Alba needed. It was clear Russell wanted this case solved soon for all his go home and rest speech.

It took a few goes, but soon they were in. Greer put her good hand into a pocket, pulled out her torch and turned it on.

"What are you doing?" asked Alba.

"Putting light on the situation?" Greer's body was tingly. Maybe she had imbibed more wine than she thought, or the painkiller wine cocktail was having fun in her system.

Alba reached out and flipped a light switch.

"That's what light looks like. Put that stupid torch away," said Alba.

If Greer had been less buzzed, she would have been offended.

Two-metre-high metal shelves packed to the brim filled the store. Greer hated herself for wanting some of it. Shelves and shelves of cocktail makers, coasters and retro memes spread out before them. She didn't even know where to start.

"The stuff we're interested in is probably out the back or behind the counter," said Alba.

"Thank goodness." Greer headed to the counter. Sitting in the seat behind it, she reached out with her working arm and started opening boxes and pulling out drawers.

Alba leaned against a shelf, watching her.

"Find anything?" asked Alba.

Greer flicked up a glare.

"There's an office out the back." Alba navigated through the shelves, heading for a small door and Greer followed her into a room drowning in a sea of paperwork, cables and power boards.

Greer sat in one of the office chairs and did a spin. A drawing of a flower with the words "believe you can" carved over it hung on the wall. Tanya would not approve.

She angled herself so she could open drawers with her good arm.

"What did the police find last time they came through?" asked Greer.

"Just the usual receipts, inventory records, some print advertising and a bunch of mail."

Greer and Alba were silent as they checked for hidden spaces.

"If you're going to kill a blackmailer, what do you do?" asked Greer.

"Make sure you have everything they were holding over you."

"True," said Greer. "However, the use of the statue suggests impulse."

Alba clicked the pen she had picked up. "Maybe, okay, once I've killed them, then I would focus on finding whatever they had over me."

"But they haven't been. They've been trying to kill me."

"So *you* have it?"

"But I don't." Greer sat back in the chair with a sigh. "I barely even knew Michael."

Standing up and walking into the main part of the store, she looked at it. Everything she knew about Michael, from meeting him and what she had learnt, meant she knew he would keep his power close.

Somewhere he could peek at it regularly. It wouldn't be on his own phone. He wouldn't risk it. A phone with its own online account. He could text, email, and store whatever he had on people. That meant a credit or debit card.

"Did any of the bank accounts Stephens found have a credit or debit facility? Something he could have used to create a separate phone account?"

Alba was leaning in the office doorway watching her.

"He only mentioned savings accounts."

"I think there's a phone here. If we can find it, we'll know the details of the online account, and then it's just a matter of a warrant, right?"

"Maybe." Alba glanced around the store. "They aren't actually things you can buy from a candy store." Greer opened her mouth, but Alba raised her hand. "However, yes, it's possible."

"Okay, so we need to imagine we're Michael," said Greer.

Alba rolled her eyes. Greer, suddenly tired and in pain, wasn't able to disguise her glare.

"Sorry, go on."

"You've a secret...a secret phone and a secret identity, almost. It's the only thing that keeps you going while being trapped in this small town."

"Okay, well, the shop is full of stuff...so where would he put it?" asked Alba.

"He would've been sitting at the counter most of the time." Greer sat there again. Instead of focusing on what she could reach this time, she scanned the store.

Diagonally to her left, a small area had a map theme and a lamp similar to one she had seen before. This one had three round plastic shades, a world map and the sun and the moon. The last one had been the full solar system. She remembered when she had first seen it on one of her rare visits to the store. She had been both horrified and fascinated and immediately bought it, much to Victoria's disgust. It kind of worked in a kitsch way when she paired it with science fiction books.

Greer pointed at it. "Check that lamp."

Alba raised her eyebrows, however followed Greer's order and tilted the lamp this way and that, trying to see if it had anything attached inside the lampshades.

"Nothing."

Greer frowned. There was something there—she knew it.

"Check the base."

Alba had already unplugged the lamp. With it on its side, she wrestled to get the base off. Greer heard a thud on the carpet.

"Fuck me," said Alba. She grabbed a piece of cloth with a picture of the lake printed on it and used it to pick up the phone. Good to see Alba was still keeping her inspector hat on.

"I've a similar lamp," said Greer.

"Why? This is the ugliest lamp I've ever seen." Alba put the lamp back together and righted it. She stood examining the phone with a slight crease between her eyebrows. "Is this why you're being attacked? They knew the phone was in a lamp and thought it was the one you had?"

"It's the only thing that makes sense." Greer frowned, well it did, and it didn't.

"But why wouldn't they just check out the store?"

"Maybe they assumed it was in that specific lamp not re-alising Michael had moved it? When I bought it, I got the only one he had. I remember Michael asking me if I was sure, which was a strange thing for a shop owner to say. He ended up insisting on delivering it the next day."

"Giving him time to get the phone out... and what... he ordered another? Why this style?"

"I suspect when he saw this lamp, he felt a potent dopamine hit. Maybe it symbolised a bigger world or its kitschiness—"

"Ugliness."

"—added to the feeling for him."

"Okay, so we're assuming the killer knew the phone was in the lamp. Confident that they could find this, they killed Michael?"

"I had the lamp in the bookstore and moved it home."

Greer looked around and realised that there was no kitchenette. She was thirsty and had forgotten to bring any water with her.

"Why?"

"Victoria objected to it."

Alba laughed, however, a sigh immediately followed it. "It isn't turning on." Alba put the phone wrapped in the cloth in the front pocket of her jeans. "But if that was the reason, why the poison? I mean, I get the home invasion. Knock you out. Check out the lamp. But why come back and poison you?"

"Maybe they didn't have time to find the lamp the first time?" Though if they had spent more time looking and less time trying to break into the bathroom they probably would have.

"But they had a free run of the place when you were at mine."

Alba was right, to a degree. There had been a lot of trades people and security people working on the property which would have been hard to navigate. However it was not what worried her.

"To go from physical violence to poison is rare." Exhaustion suddenly flooded her. "Maybe I'm mistaken."

"Or there's something else you know."

Greer rubbed her eyes with her right hand. The adrenaline, painkiller and alcohol combo were wearing off and her left shoulder ached.

"You alright?" asked Alba.

"I'm fine. The shoulder is hurting a bit, that's all."

"We have the phone." Alba walked over to the counter with another evidence bag to where a group of phone chargers were plugged in and grabbed them all. "And hopefully we have a charger. The rest can wait until tomorrow."

Greer gratefully agreed. After securing the shop, they walked back to Alba's car. Greer collapsed into the passenger seat and gingerly pulled the seat belt on, ensuring it wasn't hitting any sore parts. As the engine started, she could feel her body relax and her eyes drifted shut.

Alba put the indicator on, and the car started moving.

"Don't fall asleep before we get home. I'm not carrying—"

A scream ripped out of Greer as her shoulder connected with the passenger door, the seat belt pulling tight across her neck. Another blaze of pain rushed through her body as she crumpled back into the seat. She turned towards Alba and found her hanging unconscious in her seat belt and the grill of a car pressed against the driver's window. It was pulling away. Someone must have come through the intersection at the same time. Considering how slowly she and Alba had been going, they must have been speeding not to see them. As she watched the car rapidly reverse, she hoped they at least called the ambulance.

The other car had pulled back enough to run when instead it sped up and headed straight back towards them.

Greer screamed and dragged Alba's head and upper body over to the passenger side. She could see the other car's grill clearly framed in the driver's window just before it slammed into them. Then there was nothing but pain.

The smell hit her first. A mix of chemicals and sadness that seemed to permeate the walls. The machine that goes ping hinted at her location as well. Greer opened her eyes. The room was dark, but light haloed the blinds on the windows, so she assumed it was daytime.

Greer did a mental body check. Head seemed okay, left shoulder numb and strapped, so okay for now. She wiggled the fingers of both her hands and toes, pleased that they responded. Her right arm and both legs moved on command, so overall, it didn't appear to be too bad. With extreme care, she turned her head to find a button to push for help or to put her bed up. It took her longer than she would like to admit, but she eventually found the buttons on the inside of the bed's handrail, next to her hand. After pushing the assist button, she pressed the up button, only going one degree at a time. There were no stabbing pains, and eventually, she was upright enough to see the room without lifting her head.

The door opened, and a nurse walked in.

"Welcome back, Greer." He smiled at her and picked up her chart from its pocket on the wall. "Good to see you're awake." The nurse was a middle-aged man with wispy brown hair and a bit of a stomach. He looked familiar, probably a member of the book club. "How are you feeling? Any pain?"

"I'm okay. How's my shoulder?"

"It was dislocated again, but the X-rays don't show any other damage. You were lucky."

"Will it...will it heal okay?" How many times can you dislocate a shoulder before it stops trying to go back together?

"Dr Yardley will come in later and discuss the best way forward."

So probably not.

He tapped her chart and then brought over some pills and water.

"Alba?" The memory of a grill ramming into the driver's door crashed through her. "Is she okay?"

"Inspector Mauzer? She's awake and in the next room over."

Greer swallowed what she could only assume were painkillers and then tried to sit up straighter. The nurse put up his hand.

"Best to wait until Dr Yardley sees you. You might not be feeling any pain right now, but you need to keep that shoulder as still as possible."

"Can I have my phone? I need to check in with Victoria and on my cat Miles."

"Yes, of course, I'll get it for you. Though I would imagine Victoria's already aware of what happened."

Of course he knew Victoria. For someone who didn't like people everyone sure seemed to know her.

"What time is it?"

"It's ten o'clock on Saturday morning."

"The day after the accident, right? I haven't been unconscious for a week or anything?"

"No." He smiled warmly at her. "You were both lucky. One ambulance had just left the hospital and saw the crash."

"The other driver?" Greer wasn't sure how much the ambulance had seen. Was it the first or the second crash?

The nurse frowned. "I'm afraid they did a hit and run. It was too dark for the paramedics to see a licence plate, but they said it was one of those large SUVs. The police are doing their best to track them down." He smiled at her again. "We can't lose our favourite book dealer." Definitely a book club member. It was getting creepy. Maybe it should register as a cult. She could imagine Amos as a cult leader.

"Hey, that's my line." Isaac stepped into the room, pushing the smiling nurse aside. "Greer, how are you feeling?" He walked around the bed and pulled up a chair next to her good arm and gave her hand a brief squeeze. "You're going to give me a heart attack if I keep finding you broken."

"It was you?"

"Yes, Lucinda and I'd just done a drop-off at the hospital when we saw the crash. Our sirens must have spooked the other driver. They ran."

Isaac's expression clearly conveyed what he thought of them and Greer promised herself she would never think negative thoughts about living in a small town again.

"I can't believe we didn't get their number plate," said Isaac, hanging his head.

"Isaac." Greer turned her palm up, and he took her hand. "I'm just grateful that you were there."

"Me too," said Lucinda, entering the room with her usual flash of energy. "That maniac might've killed you if we hadn't shown up." She slapped the nurse on the shoulder. "Hey Lars, how's our favourite book pusher doing?"

"She'll be alright. Just don't go slapping *her* on the shoulder." Lars rubbed his own meaningfully.

Lucinda laughed and draped herself across the bottom of Greer's bed, just missing her feet. Lars left, telling Greer he would let Dr Yardley know she was awake.

"Greer..." Lucinda shook one of her feet. "Just what have you gotten yourself into? Smashing of shoulders...poisoning of Miles...someone trying to ram you out of existence with their car..."

"You saw that, did you?" Greer looked at both of and felt a warm glow move through her. She supposed it could be gratitude or the drugs kicking in—it was hard to tell.

"We were a few blocks down, but we saw the crash...and them come back for another. Once we find them, they'll have a hard time explaining that one." Lucinda patted her foot a little more gently this time.

Greer closed her eyes and tried not to think about what would have happened if they hadn't been there.

"Have you seen Alba?" Greer's throat tightened. The nurse had said she was okay but there were different levels of okay. "She was on the driver's side."

Isaac squeezed her hand again. "A knock on the head and her right leg took a bit of a beating, but nothing broken. Good work, bringing her over to your side. Probably saved her from a cracked skull."

"My side?" asked Greer. "I don't remember that."

"I don't know how you did it. Even with the seat belt on you managed to pull her upper body over you, with one arm, I might add." Isaac sounded impressed while Lucinda gave her leg another pat.

Greer didn't miss the concerned look she shot at her brother. She closed her eyes and tried to remember, but all she could see was the grill of the larger car framed by the driver's window.

"Don't worry if you can't remember," said Lucinda. "It's not uncommon. Bro, we have to head." Lucinda slid off the hospital bed. "Greer, look after that shoulder this time."

Isaac gave her hand one more squeeze before following his sister.

Greer thanked them again.

He paused at the doorway and regarded her.

"I'd like to get through this shift without you being attacked...think that's possible?"

"No guarantees the way this week's going."

He sighed but nodded, giving the doorframe a couple of taps as he left.

Greer wasn't on her own long before Clement and Alba came into the room. Greer could see the bruises from Jayden's attack were now covered by new ones and Alba was using a walking stick to keep the weight off her injured leg.

"Should you be walking?" asked Greer.

"No, she shouldn't," said Clement, showing signs of being tired himself. "But she insisted, so I escorted her to prevent a fall."

"Are you okay, Clement?" asked Greer. She had gotten to know Clement over the last week, and she knew he avoided working Saturdays. "Why are you working today?"

"Warren had to travel for work, so I picked up an extra shift. It always makes it easier to ask for favours on the roster if you volunteer where possible."

Greer wondered whether after all this was over, she should engage his partner, a travel agent in Mountview, and take a break. Or she had been right before, maybe it was time to leave Lakes End more permanently.

"I hope you get at least one day off," said Greer. She contemplated Alba, who appeared to be in pain or constipated. It was hard to be sure. "How are you Alba? I heard your leg took a beating."

"I'll live." Alba walked with only a slight limp to the chair vacated by Isaac.

She didn't take Greer's hand however for which Greer was grateful. She didn't really like people touching her. Except Isaac. She wasn't quite ready to think about what that meant and focused on Clement who picked up her chart and moved closer. She wondered what it said. Was her shoulder ever going to be right again? She had heard horror stories about dislocations never fully healing and she had dislocated it twice in almost as many days.

"What are the pain levels?" he asked.

"I can't feel anything really, thanks for the drugs."

"I'd say anytime...but the police are listening." Clement grinned at Alba.

"I hear nothing," said Alba. "Though that might explain why she isn't in pain, and I am."

"You're in pain because you refused the good drugs," said Clement.

"Someone tried to kill me yesterday, so forgive me if I want to keep my wits about me."

Clement shrugged and put down Greer's chart.

"Greer you can go home today. There's nothing concerning on the x-ray, and it's just a matter of keeping that arm as still as possible. Avoid any more midnight raids on stores if you can." He turned to Alba. "You took quite a blow, and while everything presents as okay, I would strongly recommend you stay another night too."

Alba frowned at him, and he raised his hand.

"I know you're going to ignore me. I'm just giving you my professional opinion."

"Thanks Clement," said Greer.

"I have to get to it. Text me if you need me."

He nodded to both of them and headed back on his rounds.

"Did you see the driver?" asked Alba, sitting back in the chair with her legs stretched out in front of her.

"No. My focus was on the car." Greer sighed. With this many attacks, she should really start paying attention. "Did you?"

Alba didn't answer straight away, and her eyes tracked her walking stick as she tapped it against the bed frame. Greer listened to the tick-tick of hollow metal on hollow metal.

"I don't know," said Alba, ceasing the tapping.

Greer saw the frustration in Alba's eyes.

"But you think you recognised them." Maybe something would come out of this attack after all.

But Alba turned her face away and swallowed.

"Not enough to identify them in court, but the shape of the shadow, the height of the person behind the wheel...." Alba started tapping her walking stick again, and they both watched it.

She shifted in her bed. "Who—"

"Greer," said Nurse Lars, coming into the room. "Dr Yardley has just advised me you are free to go home if you want to. Inspector Mauzer, he asked me to give you the paperwork for discharging yourself against doctor's orders."

Greer looked at Alba. "Maybe you shouldn't—"

Alba waved her hand and took the papers from Lars. Greer stifled a sigh and left her to it.

Lars cleared his throat. "I'm afraid the police have taken your clothes..." He looked uncomfortable, and Greer wondered if they were expected to exit the hospital in their paper-thin gowns.

"Our clothes, why?" asked Greer. She glanced at Alba, who frowned but didn't look up from the paperwork in front of her.

"Not sure. However, they said they needed them for the investigation. Seems harsh to me," said Lars. "I mean, leaving you with nothing to wear." A small smile slipped through his serious expression. "However, you're in luck. I'd already taken out your phone." He handed Greer a mobile. He coughed. "No need to tell them that?"

Greer shook her head while trying not to stare too intently at the mobile that wasn't hers, and Alba, glancing up from her paperwork, stilled. Greer reached for it trying to keep her hand steady.

"Since neither of you can drive, I recommend you have Victoria come and pick you up with some clothes." His gaze flicked to Alba, who was still in her hospital gown, signing her discharge paperwork.

"Thank you, Lars. I'll call her," said Greer.

He left after checking to see if she needed anything else.

Greer looked at the phone, not sure what to do. It still didn't have any charge, and she didn't have her own phone.

Alba handed over the landline phone in the bedroom.

"Err..." Greer looked at the phone. How long had it been since she had used one that was actually attached to a wall? "I don't know Victoria's mobile number."

"You know the bookstore's number though, right? It's Saturday morning. What do you think the chances of her being there are?"

Greer nodded and dialled.

"And make sure she brings some loose clothing for me," said Alba, collecting her paperwork into a pile and putting it on the end of the bed. "There's no way I'll fit into hers."

"Why do you think they took our—"

"Talk when we get home." Alba flicked a glance to the open bedroom door.

Victoria was at the bookstore and brought them clothes, finding the most unflattering pair of sweats for Alba that Greer had ever witnessed worn in real life. Apparently, Victoria's late husband had a taste for fluorescent green.

Greer had also contacted the vet. Miles had survived the night. The vet had said he was lucky so many times that Greer had teared up but was grateful that he was well enough to come home.

Not that she had a home to go back to. Alba insisted they were safer at her place and so with three injured passengers and Victoria joking about starting a hospital ferry service they headed back to Alba's place.

Victoria helped them inside, poured herself a whisky, and settled into an armchair.

"You don't need to stay, Victoria," said Greer.

"What? With the two of you, the walking wounded? I'm not going anywhere. You couldn't protect a glass of whisky, let alone yourselves right now." Victoria took a sip.

"You know it's only the middle of the day, right?" asked Alba.

"Hey, it's Saturday. Someone tried to kill my best friend, and my bookstore might close, so forgive me if I need a bit of fortifying," said Victoria.

Greer was quite moved. It wasn't like they had exchanged words.

She poured herself and Alba shots that a bartender would charge the price of four for and settled into the armchair next to Miles' cage. He was still recovering and was lying there so quietly that she had to keep reminding herself that he was alive.

Greer reached down to let Miles out.

"What are you doing?" asked Victoria, pulling herself forward so she could reach the front of the cage. "Just ask, you silly girl."

Victoria opened up the cat carrier. Miles wobbled as he pushed himself to his feet and took a couple of steps forward. Stopping, he sniffed the air. It took him a bit of effort, but he eventually got himself up on the chair with Greer. His weight was heavy against her, and she tried to stop the tears in her eyes as she ran her fingers over his fur. The purr reverberated throughout the room.

"Poor boy," said Victoria, getting teary herself. "Who would hurt an animal—a monster, that's who." Her gaze darted between Greer and Alba. "What are we going to do about it?"

22

Alba

Alba dropped onto the couch, trying to angle herself so she could stretch her leg out but still face the others with mixed success.

"So..." Greer's fingers stroked the purring killer on her lap. "Who do you think it was?"

Alba shifted awkwardly so she was facing her.

How much should she tell them? She had gotten to know Greer true, but she had only spoken to Victoria twice, maybe three times.

"You know?" asked Victoria, sitting forward.

The pain in her leg, not to mention the destruction of her car, made her want to crawl into bed but Greer and Victoria's expectations weighed on her, forcing her to fill the space.

"Nothing definitive. I think I glimpsed the driver for a second and..." Alba looked away from them. "I believe the driver had a similar body shape to Superintendent Russell." There, she had said it.

Greer and Victoria both sat back, frowning.

"Are you sure?" asked Victoria. "I can imagine Bana Russell killing someone sure. I'm just not sure that he would be this bad at it."

Alba couldn't help but smile.

"I know. I've been going over this in my head repeatedly. If he committed Michael's murder, it was on impulse. But since then...there's been a level of desperation..."

"Do you think he followed us from your house to the store?" asked Greer.

"Yes...maybe...and then fearing we had found something...he acted quickly," said Alba, rubbing her leg.

"The mobile." Greer pulled it out of her pocket. Somehow Victoria had found Greer a soft white jersey tracksuit which, of course, looked great on her, unlike the green monstrosity she was wearing. Few people could pull off fluorescent green, and Alba was not one of them.

"How hard is it to hack a mobile phone?" asked Greer.

"I don't know." Alba examined the phone. It wasn't something she had ever had to do before. "The tech unit at the police department does it."

Greer pulled the mobile closer to her. "You can't take it to the police if the super—"

Alba laughed. What did she think was going to happen? "We need to. It is part of a formal investi—"

"Have you logged it in yet?" asked Greer.

"No, a car crash interrupted me, remember?"

"So, we hack—"

"It's called tampering with evidence."

"Err, I don't want to interrupt you both," drawled Victoria. "However, that ship has sailed."

Alba examined the phone. Victoria was right. It had been floating around the hospital and handled by who knows how many.

Leaning her right shoulder against the back of the couch, Alba dropped her head sideways onto it. This wasn't what she'd signed up for—investigating her own people. All she'd wanted was to be a police officer in a small town, part of a close-knit team. Was that really too much to ask?

"Do you think it's Russell and Amos working together?" asked Victoria.

Alba lifted her head and stared at her.

"It would explain the physical attacks and poison," said Greer. "If I were doing an assessment, I would say Amos was much more likely to use poison than Russell. It would also explain why, out of the blue, he isn't renewing my lease."

"So, what pushed Amos to poison you?" Alba's mind and body were both moving slowly. She looked at the whisky that Greer had given her. She didn't know if it would help or make it worse. She took a sip.

"I don't know, but I must have said something." Greer exhaled.

"The person walking the dog," said Alba. She had returned her head to the couch and didn't bother raising it this time.

"But I couldn't identify—"

"Yet, you can't identify them yet. Maybe if you saw them again, you would. Maybe it would be the person, or maybe it would be the dog, the superintendent's dog…"

"Shit," said Victoria, sitting up straight. "What are we going to do?"

"First, we need a charger." Alba looked around the room. "I'm going to assume the phone's locked, so we'll take it into the tech unit and see what happens."

"We can't," said Greer, her voice getting a little sharper.

Alba remembered she was in pain too, though perhaps less so because of the painkillers. But neither of them was firing all cylinders at the moment.

"The longer we hold on to it, the worse it gets. Today we can claim that with the trauma of everything that we forgot…tomorrow?"

"We just need some time," said Greer. "If you can look up how to make a bomb, you must be able to look up how to hack into a phone."

Alba looked at the ceiling. What had she done that was so bad she had to relive betrayal and suspicion all over again? She knew that if she pursued this, her career was over. No one would want a colleague who kept finding corruption at every station they went to.

"Putting aside the guesswork, what do we actually know?" asked Alba. "That I think the driver may have resembled the superintendent? That's all we have."

"We have the phone," said Greer.

"Which we probably can't use as evidence… not to mention we don't even know how to get in—"

"Yet—which we don't know how to get into yet," said Greer.

"Alba's right," said Victoria and took a large drink of her whisky. "We can't go in swinging. Despite all his desperate nonsense this week, Russell's not stupid. But if that phone has evidence? Once you hand it over, you will never see it again. That's the problem with people today—too trusting."

Alba's stomach twisted. "I'm reluctant to risk my career on conjecture. I have already restarted once. In fact, I'm still in the middle of trying to do that." She glanced at Greer who had stilled.

Miles shifted in Greer's lap and stretched out his paw towards Greer's chin. Greer visibly forced herself to relax and went back to patting him.

There was a knock on the door. Victoria put down her whisky and stomped over to it. She opened it to reveal a stiff Constable Grimaud. Grimaud looked through the doorway to where Alba was seated on the couch.

"Sir, the superintendent has asked if you and Ms Roberts could come in and make a statement if you are up to it," said Grimaud. "He sent me to give you a lift."

Alba nodded but didn't get up. Grimaud clocked her tracksuit.

"I'll wait if you want to change first." Humour coloured her otherwise professional tone.

"Thanks," said Alba with a drawl.

Grimaud nodded dand went back to her car.

Alba wasn't up to the stairs, so she asked Victoria to grab her own neutral-coloured clothes and a jumper and changed in the laundry room with a minimum amount of swearing. With her coat on, she looked almost civilised.

Before leaving, Alba turned to Greer and took the phone.

"Don't—" said Greer.

Alba put it in the inner pocket of her coat and straightened, facing them both.

"I'm already outside the lines. I won't go further."

Greer rose slowly, shifting Miles off her lap deeper into the armchair. Victoria refused to leave and said she was going to stay with Miles. Alba knocked on Henri and Eli's door to ask if they could check-in. She made sure it was loud enough that Grimaud, and anyone else listening, could hear.

The icy wind and heavy cloud cover gave the police station the gothic atmosphere that it craved. Alba tried not to let the weather affect her mood, but dread rose as she hobbled into the station. Her face was grim, and she did her best to minimise her limp. Alba had barely spoken to Grimaud. She didn't have any proof it was her, but the last thing she wanted was another complaint right now, so she had left the small talk up to Greer.

She paused in the foyer. She was here to give a statement, so she wasn't sure if she should go to the conference room or one of the interview rooms. She turned to ask, but Grimaud had disappeared, and everyone else seemed to avoid looking at her. Her stomach did a dip and roll.

Stephens approached them, and his face twisted in a concerned expression. "Inspector, Greer, glad to see you are both okay, if a little worse for wear."

Alba could feel the paranoia set in as she wondered whether the concern was real and had to stop herself from peering at him to see if it reached his eyes or not.

That way led to darkness.

"Let's get this over with," said Alba. "Where do you want us?"

He grimaced. "We'll use the interview rooms."

Alba didn't respond and headed to the one closest to her.

Stephens led Greer into another one, and Constable Beitean joined Alba. The usually chatty Beitean was subdued, which did little for the dread knotting Alba's stomach. Still, she stayed focused and gave her statement of what had happened yesterday evening to the best of her ability.

"You had just left Michael Williams' store...at what time?" asked Beitean.

"I'm not sure. I think we headed there about nine, so it would have been close to nine-thirty when we left. We weren't there long."

"And why were you there?"

"Ms Roberts thought we might lose evidence as the family was coming on Saturday, today, to pack up Michael's papers."

"And did you find anything?" asked Beitean.

She opened her mouth to tell him about the mobile phone.

"No," said Alba.

Fuck. Just say it. *Phone* wasn't that hard a word.

"Nothing?" asked Beitean.

Was he too eager? Were they all in on it? Her stomach twisted as she realised she wouldn't tell them. She really hoped Greer was saying no as well. How more thoroughly could she fuck this up?

"The incident occurred as we headed home," said Alba, trying to get the statement back on track.

Beitean let her change the subject. "What happened when you left?"

She and Beitean went through the crash a few times. As the first hit had taken her out, she didn't remember the car going at them again.

Once they captured everything she could remember, she shuffled back into the main area and, seeing Stephens with Greer in the conference room, headed there. She wished she could pull Greer aside to check whether she had mentioned the phone. Alba suspected she was going to need valium before the day was out.

"Have you had any luck in finding the other driver?" asked Alba on entering the room.

"No, not yet," said Stephens, he glanced at the board with a despondent look on his face.

There were no new cards up there.

"Were there any CCTV or cameras at that intersection?"

"Inspector."

The superintendent's voice caused Alba's stomach to lurch. It surprised her she wasn't on the toilet with the way it was spinning like a front-loader washing machine. Alba turned towards where Russell was standing in the doorway.

"Stephens and Savas are putting in every effort to find out who did this."

"Yes, sir."

"Can we speak for a moment?" He turned and headed back to his office.

Alba hesitated and glanced towards Greer's anxious face and Stephens' grim one before turning and following.

"Inspector," said Stephens.

Alba paused and looked back.

"If there was CCTV footage, it's gone. We aren't sure how. Either it wasn't working that night, which is possible, or they destroyed it afterwards."

Alba's throat tightened, but she thanked him and continued into the superintendent's office.

Russell gestured to his visitor's chair, and Alba gratefully took a seat.

"How are you feeling, Inspector?"

"The leg's sore and stiff but no lasting damage...according to the doctors anyway."

"I'm glad to hear it."

Russell's fingers started drumming, and Alba couldn't stop her gaze from shifting to the picture of his dog, Charlie.

"Inspector, I know you've had a rough twenty-four hours. However, I need to talk to you about what went down last night."

Alba shifted her eyes back to Russell in surprise. Was he going to confess?

"As you know, it's routine for any drivers in a car crash to be tested for blood alcohol levels afterwards. Last night you and Ms Roberts tested positive."

"Positive? We barely had any—"

"You weren't over the limit, but you had enough alcohol in your system to show that you had at least a couple of drinks and Ms Roberts even more."

So what's the problem? Alba imagined her lips glued shut to avoid voicing her thought.

"I'm concerned, Inspector, because you and Ms Roberts took it upon yourselves to use a search warrant at nine o'clock at night after drinking."

Alba could feel her eyes widen. This was not how she expected this conversation to go at all.

"Superintendent, as you said, I was under the limit. Ms Roberts and I had discussed the case and concluded that there was a risk of evidence being lost when the family arrived the following day, and it was best to—"

"Were you and Ms Roberts alone when you had this discussion?"

What the fuck was this?

"While my neighbours had been over for dinner, that discussion occurred after they left. Which was one reason for the lateness of the hour."

"And did you seek approval to conduct this search?"

"As the search warrant was still active and I'm the lead investigator, I didn't think it necessary."

"And how did you enter this property?"

Alba sat there, not moving. *Fuck.*

"I had the keys with me."

"Keys...evidence...from the case...taken to your home."

Alba forced herself to nod.

"I don't know how you ran your investigations in your previous unit, Inspector. But here...we don't take evidence home."

"No, sir."

Russell exhaled and stood, looking out his window. Alba followed his gaze, watching the wind move the branches in the park across the road.

"This is a serious matter, Inspector."

"Yes, sir." Though considering how often he had broken protocol on this case she thought it was a bit rich to be suddenly a stickler for the rules. But perhaps he had reason to be.

"Even though you're a victim of a crime, I can't have my officers breaching procedures like that."

"No, sir." *Only yourself apparently.*

"Considering these significant breaches and the complaints received about you..."

Fucksticks, all of them.

"I'm afraid, Inspector, that I'm going to have to suspend you while we investigate this matter."

"Sir?" He had to be fucking kidding.

"I'm giving you paid suspension on top of the leave you need to recover from the crash. Once the doctors sign you as fit for duty, we'll contact you regarding the investigation."

It wasn't like she hadn't done it without reason. The weight of the phone in her pocket dragged at her.

"I'm sorry it has come to this Inspector."

Alba's blood hummed in her ears.

"I suggest you focus on recuperating for now."

The yes sir whispered between her lips. She pushed herself into a standing position. This time, she didn't bother trying to hide the limp as she walked from the office back to her desk. Rage turned the hum of blood in her ears into the sound of war drums. She looked around the room, and everyone's gaze dropped as hers came near them.

Fucking fucksticks, the lot of them.

It was the first time that Alba could understand why someone might burn a place down. The injustice of it consumed her. She could feel the heat from the imaginary flames consuming the walls, desks and people inside.

As she passed Stephens, she examined him. He was the only one with the courage to meet her gaze. For the first time, his eyes look cruel. No doubt he had been working with the superintendent to set this up. He was probably the one to wipe the CCTV footage.

Asshole.

She didn't know what the others could see in her expression, but everyone was quiet, watching her from the corner of their eyes. She wouldn't have been able to hear anything anyway, as the bloody drums in her ears reached their crescendo.

She made it out onto the street in front of the station and turned towards the car park before remembering Grimaud had driven them.

"Alba."

She turned towards the park across the road and headed towards it.

"Alba."

As she stepped off the kerb, not bothering to look for non-existent traffic, she felt a hand on her elbow. She swung around with a snarl on her face.

"Fuck off, Dad."

"Are you okay? I heard—"

"What did you hear? Did you hear I got hit by a fucking car? Or did you hear I got suspended?"

He just stood there, taking in her bruises.

"What?" she snarled. "What do you want?"

"I wanted to make sure you were okay. I want you to know you can always come back and—"

"There's no fucking way I'm living with—"

"When injured, body and soul, it's not unheard of to return to your home to heal."

"It is when it was home that landed the first blows."

"Don't talk like that. I never—"

"I'm talking about the gut-wrenching betrayal." Her lips were stiff, and the snarl seemed to have deepened. For the first time, the hurt hardened into hatred, and she could feel the drums pick up their pace again. "Since you seem to have forgotten."

"Mr Mauzer." A soft voice broke through, and they both turned to see Greer standing there with a bloodless face, one arm in a sling and the other holding two crumpled paper bags in white knuckles. "Mr Mauzer, this is not the time."

Her father inhaled deeply and examined Alba's face. His shoulders slumped, but he gave Greer a nod and stepped back.

He glanced at Alba. "When you've finished burning all your bridges, just know my door's always open."

Neither Alba nor Greer responded, and after a moment, he turned and walked away.

"I need to get home," said Alba.

Greer pushed a bag of their stuff from the hospital at her. "I've organised a lift."

Alba just nodded. What was she going to do? *Fuck them all.*

A car pulled up in front of them. She wasn't up to speaking, so left Greer to take the front passenger seat and thank Julius for the lift. Alba got into the back seat and slumped for a second before her breath caught.

Alba leaned forward. "Did you mention the phone?"

"No."

Alba let out a breath she hadn't even realised she had been holding.

"Did you?" asked Greer.

"No."

"What happened?" asked Greer.

Alba sank into her seat but could see Greer's face pinched with concern in the rear-view mirror.

"He suspended me."

"What? What for?"

"Taking the keys home."

Alba closed her eyes and dropped her head back on the car seat. Her eyelids were hot and wet, and she refused to open them until she had her anger under control. When she did, she was sitting on her couch, her leg up, a whisky in one hand and an enormous cat in her lap. She looked down at Miles. He must have been more drugged up than she thought as he reached out a paw and tapped the hand lying closest to him.

She ran her hand down his back as she had seen Greer do earlier. He didn't purr, but he dropped his head on his paws, content to stay. She lifted her other hand up to her mouth and took a sip of whisky. She felt shaky and wasn't sure she should be drinking alcohol, but it was there.

Looking around, she found an entire room of people looking at her with concern.

Victoria, as always, summed it up perfectly.

"So, how do we get this fuckcouple?"

23

Greer

Greer needed more painkillers but wanted to eat something first. She wondered if it would be poor form to
stop the investigation for a late lunch. From all the eager
faces in the room, no one else was thinking about food.

"What?" asked Alba.

"I think Alba's in shock." Greer smiled at the crowd.
"Food would help, maybe some sandwiches, and water, or at
least something other than whisky. Then once we are all fed
and watered, we can discuss the...couple."

"Sandwiches," said Eli, frowning.

"Not that your food isn't amazing," said Greer, realising
she might have hurt Eli's feelings. "However perhaps now is
not the time for a full dining experience?"

Eli sighed.

Victoria pulled out her phone. "I'll put in an order for
some burgers and fries. We need some fat and carbs after a
day like today."

It hadn't quite been what Greer had in mind, but food was food. With the order made, they returned to the problem in front of them.

"Where are we with the phone?" asked Greer.

Victoria held up the phone which was connected to a charger.

"I found a cord that fit. It's powered up but locked."

"And I've researched how to unlock it," said Henri. "We're downloading some software onto Eli's laptop. Once we hook it up, we'll be in."

"I have to say Henri's very impressive with all the computer stuff." Victoria looked over at Henri and her face shifted, for a moment, out of dour.

It did not surprise Greer that Henri and Victoria had bonded. She was only surprised that they hadn't become friends before. Victoria was like her though, preferring to keep the number of people she interacted with to a minimum.

"You don't work in ICT for twenty years without learning something," said Eli with a proud pat on Henri's back. "Why do you think I asked her to be my video editor?"

"ICT? What does that even mean?" asked Greer.

Her head ached, and the shoulder throbbed. How had this happened? She wished it was Saturday—a week ago—and the paperwork was getting done.

"All you need to know is that it means I know how to connect a phone to a laptop," said Henri.

"Fuckcouple?" said Alba, her eyebrows low.

"Superintendent Russell and Amos Beecher," said Greer.

"You think they're in it together?" asked Alba. She was looking at the empty glass of whisky in her hand, and Eli replaced it with water.

"Let's see..." said Victoria, holding up her hand with her fingers curled down. "One Amos is not renewing Greer's lease." One of her fingers uncurled. "Two, Russell has suspended you. Three, twenty years ago, Amos' father died under suspicious circumstances. Four, you thought you saw Russell driving the car that hit you."

Only the thumb remained tucked in. Greer wondered what Victoria's plans were if she had over five points to make.

"And five." Victoria's thumb straightened. "Michael, and possibly Tanya, ran a fraud racket in Lakes End for years with no one noticing. Blackmailing the superintendent, that would certainly explain how they got away with it for so long." She shook her head. "Michael's not bright enough to run a scam that long without getting caught, not without some help."

Greer was pretty sure there were seven points there, but Victoria wouldn't appreciate her pointing that out.

"No, he wasn't," said Stephens.

Everyone looked towards the front door and saw him, wrapped in multiple coats, scarves and a hat, standing there. Greer hadn't even heard the knock. However Julius, who had been fairly quiet until now had gotten up and let him in.

Alba growled, and Miles, sensing a threat to his new friend, echoed it.

Stephens held both his hands up and stepped inside.

"What are you doing here?" asked Alba.

Stephens took a deep breath. "I heard about the suspension and I know you aren't just going to walk away from this, so I thought I could...help."

"Let him in," said Victoria. "I think we're going to need the assist."

Greer ignored Alba's mumbling and invited him to take a seat near her. Stephens headed towards it and unwound a scarf and even taking off one of his coats.

"Thank you for coming Hugh," said Greer, smiling at him.

Stephens nodded, however his gaze stayed on Alba, who ignored him.

"What if this is all about a murder?" asked Henri.

Everyone looked at her.

"It *is* about a murder," said Victoria, staring at Henri, her expression hitting scorn levels.

Henri frowned at her. "Not Michaels, and another murder." Henri looked towards Stephens. "Sure you want to be here?"

Stephens slumped in his chair but nodded.

"Right-o," said Henri. She glanced around the room. "We've hit the mother lode."

"What do you mean?" asked Alba.

"The documents in Michael's account are the old investigation files on Amos' father."

Victoria received a notification that the food was ready, and Julius offered to drive. Soon they had a mountain of burgers and chips. The conversation paused as everyone devoured their food.

After they finished eating, Henri shared a link to the investigation files with everyone except Stephens, who also hadn't gotten a burger. Greer would have shared half of hers if she had been less hungry, however today was not a food-sharing day. The comforting weight of too much food in her stomach made all of this unpleasantness seem even more distant.

"Come on, Henri," said Greer, still feeling guilty about the burger. "How can he help if he doesn't have a copy?"

Henri grimaced. "Fine, but I'm giving him view-only access."

Stephens' phone beeped.

"Thank you, Henri," said Stephens. Eli pulled up a chair next to him and patted his knee.

"Don't take it personally," said Eli. "The trust in the police is a little low right now is all."

No one said anything while they read. The file included witness statements, evidence logs, and test results, but no smoking gun.

"Would there be evidence of money?" asked Greer. She wasn't sure why Henri had been so excited about these files.

"Money?" asked Julius.

"Surely Michael would have asked for money...if he was using these for blackmail?"

Stephens looked up from his phone. "If we could find a series of payments coming in regularly over the years..."

"Assuming we can find the money, what then?" Alba threw her phone onto the couch and pushed herself off it. "These fucking files have nothing in them." Miles yowled and dropped to the floor. He glared at everyone before making his way to Greer and collapsing in her lap, exhausted from the effort of moving chairs. Waving off everyone's offers to help, Alba hobbled into the laundry, no doubt to use the same toilet Greer had thrown up in only a few days ago and slammed the door.

"There has to be something," said Victoria. "Surely they would have insisted on seeing it before they paid for twenty years?"

"How did he die?" asked Eli. "I can't see the pathologist report." He continued swiping through the files.

Greer turned back to her phone and went through them again. She couldn't find it either.

"Henri, are there any other files in there?" asked Greer.

A knock rattled the door as Alba stepped out of the laundry.

"This house is turning into a bloody train station," said Alba.

She shuffled over to the door and opened it to find Amos.

"How do you know where I live? And what the fuck are you doing here?"

Amos' face—naturally shaped to frown—made his attempt at a smile look like a dog baring his teeth.

"Everyone knows where you live...and I need to talk to Greer."

"For fuck's sake." Alba stepped back, and Amos saw the number of people in the room for the first time. He started back, however scowled and dragged himself forward into the room. Alba locked the door behind him.

Greer, surprised to see Amos, was too tired and in too much pain—she really needed to find her painkillers—to stand.

"Amos, why are you here?"

"I just wanted you to know that I didn't do it."

"Didn't do what?" asked Victoria. "Cancel her lease...try to poison her...or hit her with a car?"

"The poison and car thing." Amos smoothed his already perfect beard. "Look, I know it doesn't look good, with the not renewing the lease, and well, we've never really gotten on..."

Greer's eyebrows raised. "Julius, I've a cat on me. Would you mind bringing me some whisky? I think I'm going to need a drink for this."

"I don't like you," said Amos.

"I'm aware of that," said Greer, gratefully accepting the glass of whisky Julius put in her hand as he perched on the back of her armchair. Miles raised his head but dismissed him and went back to pretending to sleep on Greer's lap, however she could tell he was watching the room as he wasn't his usual purring dead weight self.

"But I don't want you dead. I just got a better offer and wanted to break the lease. I heard about the car and about Bana suspending the inspector." With each word he became more agitated. "And now everyone at the pub, and the book club, thinks we've been trying to kill you!" He threw his hands in the air.

"Haven't you?" asked Alba. "Twenty years of being blackmailed by Michael seems a pretty good motive to me."

If she could have reached her, Greer would have whacked Alba on the back of the head.

"Blackmail? What for?"

Greer's stomach sank as she took in the genuine confusion on Amos' face.

Alba's frown deepened. "The murder of your father."

"What? No, I mean sure Michael was always going on about that, tried to hint he knew things. But it wasn't murder. Dad committed suicide. He had cancer and didn't want to go through the treatments."

"Why hide it?"

"Suicide was a big deal back then, shameful. We didn't want him remembered that way. Those who knew agreed to lose the pathologist's report and close the case once they found the fourth-stage bone cancer. Everyone knew he only had a few months to live, and it was going to be brutal."

"What about the life insurance?" asked Julius. "Some of them have anti-suicide clauses."

"No insurance. Dad had transferred everything to me once he got his diagnosis." Amos snorted. "Believe me Greer, you're very annoying and have terrible taste in books but I wouldn't kill you for it."

"Fuck," said Alba. "But even if *you* didn't...what about the Superintendent? I saw someone who looked like him behind the wheel last night."

"Can't have been." Amos shook his head, his shoulders straightening, his usual confidence returning. "We had drinks at the Cobbler. He felt bad about how things were going with you, so I took him out. Check with the staff, they'd remember him." A faint hint of a blush above his beard was visible. "There was singing."

"Fuck."

"The book club is holding a meeting tomorrow and is threatening to have me kicked off it." Amos smoothed his beard again. "Me! I founded the blasted thing."

Greer almost laughed. She had wondered what had brought Amos here. Could someone really care about a book club that much?

"And you think we can change that?" asked Greer.

"Yes, they'll listen to you...and them." Alba gestured towards Henri, Eli and Victoria.

Who knew they were such powerhouses?

Henri stood up. "Don't think we won't check it out, but we will let people know if it wasn't you...if you let Eli and me back in the book club."

"Err Henri," said Alba with what Greer would describe as an air of exasperation.

"Fine," said Amos, "but no more bloody salmon."

"Does that mean you'll renew my lease?" asked Greer.

"No," said Amos. "I mean, obviously I would if I could." He appealed to the audience in front of him and then turned to Greer. "I've already signed the new one."

Greer's body deflated. Of course he had.

Victoria stood up. "Well Amos, I just hope you are okay with there being two bookstores in town, and maybe two book clubs?"

Amos frowned at Victoria, however Eli stepped in and reassured Amos that they would clear his name before his precious book club meeting tomorrow and led him out the door.

"Are we seriously going to spend the evening clearing Amos' name so he can stay on in the book club?" asked Victoria. "That asshole's still kicking Greer out of her shop."

"Well, if it wasn't him and it wasn't the superintendent...we need to find out who it is," said Henri.

"You just want back in," said Victoria, scorn dripping from her.

"It has all the best events," said Eli, his eyes pleading with Victoria for understanding. Greer was surprised Victoria's face shifted to extremely dour, she must like him.

Alba slumped on the couch.

"I really got suspended," said Alba. Eli took in Alba's expression, and soon she had her own glass of whisky.

"Sorry kid," said Henri. "I've been fired a few times myself. You think it's the end of the world, but it isn't. A new opportunity awaits."

"After we find out who's trying to kill you and Greer," said Victoria.

"If the file on Michael's phone isn't a blackmail file. What was the phone for?" asked Greer.

Henri had plugged the phone back into the laptop.

"All the texts and phone calls are to one number," said Henri.

"Can you see what the texts say?" Alba got up off the couch and limped around to look over Henri's shoulder. "What do you know...another fuckstick."

24

Alba

Alba wanted to stomp around the kitchen and bang things, but her leg ached. Even standing hurt. She grabbed a stool and sat next to Henri. She needed to keep her leg up, but she didn't have time for that right now.

"Whose is it?" asked Greer.

Alba looked up. The entire room's attention was on her.

"You won't fucking believe it. It's—"

A knock on the front door interrupted her.

"Oh, come on," said Julius.

Eli grinned and went to answer the door.

"Clement, come in," said Eli, he stepped back and looked around the room. "Have you met Victoria?"

Alba scanned her space., they were almost out of chairs.

"Of course Clement knows me," said Victoria with a nod in his direction. "What *I'd* like to know however is who killed Michael and is trying to kill Greer? If it's not too much of an inconvenience?"

This request was ignored for a few minutes so chairs could be rearranged, and despite the hour, wine found. Alba was going to have to put another order in with the local vineyard. They had worked through an entire case in a week.

With everyone settled, ready to hear what Alba had to say, she felt more like the evening's entertainment than a police inspector about to identify a killer. But she wasn't on duty, was she? That was future Alba's problem. Right now, they had a fuckstick, or potentially a pair of fucksticks to deal with. Then she would handle the rest of her life.

"It's Hilary," said Alba.

A chorus of—what—how do you know—and one why—echoed back at her.

"Because the night before he died, Michael stayed at Gregory and Hilary's house. This is a text telling her to get ready for when Gregory falls asleep."

"What?" asked Victoria, sitting up straight. "Michael and Hilary? Eww."

"Are there dirty texts?" asked Julius, his expression a mixture of fascination and horror.

Alba pretended she hadn't heard that.

"And sharing in the fraud's abundance," said Henri.

Alba glanced at the text she was reading. Michael had shared what the valuation of the bronze pigeon was.

"Wait, I thought Gregory or Tanya was the fraud partner?" said Julius.

"So did we," said Stephens. "The bank accounts were in Michael and Gregory's names."

Stephens' phone started dinging. He pulled it out and frowned at it.

"They were all in it?" asked Eli.

"It doesn't make sense," said Henri, with a puzzled frown on her face. "If Hilary and Michael were having an affair, why would they include Gregory in the fraud? And how does Tanya fit into all of this?"

"Maybe she really did just let him use the equipment," said Greer.

"Or...Gregory left all the finances in Hilary's hands," said Julius. "Just because it was in his name doesn't mean he actually knew about it or had access to it...if she managed everything, she would have all the details needed to set up the online account."

"But why his name and not hers?" asked Victoria. Her voice sounded quite horrified at the idea of putting money in someone else's name.

"Distancing herself from the crime?" asked Greer.

"Potentially," said Alba. "What if we have Gregory thinking he's helping Michael with his store and Tanya, that she is making a few bucks on the side. But really it is all just a front to hide the fact that Michael and Hilary are running a scam and having an affair?"

"That would make more sense than Gregory being part of the fraud," said Greer. "It always puzzled me...the idea he was some sort of criminal mastermind. I would suggest that his greatest ambition is to have a pleasant and quiet life."

"A noble ambition," said Henri with a smile. Those with wine raised their glasses.

"What about the attacks on Greer?" asked Victoria.

Greer shook her head. "Hilary? The poison, yes, maybe. The hit on the head, or in my case shoulder, in the laneway, also maybe. The break-ins, trying to get into my bathroom and ramming us with a car? I just can't see it."

"I'm glad it's not the superintendent," said Henri. "It upset me he would be so bad at it."

"So, who in our cast of players would be reckless and use violence, ineffectually, to resolve the issue?" asked Eli.

Alba slapped her forehead. "Alfie." She winced as her hand contacted layers of bruises, but the pain helped get her head working again.

"But he's in hospital...because of Jayden," said Eli.

"Released yesterday afternoon," said Clement. "A bit bruised but not too worse for wear."

"That's an interesting point," said Victoria. "What about Jayden?"

Alba looked at her empty wineglass, which at some point had replaced the whisky. She was thirsty but knew she should have some water first. Then she remembered she wasn't working anymore, so she poured herself another glass of wine.

"I think he played the role he said he did," said Alba. "He found the estate sales for them. It also explains why he attacked Alfie and not Gregory."

"I thought he was working for Gregory and Michael?" asked Stephens, glancing up from his phone for a moment.

Alba turned towards him. She was still pissed, pissed at all of them. But maybe she had it wrong, maybe Stephens wasn't as much of a fuckstick as the rest.

"I'm not sure." Alba sighed. There were still so many unanswered questions—and she was stuck here rather than at the station with the resources she needed. Though to be fair, having food, friends and wine around her wasn't all bad. "But before Jayden stopped talking, he just talked about *them* cheating him out of the money. He didn't use Gregory's name." Another mistake on her part. The superintendent had been right to suspend her. She had made a hash of the entire case.

"Makes sense," said Stephens, sitting forward. "I just found out—"

"I still can't see what Alfie got out of it," said Julius. "I mean, two million is barely enough for two people these days, let alone split three ways. My guess is there are more accounts, probably under Alfie's name if Hilary's avoiding using her own."

Stephens nodded. "You might be right. In fact we've just—"

"Hilary"—Victoria's tone was withering—"would've known about the lamp, which meant she was probably the one to poison Miles." Victoria's nostrils flared.

Alba had never seen someone do that in real life before and was impressed.

"The thing that's annoyed me all along..." Alba shifted on the uncomfortable stool. "Was how did Michael's car get home? If Alfie and Hilary were in it together, it makes sense." Her being asked to leave the station played on repeat in her mind. She hated she needed him to finish this. "Stephens, tomorrow—"

"We've some more information." Stephens cleared his throat. "Jeffrey can be overenthusiastic about enforcing traffic laws—"

"We know," said several people in the room.

He glanced at them all with slight amusement. "*And* apparently, he put in a request for extra cameras and CCTV for the intersection Alba and Greer were hit. Savas signed it off but forgot to tell anyone about it."

"I thought the CCTV wasn't working?" asked Alba, leaning forward.

"The one that everyone knew about, but not the new one." A small smile broke across Stephens' face. "Jeffrey took it upon himself to track down the person who crashed into another police officer, even..." He coughed. "Anyway, it isn't the best picture, but he just sent through a screen grab that looks an awful lot like Alfie Jones."

"So, we have them?" said Henri.

Apparently, when seated behind a car wheel, Alfie had a very similar physique to the superintendent. Her throat tightened and for a moment she wished time travel were possible.

"We have Alfie..." Stephens let out an enormous sigh. "We just don't have Hilary...not yet. All roads lead either back to Alfie or Gregory."

"So, she might get away with it?" asked Greer, her hand resting on Miles.

"Even with Alfie involved, it doesn't mean we won't pursue Hilary as well. At the very least, she must have known something, and there ought to be some professional breaches there somewhere."

Victoria made a scoffing sound. "What? She organises to have Michael killed, potentially almost kills Miles, and the only consequence is she can't work as a lawyer anymore?"

The crowd went wild.

Alba spent almost an hour calming everyone down and getting them out of her house. By the time it was done the weight of exhaustion pulled at her, sending images of soft beds that would take the weight of her body and the world away for a few brief hours. Sadly, she had an injured houseguest, two if you counted Miles. After loading the dishwasher with an impressive number of glasses, Alba helped put out some food for Miles. Raw meat and water were a gross combination, however he seemed to enjoy it. Looking at the bits left behind, she was sure the cockroaches would too.

She triple-checked all the locks and left one lamp on downstairs. It was still early but the winter sun was setting and both of them were exhausted.

Between her limping and Greer's struggling with one arm, she wasn't sure who was helping whom up the stairs.

"What next?" asked Greer as she sat down on the edge of her bed. She patted next to her and Miles rocketed past Alba and onto the bed for a pat. Alba was glad to see him feeling better.

"We sleep."

If only because she wasn't much good for anything else right now.

"And tomorrow?"

"Tomorrow, we take the psycho-fuckstick down."

Greer smiled and gave a happy sigh. Alba wished she felt as content, but as she hobbled to her bathroom for a shower, a headache grew. Her thoughts swirled with all the pieces but no matter how she twisted them, there didn't seem to be a way to resolve this. Or at least not a way that would end with a conviction in a court of law.

She didn't think Hilary was crazy enough to try anything tonight. Still, the vulnerability of sleepwear was too much, and she chose a tracksuit. Comfortable enough to sleep in but without embarrassment if she had to run in it.

Not that she could move, quickly that is. Her leg throbbed, and she lay there for a few minutes before finally giving in and taking some painkillers the hospital had given her. Nothing too intense, just enough to numb the pain so she could go to sleep.

An hour later, Alba lay there, her mind churning. What could she do? She had no police powers. Walk up to Hilary and accuse her of murder, hope for a sudden attack of conscience?

Fuck that for a lark.

The morning was worse. Alba's right leg barely bent, and she cursed the doctors for sending her home—conveniently ignoring that she'd discharged herself. Her sheets trapped her when she tried to sit up. A few tugs and she was able to slide out the left side of the bed, gingerly swinging her legs out, but her right leg protested. She swung it back. A considerable furry weight occupied the middle of the bed and for a moment Alba imagined crawling back in, letting his warmth and purrs soothe her and leaving the Hilary's of the world to someone else.

But she was not a cat. Instead she tensed and focused on standing.

It took her half an hour to be able to move—with the walking stick. She didn't bother changing out of her tracksuit but grabbed some clothes for later. There was no way she was coming back up the stairs.

Clouds and some soft rain had settled in, making it hard to tell the time, but the clock showed it was just past eight in the morning. The horror of being out of coffee trumped any sense of relief she might have felt from not being killed in her sleep. She hadn't had time to shop. Now here she was unable to drive and unable to walk. And no coffee.

The squeak of the stairs preceded Greer's descent and revealed her once more neatly dressed for the day ahead.

"We're out of coffee," said Alba.

Greer for some obscure reason didn't seem too perturbed. "Do you have tea?"

"Probably, but..." Alba wasn't sure what to say that wouldn't be insulting.

"A visit to Elvira's Cravings?" Greer appeared to be amused. "It's a Sunday morning and Alfie's in custody. I wouldn't mind some coffee and doughnuts without the threat of someone trying to kill me."

"Neither of us can drive, and I can't walk that far," grumbled Alba. She glared at her empty kitchen cupboard.

"I'm sure that of the thousands of people who have attached themselves to you, we can find someone to give us a lift."

It took a bit of a phone tree, and in the end, the only person who was free was Julius. Of course he was. Alba changed in the laundry while Greer went back up to put on an outside outfit as apparently what she was wearing was only for lounging around inside, though it looked perfectly fine to Alba.

On a typical Sunday, Alba probably wouldn't have even changed out of her PJs. But today was no ordinary day. Today, they needed to find out how to link Hilary to everything.

After coffee.

Julius turned up and chatted with Greer at way too high a volume for a pre-coffee Sunday morning. Greer just smiled and nodded, but he seemed to take that as a sign of attention rather than disinterest. Who knew with Greer? Alba took the back seat, stretching out her right leg and practicing flexing it.

With rain shifting down steadily, only a few hardy souls with large coats and larger umbrellas stood waiting outside Elvira's.

"Julius," said Greer. "You like lattes, don't you? My shout for driving us out here."

He smiled at her, his gaze warm. "You don't have to do that. I'm happy to help."

"No, I insist, this is above and beyond the call of accountancy services."

"But not of a friend, I hope?"

For fuck's sake.

Alba was just wondering whether she wanted to kill herself or them when they were all saved by reaching the counter.

"I'll get the coffees," said Alba, a small price to pay for the end of that conversation. "A long black, a latte and an oat latte."

"And doughnuts," said Greer.

"And three doughnuts," said Alba.

Elvira started making the coffees. "Good morning, Greer, Julius. What brings you both in on the weekend?"

"Alba's out of coffee," said Greer.

Elvira seemed to throw an involuntarily sympathetic glance towards Alba but caught herself and changed it to a frown.

"Wasn't my fault," said Alba, interpreting the frown as Elvira blaming her for arresting Fran.

"Whose was it then?" asked Elvira as she put three doughnuts in a bag and handed them to Greer. "I'm just pleased that common sense prevailed in the end."

Alba didn't have an answer to that, so she said nothing. After paying, she took a step to the side out of the queue of those waiting to order. As Greer stepped away as well, Elvira gestured for her to come closer.

"I've done some digging, and it looks like Amos was telling the truth. He has an offer from one of the big chains."

Greer looked sad—but resigned. "It's his property, and his choice to make."

"He's also put a change of use application in," said Elvira, her tone sharp. "Which probably means a café as well."

"I'm sorry," said Greer. "I hope it won't affect you."

"It's poor form of Amos." Elvira sniffed. "I've spoken to my landlord."

"Your landlord? I thought you owned this building?" asked Greer.

Alba scanned the building the café was in. It was an old two-storey brick building. The café used two rooms and the area off the back for the small outside seating space. Most of the ground floor next to the café, which had the traditional frontage, was empty.

"Why don't you have anyone renting out the space next door? Or why don't you expand?" asked Alba.

Elvira threw a glare at her.

"The last tenant left a few months ago and I've been thinking about it. But I don't really want a larger space. That means more staff." Elvira turned towards Greer. "It would be good to have a little more seating space though, which means if the new tenant was say...a bookstore, we could work something out."

Alba's eyebrows rose, as did Greer's. It made sense, but they didn't have time for it today.

Elvira slid the coffees across the counter.

"Great idea." Alba grabbed hers. "You and Greer should talk about it. Tomorrow."

Elvira frowned at Alba again but kept her attention mainly on Greer.

Greer smiled warmly back at her. "I like it. I love this building, and it would give us a fighting chance. Alba's right though...tomorrow?"

Alba left Greer and Elvira to work out the details and hobbled out of the café with Julius, to find Gregory standing outside.

"Mr Williams, I believe the police are looking for you," said Alba.

"Inspector, I didn't do it."

Alba could feel the curiosity of the people in the queue. Who was about to double their money on the pool?

"Get in." She gestured to Julius' car. At least it was dry and out of earshot.

Julius looked at her with a raised eyebrow and kindly offered her his arm but didn't say anything. With more people piling into the car, Alba was forced to take the front seat so she could keep her leg straight while Gregory got in the back. Greer seeing them as she came out of the shop, joined him.

"Where to?" asked Julius.

"The bookstore," said Greer.

"The station," said Alba.

"I didn't do it," said Gregory, his voice high. "Please, you need to hear this."

Alba twisted around to find Gregory's pleading expression.

She might regret this. "Fine, the bookstore."

At least the store was closed, so they sat in the middle in a circle of chairs that Julius put together. With Alba and Greer injured and Gregory in a state of distress, Julius had been on his own. Not that he seemed to mind. Alba considered asking Julius to leave, but one, she wasn't sure if he would go, and two, she might need a ride soon.

"Okay, Gregory, you have our attention. What do we need to know?" asked Alba.

"I didn't do it."

"Yes, yes, you said that," said Alba.

"None of it. I didn't attack you, and I didn't know about the money."

"That's great. You could have told us that in the car." Alba stood up.

"It wasn't just Alfie," said Gregory. Alba couldn't help rolling her eyes. It was like pulling blood from a stone.

"All the accounts and phones are in your and Michael—"

"Who do you think it was, Gregory?" asked Greer.

Alba looked over at Greer as she cut her off. Would she have done that if she was still the inspector on the case?

Gregory turned to Greer. "Hilary, it was all Hilary."

The room probably didn't react the way Gregory thought it would, and he looked confused.

"Assuming we believe you," said Alba with a slight drawl. "How do we prove it...with so many roads leading to you?"

25

Greer

Greer was exhausted. The pain in her shoulder should have been lessening by now. Instead, because Alfie thought it would be fun to ram her with a car, it was more painful than ever. She looked at Gregory. He looked tired too, and she could smell his day-old sweat.

She had spent so much time thinking about what had been happening to her and, to some extent, to Fran, that she had forgotten about Gregory.

"I have her phone."

Now that he had the attention of everyone in the room, Gregory shifted in his seat, unable to stop moving his hands.

"Hilary's phone?" asked Alba.

"The one she used to talk to Michael."

Greer's heart hitched. "Gregory, did you read...?"

"I...I...a few...I...couldn't..."

"It might be tempting, but it won't be helpful," said Greer.

Gregory's eyes dropped to his hands and his shoulders folded forward. "I can't believe that Michael would do this to me."

Greer found it interesting that he mentioned Michael rather than Hilary.

"I'm so sorry, Gregory," said Greer.

"Don't be sorry for him yet," said Alba.

Gregory slumped further in his chair. "I told you I didn't do anything."

Alba grunted. "We're just meant to believe you?"

Julius glared at her. "I believe you, Gregory," said Julius.

Alba glared back.

"You said you had Hilary's phone," said Greer, hoping to get the situation back on track. "Do you have it with you now?"

"I fucking hope so," muttered Alba.

Greer wished she were close enough that she could kick her in her sore leg.

"Yes." Gregory rummaged around in one of his pockets and pulled out a phone. It was the same kind as the one that Greer and Alba had found in Michael's store.

Before Gregory could hand it over, there was a ringing sound, but not from the phone in his hand. He fumbled with Hilary's phone until Julius took it off him, freeing Gregory to pull out his own.

"It's Fran," said Gregory, looking at the screen.

Alba leaned forward, her whole-body vibrating. "Answer it. On speaker."

Gregory swallowed and accepted the call.

A faint voice was heard. "Gregory?"

"One sec, sorry, just need to, right..."

"Gregory?" The voice was clearer now, though still soft, almost a whisper.

"Fran, are you okay? Why are you whispering?" asked Gregory.

"Gregory, I need you. Can you come over? I...I think Hilary's gone crazy."

"Hilary? What's happening?" asked Gregory.

Greer reached out, put her hand on Gregory's shoulder, and leaned forward.

"Fran, this is Greer."

Her blood thrummed in her ears. Was Hilary listening? Had she made a mess by revealing herself?

The voice dropped out of its whisper. "Greer?"

Greer frowned. She recognised that voice. But it wasn't Fran's. "Tanya?"

A woman's scream was abruptly cut off.

Greer hit call on Fran's number, and they all watched it ring out.

"Come on!" Greer jumped up and headed to the door, only stopping when nobody followed. "What if she's hurting Fran or Hilary?"

At that, they all started moving. Alba could barely walk, and Julius ended up having to help her to the car. Eventually, they were all packed in the vehicle and Julius took off, breaking several traffic laws along the way.

However from the look of almost excitement on his face she didn't think he was too concerned about future fines.

"Call Stephens," said Greer. It had been a long time since she had heard that tone in her own voice. Dale had always called it her *in command* mode. It felt strange, like it needed warming up or dusting off.

"What?" asked Alba, twisting to stare at her with wide eyes.

"Call him, let him know we think Tanya's at Fran's house and possibly hurting her."

Alba snorted but dutifully pulled out her phone. "If I call they'll ask a bunch of stupid questions." Alba tapped out a message on her phone and then put it away once it started to beep with incoming messages. "They're on their way."

With Gregory directing Julius, they were soon in front of Fran's house. There were no signs of the police.

They all got out of the car. The clouds were heavy but thankfully the rain had eased for the moment. However it was only Greer and Gregory that immediately headed up to the house.

"Wait a minute," said Alba, leaning against the car. "Just wait, the police are on their way. There's nothing you can do that won't make it worse—"

A scream and a crash cut through the air.

Gregory took off.

"Stay here. Let the police know what's happening," said Greer. She followed Gregory into the house, colliding with him in the entrance to the living room.

Around him, she could see Hilary lying on the floor with a heavy vase covered in blood next to her, and Tanya holding Fran by the hair with a knife at her throat.

"Thank you, Greer," said Tanya, tightening her hold and pressing the knife so it dimpled Fran's skin.

"Happy to help," said Greer. She could not tell if Hilary was breathing, but Fran was still very much alive, so she focused on getting the knife away from her throat.

"Aren't you going to ask what for?" Tanya shifted her grip on Fran's head, pulling it further back to keep her off balance.

Greer shrugged. "For bringing the police?"

"Police?" She snorted. "I don't see any with you. And I heard about Ms Inspector being fired. Such a shame." Tanya shot a glare at Gregory. "Don't take another step."

Fran's hand slowly inched up her front.

"You need Gregory?" asked Greer. "You think he can tell you where the money is?"

"I know where the money is," Tanya snorted. "I just don't know the passwords and Gregory here, as the official owner of the accounts, is going to help me get them."

"I'm surprised you didn't hear." Greer tried to shift to the side so she could see the front door, and hopefully the arrival of the police. "There's a freeze on all the accounts."

"Only the ones they know about my dear Greer," Tanya snarled. "Now Gregory, this is what's going to happen. If you don't want serious injury to happen to Fran here, you're going to get Fran's car and then we are all going to take a trip, is that clear?"

Gregory glanced over at Greer, who nodded. There wasn't much else they could do but agree and stall for time.

"Don't look at her," said Tanya. "I'm the one with the knife."

Fran's hand finally landed on the knife and then, in a move that Greer wasn't sure she would have been brave enough to do, Fran fell back into Tanya and shoved her hand up between the knife and her neck.

Tanya sliced downwards, and Fran screamed as it cut into her hand. Blood covered the knife and Tanya pulled harder on Fran's hair, over-balancing her.

"Fran!" Gregory threw himself at Tanya, who swung the knife around and cut at his face. He flinched back, and she shoved the knife into his shoulder. Gregory screamed and stumbled back. Tanya took advantage of the opening and kicked at his legs, causing him to stumble into a coffee table and fall over. She pulled Fran back up and pressed the knife into her neck, cutting the skin.

Greer took two steps forward. "I bet this is not how you thought this would go?"

Tanya kicked at Gregory's head, but took a step back, dragging Fran with her. Fran looked dazed and her right hand trailed blood next to her.

"I just want what is owed to me," said Tanya, giving Fran's hair another yank. "I'll not be screwed over again."

Greer took another step forward. "Give—"

"Don't fucking try to shrink me, you stuck-up dipshit."

Greer held out her hands, palms up. "Think about it, Tanya. The police are on their way. What's your next step?"

Tanya's gaze dropped to Hilary's still body. "Not much difference between two and three."

The hair stood up on Greer's arms and she watched as Tanya's elbow moved backward, dragging the knife further into Fran's neck.

Fran screamed and jerked her head back once more sacrificing her hand to keep the knife from cutting deeper into her throat.

Greer ran forward and locked her right arm through Tanya's elbow. She tried to use her weight to pull it away from Fran, but she was too weak. Her arm slipped as Tanya kicked out at her.

And then Tanya was gone.

Greer dropped to her knees before sitting down on the carpet. Fran, on the floor next to her, had blood flowing from her neck and hand. Gregory crawled towards Fran and reached out trying to stop the bleeding in her neck while his other arm hung useless beside him and every move made his face paler.

Thump.

Greer looked over to find Tanya lying on the floor halfway to the door with Alba sitting on her back, both their faces twisted in pain.

"I don't suppose anyone has any zip ties?" asked Alba, examining the woman beneath her who stared balefully at the knife just out of reach.

Alba told Greer that she had convinced Julius to wait for the police, however, it had taken her a while to get into the house, even using her walking stick.

Tanya had been too busy to notice her arrival, which allowed her to get close enough that once Greer had pulled the knife away from Fran's neck, she could knock her feet out from under her with her stick.

They had both sat there, happy to let the police, who had finally arrived, take Tanya away and wait for medical assistance. After the police had taken over caring for Fran, Gregory had collapsed next to her.

Two ambulances arrived and of course, Lucinda and Isaac who were apparently always on duty, immediately headed over to Greer.

"Book pedlar!" Isaac stood in front of her, shaking his head. "Why do you do this to me? I'm going to have anxiety about going out on calls if every one of them ends up with you covered in blood."

He knelt down next to her, and Lucinda joined him.

"I'm pretty sure the others are in a lot worse condition than me."

Lucinda looked across at Fran, who still lay on the floor bleeding, though at least the wound on her neck looked minor from this angle, and glanced at Gregory, nodding. "She's right brother," she said. "Come on, you can check on Greer later."

Isaac held Greer's right hand for a moment longer. "Are you sure you're okay?"

"I'm fine. Only my pride's hurt I promise."

He patted her hand and left to help the others. Greer stayed seated on the ground, too tired to move. Fran and Gregory were loaded into Isaac and Lucinda's ambulance while the other paramedics called out that Hilary was still alive, though Greer could see no movement. With shouted advice for Greer to see a doctor, Isaac and Lucinda put on their sirens and joined the other ambulance racing to the hospital.

Julius, who had been a traffic controller during it all, helped them back to the car and drove them back to Alba's.

Greer realised she had never gotten to eat that doughnut and her stomach rumbled. She walked over to open Alba's fridge. It was clean. She could tell that it was clean because it only had a tub of butter and a block of cheese. Greer wasn't entirely against the cheese and butter combo, but she was looking for something more substantial. And to be honest, she didn't want to eat cheese and butter in front of others. She suspected there would be judgement.

"You'll find some stuff in the freezer if you're hungry," said Alba, who immediately took a seat on the couch with her right leg up. It must have been excruciating for her to voluntarily sit still. She touched her own shoulder. Maybe some painkillers were due all-round. After food.

Greer reached up and opened the freezer. Alba was correct. There was food in there. Four frozen meals and a couple of hash browns, to be exact.

Julius peered over her shoulder. "You don't have to make that sacrifice. We all need food. I'll get some sorted." With that, he left to go foraging.

Greer's lips curved upwards. Julius was a good sort. He had been her accountant for over four years, and they had developed a kind of friendship. Or as much of a friendship as she allowed. This last week with Alba made her realise how controlled she was with people. How superficial her relationships here at Lakes End really were. Alba just threw open her door and let them all in. Greer wasn't sure she could do that, especially as one consequence seemed to be that they didn't leave. They did bring food though.

Trusting that Julius would take care of it, Greer collapsed into an armchair. With the sixth sense of a cat that told him a lap was available, Miles sprinted down the stairs and onto her. She gave him a cuddle as she checked him over. He seemed to have his energy back. Exhausted from his dash, he turned twice to make himself comfortable against her. He was too big to sit entirely on her lap, so he was half on the chair and half on her, trapping her.

She should have poured herself a glass of water before sitting down. Accepting that no one was interested in moving right now, she rested her head against the back of the chair and waited for Julius to return.

The front door opening woke Greer up. Alba had caught a quick nap too, and Greer watched her sit up and blink vacantly at the kitchen.

"What—"

"Julius has food," said Greer.

Alba rubbed her eyes, and Greer wondered just how much sleep she had squeezed in this week.

"Thank you, Julius," said Greer, smiling at him.

He smiled back as he made himself at home in the kitchen, pulling out bowls and forks.

"Not a problem. It's just going to be a fruit salad. I hope that's okay?"

It wasn't, really. Usually, that would be exactly what she wanted. In this moment though, she had been hoping for something heavy, maybe an early lunch even. But despite that, there was only one thing to do when someone else makes the food.

"Of course, that sounds delightful."

"Do you need a drink?" asked Julius.

"Water would be wonderful," said Greer. Though she had never gotten around to finishing her coffee but it was probably too much to ask him to go out again.

A loud exhalation came from the couch.

"You alright?" asked Greer.

"No." Alba rubbed the back of her neck and flexed the leg she had up on the couch, grimacing. "I'm pissed."

"About?" asked Greer. She was curious, after all they had caught the murderer right?

"Oh, you know, a botched murder investigation and potentially losing my job?" Alba slammed her hand down on the back of the couch.

Greer snorted. "Do you want my opinion?" she asked. Very early in her career, she learnt always to check first.

"No, not really, but give it to me anyway."

Julius gave each of them a bowl of what looked like a lovely fruit salad, which he had obviously prepared himself, and a glass of water.

"It looks delicious," said Greer.

Alba picked up the fork and stabbed into the bowl and looked at the fruit on the end of her fork with a confused expression. Greer commiserated with her.

"What's this opinion?" asked Alba.

Greer examined Alba. She was tired, but her body language was open.

"First, Tanya. I think you went further with that investigation than anyone else. If it hadn't been for you she would've walked free and we might not have even known about the rest of the money. What if Hilary and Alfie had continued the scam? Or what if Tanya had killed both of them and anyone else she saw as a threat?"

Alba just shrugged.

"None of them really helped, did they? Just made everything more of a mess," said Julius.

"Exactly," said Greer. "It's hard to pick who's guilty when they all have something to hide." Greer took a sip of water. "I also think you went back to work too early."

Alba frowned at her and opened her mouth.

Greer was grateful there wasn't food in it. "Before you say anything, hear me out."

Alba sighed and went back to poking at the food in her bowl.

"Your partner and your father, who was the whole reason you joined the police, betrayed you. This is a significant event. Just moving locations doesn't make the hurt go away. Would you have suspected the superintendent before that event? Say if you had been working here two to three years ago? Would you have taken those files home?"

"No, I wouldn't." Alba gulped down her water. "I would've assumed there was another explanation and talked to him."

"See, but you didn't. It is understandable considering the circumstances. I know you've bought this house—"

"You bought this?" asked Julius, his tone horrified.

Greer glared at him.

"Sorry." Julius picked up his own fork and tried to look interested in his bowl's contents.

"You bought this house, which says to me you don't want to go back."

Alba gave a laugh. "Well yeah, der."

Greer struggled not to roll her eyes. "What I mean is…I think you tied yourself here so you couldn't, or at least to make it harder…however that might not have been the solution you needed…maybe you should consider not working for the police anymore."

There she had said it. In the short time she had observed Alba, she could see how much she hated it. However she suspected that Alba's identity was deeply tied to being a police officer, which meant it would not be easy to move on.

"And do what?" Alba put down her bowl and slumped deeper into the couch. "It's all I've done."

"How about staying here and helping the people in the town?" Greer tried to lean forward however Miles refused to move so she settled for waving her hand towards the centre of town. "We've just found out that a bunch of people were getting ripped off. You could be someone people could go to get things checked out."

Greer had been thinking about this for a few days now. She hated Kendall had been ripped off, and as they had found more and more money, it frustrated her that no one wanted to address how it had happened.

"I don't know if there's enough of that to make a career."

"Stop thinking about a career and start thinking about what kind of life you want. Do you want to do something you hate? To drag yourself out of bed every day and to use copious amounts of caffeine to get you through the day?"

"I escaped...kind of," said Julius. "I'll never regret it."

His expression had more sympathy in it than Greer had ever seen directed at Alba before. She wondered what kind of life he had been in and an image of a large glass and steel office with deadlines on a large screen over his head flashed in her mind. Some people might love that however it was easy to imagine getting sick of it after a while.

"Take a break," said Greer. "Take a year. Explore something else."

She had, and she would never go back, but she didn't mention that part to Alba. It was her decision to make.

As it was a chilly day and the rain had set in, the doors and windows were closed, so all three of them squealed when a person appeared at the glass patio door.

Greer promised herself a house with no glass doors next time.

Henri knocked on the door, wanting to be let in, and Julius got up to open it.

"Thanks, Julius," said Henri. He grabbed one of the other seats and pulled it over near the couch. "Is it true?"

"What?" asked Alba, frowning at Henri.

"That it was Tanya Zuvic?"

Greer thought about who knew. Gregory, Fran, which meant Alex and Sam, and the entire police department. Really she was more surprised it had taken so long for it to get around.

"Yes," said Greer, looking over at Alba who sat there frowning.

"Tanya, so was Michael sleeping with her and Hilary? I mean, who knew he had it in him?"

"I don't know," said Alba, frowning. "But it looks like he was about to run off with the cash and Hilary. I suspect he made the mistake of telling Tanya."

Henri sat there shaking her head. "And she didn't take it well...understandable, really, I wouldn't have either."

Henri's expression turned contemplative and Greer suspected she was thinking of how she would have done it—and gotten away with it.

Alba tried to sit up straighter. "Stephens thinks she killed him on his way to sell the statue to the Gulbransons, drove his car home and buried it in Fran's yard. No one was looking for her, so she walked home pretending to be on a morning stroll." Alba's fingers gripped her glass, her knuckles white. "But despite all our questioning, no one saw her walking around with blood on her."

Greer examined her with sympathy. Whether or not Tanya had chosen it deliberately, it had been an excellent morning to commit a murder. "A dark coat and scarf on a winter morning..."

"So, is that it?" asked Henri, her expression almost disappointed.

Greer nodded and Alba picked at her bowl.

Henri watched her. "Is that what you're having for breakfast? If you want more Eli could whip something up."

Greer wondered if Henri had the house bugged and tried to remember if she had said the word bacon aloud before shaking her head and getting back on track.

"Maybe later, we're just discussing our futures," said Greer.

"Futures?" asked Henri, perking up.

"Yes, Alba needs to decide what she does next, and I also need to decide whether I move the bookstore next to Elvira's Cravings or maybe the Hidden Gem."

"I'm glad you've decided to stay." Julius smiled at her.

Greer suppressed the uncharitable thought that he was just grateful not to lose a client. She pushed back a bit of hair that had fallen over her face. "Though with Amos bringing in that bookstore..."

"Don't you worry," said Henri. "We'll just turn this town into one that can support two bookstores!"

"Exactly," said Julius. "It's all about supply and demand after all, and I know you can increase demand."

True, it would just take a lot of work. She had enjoyed the last five years of just running her little bookstore with little competition or effort beyond having to keep it open. Still, maybe it was time to engage more with the community.

"You're right," said Greer, running her hand down Miles' back. "Elvira and I could become *the* community hub."

"And as a bonus, it'll drive Amos nuts," said Henri. "Okay, if you're sorted. Alba, what's happening with you? I thought it wasn't the superintendent?"

"It wasn't," said Alba. "Which...which means I'm suspended because I fucked up."

"No need to sound like the world's ending. You're young...ish yet, and we all fuck it up sometimes." Henri frowned at Alba. "So, what are you going to do about it?"

"Transfer somewhere else...I guess."

"What? After you bought this house and just moved here?"

"I might not have a job if I stay," said Alba.

"Get one or make one." Henri dismissed Alba's comment with a wave of her hand. "Being a police officer isn't the only job out there, you know."

"Exactly," said Greer, pleased to find her own words mirrored in such a succinct way.

Henri had decided that after everything that had happened that week an early lunch of pizza and wine was called for and sent Eli a message.

She obviously sent it to a few others because within an hour, the house was full again. Clement and his partner Warren, who had returned from his trip early, came over with a couple of bottles of wine and some cheeses, and to Greer's surprise, so did Victoria and Kendall.

"Thanks for inviting Victoria," said Greer to Henri.

"I like her. Got a good head on her shoulders, and good taste in men and wine." Henri flashed a grin at Greer and went off to order people around arranging the chairs.

Eli came over with some pre-made pizza dough and toppings. Greer helped Henri film it, and Julius attempted once more to be his assistant. He was much better at it when sober. Victoria and Kendall seemed in charge of the wine.

"How are you both going?" asked Clement, coming over to Greer and Alba. "How's the leg?"

"Sore, but working," said Alba.

"And the shoulder?"

Greer touched it gingerly. "Throbbing, but as long as I don't move it, bearable."

"To be expected." He examined them both. "If I thought you'd listen to me, I would suggest getting it checked."

Greer laughed. He was right of course. However right now there was pizza coming.

Eli had finished making the last pizza when there was a knock on the door. Alba muttered something about the train still running.

Clement, the closest to the door, opened it to let in a damp and cold Hugh Stephens. Silence struck.

"Stephens," said Alba.

"Mauzer," said Stephens as his hello.

Greer could only imagine how much the absence of her inspector title hurt.

"How's Hilary?" asked Eli.

"She died on the way to the hospital." Stephens exhaled heavily. "Tanya has two murder charges against her now."

Clement took Stephens' coat and hung it up. Greer saw sadness flicker across Stephens' face as he noticed Kendall and Victoria sitting together. Kendall passed him a glass of wine, and Stephens graciously accepted it with a smile.

"I think this calls for a toast," said Henri.

Some of the carefreeness had left the room with the news of Hilary's death, and everyone looked to Henri.

"I know Hilary has passed away, and I wouldn't have wished that on her. But death doesn't make us angels in life. She ripped off people in this town, betrayed her husband and used her brother to try to kill Greer and Alba. I just regret that she isn't alive so they can hold her accountable for her actions. Therefore, I propose a toast. To Alfie being in jail where he belongs."

Everyone cheered and clinked glasses.

Henri turned to Alba. "I asked you to pin it on the Jones' if you could, and you did. Thank you."

Alba laughed at that.

"Here's to Alba and Greer who, almost despite themselves, have solved this case," said Eli.

Chuckles, chinks and here heres cascaded around the room.

Once the toasts started, it was hard to stop them, and everything from new bookstores, doughnuts, future pizzas to safe cats was celebrated.

Clement and Warren put out cheese and crackers while they waited for the pizzas and turned the entire space into a Knights of the Round Table arrangement. Eli's pizzas were spread over clustered tables and everyone pulled in seats where they could. Once Victoria pulled out a pack of cards, Greer suspected they were in for a long day and probably night. Good thing most of them weren't working tomorrow.

As the sun set the warm room, infused with the smell of grilled cheese, was loud. Much louder than Greer was used to—or even liked. But today, it felt comforting to be surrounded by friends.

Dale had always been the one who attracted people, with her included by default because she was his sister. His friends had reached out a few times, but she hadn't wanted to connect with them—they were Dale's friends, not hers. Not that she had thought of herself as lonely. However surrounded by people who wished her well, she realised that this was the piece that had been missing. She wished Dale was still alive. He would have loved this.

26

Epilogue

Dale,

The murderer is caught, and I am safe. For now, that is enough.

You would have liked tonight. People laughing, playing cards, good food and wine. All your favourite things.

A heavy shroud lifted and I walked with my arms swinging freely for the first time in a while (metaphorically, of course, my shoulder still hurts like a...well, a lot).

And I am starting a new era with the bookstore.

Miles is well, and I have finally found new friends. Remember I was never as fast at it as you.

I always miss you. Tonight was somehow worse though. I realised I will never get to share what I have found here with you and that hurts more than expected.

Wishing, as always, that you were still here.

Greer

Alba had a hot shower before falling into bed. Considering she had spent most of the day stretched out on the couch, she was still strangely tired. It had been a big week. And now it was over. All of it—the case, her career, her family. Hot water formed in the corner of her eyes, but she practically forced it to be reabsorbed into her body.

She thought about what Henri and Greer had said. A different life, a life without worrying if you were about to be betrayed. She couldn't work for someone else, but she could run her own business. Ex-police officer. Already she could feel herself becoming comfortable with that phrase. In fact, her whole body relaxed at the thought.

Alba thought about Greer across the hall. She had made it clear she wasn't going back to her mountainside glasshouse. Maybe she could stay here. The rent would help, and she wasn't the worst company.

Large paws pulled at her sheets as they walked up her side and a body flopped down next to her. Miles—making it clear all beds were his. The warm weight was comforting.

A cat, a flatmate and her own business. She could practically taste the future—office space over Elvira's, bottomless coffee and warm doughnuts.

Author Website

HARRIEBLAKE.COM

Chance to win an advance copy of the next release